Taking another cha
than casual interest from
and stepped in closer t
which were stretched out
his fragrance, feel his breath. Her eyes shifted away from
his and moved to his mouth.

He watched her move in to capture his lips in a kiss
that was a soft tentative touching. Captivated again by
her boldness, he waited to see what she'd do next. As she
pulled back, his teeth captured her lower lip and held it
for a second. Her eyes snapped open and met his, which
were dancing. He smiled, which she returned, and their
smiles gave way to laughter.

"See you around, Stephen Stuart," she said, still
chuckling while she walked to her truck.

"See you around, Reye."

He continued to lean on his car as he watched her
walk away. Nice body, he thought. Nice legs that led up
to a small, firm backside. Her hips tapered up to a trim
waist. He remembered how she'd felt when she'd rammed
into his back. Nice breasts, he added. She didn't look
back.

REYE'S GOLD

RUTHIE ROBINSON

Genesis Press, Inc.

INDIGO LOVE SPECTRUM

An imprint of Genesis Press, Inc.
Publishing Company

Genesis Press, Inc.
P.O. Box 101
Columbus, MS 39703

All characters in this book have no existence outside the imagination of the author and have no relation whatsoever to anyone bearing the same name or names. They are not even distantly inspired by any individual known or unknown to the author and all incidents are pure invention.

ISBN: 13 DIGIT : 978-1-58571-432-2
ISBN: 10 DIGIT : 1-58571-432-1
Manufactured in the United States of America

First Edition

Visit us at www.genesis-press.com
or call at 1-888-Indigo-1-4-0

DEDICATION

To Ronnie for 22 years of putting up with my crazy self. Love you more than you'll ever know.

ACKNOWLEDGMENTS

A huge shout out to Winnie, Linda, Andrea, Gwendy Gayle, Cassie, Lisa J, for your invaluable feedback and support.

PART ONE

CHAPTER 1

Growing up the only girl in a family of four older brothers offered mucho benefits for Reye Jackson: an endless supply of boys to ogle, protection and assistance in a fight, and four escorts held in reserve, for use only under extreme and dire conditions. Being the only aunt also offered up mucho benefits from the nieces and nephews of said older brothers, in the form of gifts, adoration, and copious amounts of hugs and kisses. Today, however, "only" was a dirty word in Reye's vocabulary, and not the dirty associated with sex, either. "Only" was responsible for her current plight, running to catch her airplane ride home.

She was late, and Reye hated, hated, hated being late. She'd overslept this morning and had to haul ass or miss her flight back home to Austin. She was returning from Fort Worth, where she'd spent time babysitting for her oldest brother, Jack, and his wife. Her sister-in-law, Neeci, had been a bridesmaid in a wedding held in New York, the city that never slept. Seeing and seizing an opportunity to turn a weekend wedding engagement into a week's vacation, the couple had called the only aunt late one night, when she was only partially awake. Somehow, the only aunt had volunteered to watch the kids for a week. Not one child, mind you, but three children.

Count them and weep: ages two, not potty trained; five, an energetic boy; and twelve, the smart-aleck diva. This week, she'd answered questions, read stories, played in the park, texted until her fingers were numb, and sat on the potty long enough to last her a lifetime.

So, now a harried, perturbed, and exhausted aunt hurried to leave for the airport. The alarm hadn't gone off, and so it was now nine-fifteen. Her flight was scheduled to leave in forty-five minutes. Seeing to the needs of three children was major hard work, and, in addition to the week's child dramas, their parents' return flight had been delayed. Her brother and his wife had arrived home at nearly two in the morning. The only aunt had waited up, and they'd all snored happily late into the following morning, kids included, until, thankfully, her mother had called.

Reye didn't spend a lot of time pampering and getting dressed, making up some time. Her short locks made at least her hair relatively maintenance-free. If only she could have driven herself to the airport she would have made it easily, with time to spare even, but her brother had slid behind the wheel of the family's minivan, turning into the world's safest driver. Of her brothers, Jack had always been the speed demon. Not anymore; his speed genes had been lost for good. He'd apparently traded in a perfectly good speeding record for the protection and safety of his kids.

Pulling up to the curb of the airport now, Reye turned to him, gathering her backpack and single suitcase. "Thanks for the lift," she said and leaned over to kiss his cheek. "Don't call me the next time you need a babysitter." He laughed while she grabbed her bags and high-tailed it for the doors.

She found the first class check-in line for her airline carrier thankfully short, and parked herself at the end of it. While she waited, she took a moment to look over her potential traveling companions, all lined up like sliced bread, waiting for assistance. An older African-American couple well into their sixties stood immediately in front of her, holding hands while waiting their turn. She hoped that when she reached their age, she would have someone that she loved enough to want to hold hands with, too. The couple reminded her of her parents, who had been together for forty-five years.

Directly ahead of the older couple stood a tall woman, whose commanding, confident manner and dress pronounced her a business executive, probably at home in any American boardroom. Reye envied the drive that women like her had. She yearned to have an innate knowledge of her life's true purpose. Life had to be easier, run smoother, if you knew where you were supposed to go.

Her eyes continued their travel, halting and resting on the next person in line. Talk about F.I.N.E.! This boy was all that and a bag of chips! GQ kinda fine! And Reye knew fine. She had always held an appreciation for men, regardless of their color. Man-child could be red, white, blue, or green, it didn't matter. She'd studied and watched them with a passion for as long as she could remember, enjoying the way they moved, the way they breathed, and even the way they smelled after a hard game of soccer.

Okay, that was her personal fetish, but so what. She loved the play of their muscles when engaged in activity, running, walking, or just plain ol' standing still.

Momentarily setting aside her rush, she paused for a minute to take in this excellent specimen of manhood set before her. *Nice!* she thought. *Very nice, indeed.* He was tall, about two inches over her height, maybe six feet, two inches or so. He was white, well, more golden, actually. He probably spent major time outdoors. She hadn't dated any white boys before, but she appreciated them nonetheless. Tall and lean this one was, with nice toned legs, not too thick but well defined. He had on those long, too big cargo shorts that all men wore these days, resting very nicely on an excellent butt, and no one appreciated butts more than she. His feet were encased in brown leather sandals that supported some nice long feet. Hmm, Reye mused, didn't feet imply a little "somethin' somethin'" about a man's appendages? Her eyes traveled back up, lingering again on his butt, before moving further up to take in a nice trim torso.

Just then he had turned to face Reye, providing her with a nice view of a well-developed chest outfitted in a snug t-shirt that must love being on that body. Squinting, she peered intently at his stomach. Was that a six-pack? Maybe, could be, the shirt would have to go to be sure. Continuing upward on her personal tour, she encountered a pair of striking blue eyes, set in a very handsome face, topped off nicely by a thick head of short, black, curly hair. Affixed to his face was a slightly wicked smile, where full lips sat surrounding perfect white teeth. She was sure it had lured many a girl over to the dark side. Wondering at that smile, she discreetly looked behind to find its intended recipient. Nope, no one stood behind her. Okay, could he be smiling at her? Not bloody likely, she thought, borrowing her favorite British term. Slowly turning around she looked to her left and right, nope, no one there either. She found his eyes again, and yes, he was still smiling, and yes, that smile was, in fact, directed at her. He'd cocked an eyebrow as if to say, "Yeah, I see you." Apparently he hadn't minded Reye's perusal, so she smiled back, because something that good should be recognized and appreciated. Her smile said "yes, you caught me, and yes, you do look that good."

He was called up next to the counter, putting an end to her peep show. You could tell the counter girl was giving him the once-over, too. Reye could certainly understand and sympathize. What must it feel like to him, to be on the receiving end of nonstop admiration? That was so not her problem. Men usually found her height off-putting, not moving beyond that point. The ones that weren't deterred usually had their own brand of issues that limited their appeal to her.

Two ticket agents, both women, worked the airline's counter. A young, petite redhead had begun to assist the golden one, Reye's nickname for the gorgeous male specimen in line, and was taking her time about it, too. The other ticket agent was much older, with short salt and pepper hair curling over a plain, nondescript face, her persona efficient and no-nonsense. The lady in the business attire moved to the counter next and was quickly helped and sent on her way. That left the older couple immediately in front of Reye, who were called and moved up for service. Only Reye remained in line, and it was now 9:45. "Okay, let's get moving," she whispered under her breath, not too loudly; the last thing she wanted to do was piss off the ticket agents. *He* was still at the counter. Reye rolled her eyes and checked her watch again, fighting against tapping her feet to show her impatience. The golden one was proving to be a distraction, and, beautiful or not, she had a plane to catch. The ticket agent helping him appeared intent on starting a conversation, fluttering her eyelashes, her smile broad, talking rather than processing.

The older couple was dispatched and finally it was her turn. "Welcome to the National Airlines. Destination?" the agent said, holding her hand out toward Reye for her ticket.

"Austin, Texas, and I'm running late," announced Reye softly, adding a hint of pleading in her voice, as she approached the counter. The golden one looked up sharply, giving her a considering look. Apparently he'd been listening and watching, passing along another smile to Reye, to the annoyance of the redheaded ticket agent.

"No problem," Reye's attendant said, examining Reye's paper work. Finding it in order, she checked in her suitcase and handed a boarding pass to her. Now she needed to make a fast and speedy trek to the gate. "I'll call ahead to inform the attendants at your gate that the two of you are running late." What, the golden one was going to Austin, too? Reye's head snapped around to find him watching her. With a small nod of his head, he confirmed the ticket agent's comment. She thanked her agent, grabbed her ticket, and proceeded to the gate.

The golden one had left the counter seconds before her, moving quickly through the terminal, his height an unknowing marker as he moved through the crowds, her personal beacon. She kept him in her sights as she took off her shoes and threw her backpack in the tub and walked through the security checkpoint. He'd cleared first, and she was not far behind. He was fast, but playing soccer and running track kept Reye in great shape, so maintaining his pace wasn't difficult. Unfortunately she'd kept her eye on him and not the other passengers, accidentally tripping over something in her path, a large canister for carrying art attached to the arm of an elderly man. Crap, she thought, struggling to remain on her feet.

Stephen had moved steadily toward the gate, keeping the pretty girl from the ticket counter in his peripheral vision. He'd noticed her at the counter giving him the once-over. Having grown accustomed to second glances and women staring, he rarely paid attention, picking and choosing among them when he was motivated. This one was tall with caramel-colored skin and beautiful long, muscular legs. He was first and foremost a leg man. Those long legs were showcased in form-fitting knee length khaki shorts, an equally form fitting t-shirt wrapped around her well-toned body. It was rare to meet women who could match him in the height department, but she was close. She had short curly hair, dreadlocks, he thought they were called, reminding him of Bob Marley's hair; only there were more of them, the strands thinner somehow, spiky even. They framed a really pretty face, which sported a charming and captivating smile, one that was slightly mischievous in its delivery, instantly inciting in him a yearning to taste. He'd heard the commotion behind him, turning in time to witness her trip over something in her path.

He decided to go back to help—a very uncommon impulse, he rarely went out of his way for strangers—but he walked back quickly and found her bent over an older gentleman, apologizing profusely and picking up items that had fallen to the floor. She looked up at him, surprise marking her face, swiftly replaced by cool. He watched her as she continued to retrieve the old man's items from the floor, her close proximity allowing him opportunity for a more thorough appraisal. His eyes roamed over mouth-watering legs that tapered into curvy hips, and, courtesy of her current bent position, a nice ass. Hers was just the way he liked them, firm, round, and visible. The view of her from the front was limited by the same bending, but she was prettier than he'd thought at first glance. Full, shapely lips circled even white teeth, long brown eyelashes fell over sparkly brown eyes, smooth caramel skin poured over a heart-shaped face. Beautiful.

Satisfied that she'd picked up everything, she apologized again and shouldered her backpack, preparing to leave. "Let me give you a hand," Stephen said, extending his hand to her. Desire warred with trust in her eyes. "I don't usually accept assistance from men I don't know."

"And I don't usually offer it," he responded, a slight smile on his lips. "I'm Stephen, if that helps any."

He watched the two seconds it took for her to reach some internal conclusion before accepting his hand.

"Nice to meet you, Stephen, I'm Reye. Thanks for coming back for me."

"No problem, but we'd better get going if we're going to make this flight," he said, turning in the direction of their gate.

"Okay, you lead, and I'll follow."

Reye, her hand in his, trailed in his wake, continuing to observe him as they resumed their journey to the gate. He was even more attractive up close. He was sexy and self-confident. His hand enclosed hers in a strong and sure grip. His long legs ate up the distance to their gate. He had to have played football, Reye thought, judging by the way he wove between people as if this were the last play of the Super Bowl and the game's outcome rested squarely on his shoulders. "Excuse me, excuse me," he said to no one and everyone, increasing his pace. Reye held on for dear life as he sprinted the last twenty yards to the counter.

As quickly as he'd sprinted, he stopped. *Whoa,* Reye said to herself as she rammed into his back. "Ump," he said as she plowed into him and bounced off, landing on the floor, hard on her butt, her backpack partially breaking her fall, her legs stretched out in opposite directions. This was clearly not how she wanted her time with him to end. She lay there for a minute testing her body parts for breakage, more than a little embarrassed. She looked up into the concerned faces of Stephen and the flight attendant, who were scanning her for any obvious injury.

"Are you hurt?" they asked in unison. Trying to catch her breath and feeling like an idiot, she laughed. "I'm fine," she said between chuckles. "Did we make the flight?"

"Yes," the flight attendant said as she grinned back at Reye. Reye didn't look over at Stephen, not wanting to see his reaction to her fall.

He helped her to her feet and the attendant handed them their boarding passes. She stepped back to allow them to proceed to the airplane, Stephen behind Reye. Entering the first class section, Reye arrived at her seat, 2B. It was an aisle seat, always her preference because otherwise she felt caged in. An elderly woman sat next to her reading a book, a good sign; hopefully that meant a quiet ride home so she could get some sleep. She put her backpack in the overhead compartment as she, out of the corner of her eye, watched Stephen take his seat in row four, making note of the empty window seat next to him. She sat down, fastening her seat belt, half listening as the flight attendant performed the mandatory what-to-do-in-case-of-an-emergency speech. The plane took off and

Reye settled back in her seat, waiting for her complementary drink and bag of peanuts.

She was bone tired. Her body was anyway, even though her mind had started racing around seeking the answer to the obvious question. Should she or shouldn't she move to the seat that was open next to Stephen? Her inner voice resisted, arguing against further invasion. *Give the poor boy a rest*, it said. Taking small, inconspicuous glances over her shoulder, she tried to gauge his interest, finally deciding to leave him alone. Recounting her morning adventures reinforced her decision to stay put. Let's see, she'd been caught ogling him, assisted through the airport by him, and then ran into his back. She had her limits.

Stephen smiled to himself as he watched Reye watch him. He had an unobstructed view of her. She had been entertaining and sexy, not a bad combination. He was intrigued by the variety of personalities she'd displayed so far, bold in her examination of him as they'd waited in line, sexy when returning his smile, and funny as hell when she bumped into him and fell on her butt. She sat there, legs sprawled in different directions, laughing at herself. He'd had to turn his head to keep from joining in her laughter. So with this image in his mind, he caught the flight attendant's attention and asked her to relay a message to the passenger in seat 2B. Fortunately, she was the same flight attendant who had witnessed Reye's fall, and the smile she gave to him seemed to indicate her approval of his request.

"My pleasure, sir."

Reye was resting her eyes behind her closed eyelids when someone touched her shoulder. She turned to see the flight attendant from earlier, now standing at her side. "There is an open seat in row four, next to the gentleman who helped you this morning. He asked if you would like to sit with him?"

"Thanks," Reye said, smiling into the twinkling eyes of the flight attendant, a silent understanding forming between them, making them co-conspirators in their appreciation of him. Reye looked back to find his eyes on her, a small smile on his lips. She unbuckled her seat belt and stood. Her sleepiness disappeared rapidly, replaced by a surge in energy. Men were such great motivators.

Deciding to leave her backpack in the overhead compartment since she wasn't moving far, she walked down the aisle toward him. He moved over to the empty seat by the window, leaving the aisle seat open for her. Reye sat down and settled back. The seats in the first-class section were larger than in the general class, so there was some distance between them. After a moment she turned to him. "Thanks for pulling me along through the airport and for letting me use your back as a stop," she said.

"You're welcome. You did a great job keeping up." It was quiet for a second between them. "So you live in Austin or are you just visiting?" he asked, breaking the silence.

She turned a little to look into his eyes, subtly scooting closer to him. She was now in full-blown get-to-know-you mode.

"It's home, I was born and raised there, I'm in my last year of school at the university," she said, answering his question, distracted a little by seeing his face up close. Who knew eyes could be that blue? And these were graced with long, black, girl-length lashes.

"We have something in common, then. I'm in my last year of law school at the university."

"Yeah?" she said. "That's impressive. What were you doing in Dallas?"

"It's home. How about you?"

"I spent the week babysitting my brother's three children in Ft. Worth, great aunt that I am." Just the thought of her nieces and nephews reminded her that she was tired. She yawned and moved her hand to cover her mouth. "Excuse me. I'm really tired. I love my nieces and nephew, but they wore me out this week."

"You could sleep on the way back."

"And miss this wonderful conversation,?" she said playfully, batting her eyelashes at him like some damsel from an old-school movie. He laughed.

"Law school, huh? What kind of law?"

"Nothing flashy, just wills and estates, trust planning. I'm the fourth-generation Stuart, my last name. Law is the Stuart family's business. After I'm done with school and pass the bar exam, I'll join my dad in the family firm."

"I see," she said. "So do you really *like* the law, or is this the path of least resistance?" He gave her a contemplative look.

"I like the law, really. I'll admit, though, my exposure to other areas may be limited, but it's what I grew up with, what I'm familiar with. I grew up learning how to argue. I argued with my dad on just about anything, from sports to politics. We both loved it. Some boys connect with their dad over sports, me it was Article III, section 4 of the Texas Probate Code."

"So you're a nerd, huh?"

Surprised, he grinned, and chuckled quietly. No one had ever called him that before.

"Yeah, a nerd I guess."

"Well, you don't look like any nerd I know. You must play sports, too, right?" She looked him over again, not hiding her attraction.

He watched her give him a scorching once-over again, charmed in spite of himself. "Yes, I did, and still do. Pick a sport and I've probably played it."

"So, you're an athletic, good-looking nerd?" she said, drawing out the compliment. "I bet your parents are really proud."

"Yes, they are."

"Are you their only kid?"

"Yep, the only kid," he said as he slid over a little further to her, until his shoulder bumped hers and his thigh touched hers. "Enough about me. What's your field of study?"

"Education. I'm going to be a teacher."

"Why teaching?"

"I'm not one hundred percent sure, but I think I want to make a difference to students like me. That makes me sound noble, don't you think?"

"Only if you mean it. What does 'like you' mean?"

"I always had to work really hard to get good grades even with the help of tutors, so I always felt like the odd person out in school. I'd like to try to help kids like me, who struggle, or maybe not, we'll see. Teaching started out as mostly my mother's idea, and, absent any other burning desire, I went along. My family would disown me if I didn't get some type of college degree. So anyways, here I am, one year away from finishing." She paused, silent for a few seconds. "Okay, no more serious stuff, what's your favorite sport?"

"Futbal," he said, pronouncing it the way that only true soccer people did.

"What's your favorite team?"

"The United States or internationally?"

"Both."

"D.C. United, Liverpool, and, during the World Cup, I pull for Germany," he said.

"You traitor," she scoffed, jabbing him in the arm with her finger. "I like your choices, except I always pull for the home team during the World Cup."

"So you know soccer?"

"A little. What kinds of movies do you like?"

"Nothing mushy, so that eliminates the chick flicks," he said, grinning at her.

"What, you don't like happily ever after?" She cupped her hands together and placed them under her chin, once again batting her eyelashes at him.

He laughed some more, thoroughly entertained.

"I'm an action guy," he said, throwing a little of his sexy charm her way, his eyes fixed firmly on hers, conveying a totally different meaning. Sex was now woven into a 150-watt smile now aimed full force at her.

"You're dangerous, you know that, especially with that smile of yours," she said and laughed. "An action guy, huh?" She nudged him in the ribs with her elbow, as she chuckled some more.

He laughed, too.

"Okay, how about music? Who are your favorite artists?"

"Maybe you should be the lawyer," he said, but he answered her question. "I like Coldplay, Simple Plan, Fall Out Boy . . . You?"

"I like all kinds. The ones you mentioned, but a favorite is Stevie Wonder. My dad played him to death at my house growing up, so I've learned to love him, too. Great lyrics. I'm in love at the moment with John Mayer's music, another guy with great lyrics. You may think this is weird, but I love to turn off all of the lights at home at night and listen to him in the dark." She watched him for a reaction but didn't get one. "Told you, weird," she said after a moment.

He studied her face for a second, taking in the humor and passion he saw there. "Not too weird, I could go for sitting in the dark listening to music with you."

"Yeah?" she said slowly, gazing into his eyes.

"Yeah," he answered back, returning her gaze, eyes slightly lowered, a sinful smile on his lips, sex personified.

"You really are dangerous," she said softly, no longer joking.

It surprised both of them to hear the pilot announce that they would be landing in ten minutes. Time had passed quicker than they'd expected. He'd felt a pull toward her, sexual for sure, but maybe more, but that could be due to the unexpectedness of meeting her. He'd enjoyed himself, though.

"Well, I guess, this is where we part company," Reye said, unbuckling her seatbelt and standing. The pilot had just given the passengers the okay to move about, and now people were filing into the aisle in anticipation of the doors opening. It was time to leave, yet they both lingered. Reye could feel him at her back, standing close behind her as they waited. Not close enough that he touched her, but enough to make her nerves tingle.

"Do you have any luggage?" he asked, his lips not far from her ear.

"Yes," she said, turning to him. Her face was close to his now, loving the way he looked up close, feeling warm all over.

"I do, too. I'll walk with you to the luggage terminal."

"Okay," she said, trying to clear her head.

Like school kids in line for lunch, they exited the airplane, stopping to let Reye grab her bag from the overhead compartment, Stephen still at her back. They followed the signs that led to the luggage area. Both were quiet on the walk over, aware of each other now. Reye spotted her bag as it rolled out of the chute, and soon after Stephen located and grabbed his duffel. They walked to the airport's exit, both moving through the sliding doors into the sunshine outside. It was good to be back home, Reye thought. Stephen moved out of the doorway, grabbing her hand to pull her along with him. He let go and turned to her.

"Do you need a ride from the airport?"

"No, I'm parked in the garage."

"Me, too. You mind if I walk you out? I couldn't forgive myself if I saw your picture on the news later and you'd been kidnapped and mutilated." His face grave, his hand placed over his heart as he pretended to be serious.

"Sure, we wouldn't want that on your conscience," she said and smiled. Crossing the sidewalk, they made their way to the parking garage, and within five minutes, they'd reached Stephen's car.

"This is mine," he said as he stopped alongside a shiny blue BMW sports coupe.

"Pretty," Reye said to him as she internally added 'really rich' to his list of attributes.

"It was an undergraduate graduation gift from my parents." Pleasure reflected in his gaze as he looked over the car.

"Nice gift," she said. "I am just over there," she added, pointing to an older red truck parked about ten cars over. "No need to walk me, you can see me get to my truck from here." She turned to face him. "So I guess this is finally where we part. It was really nice talking to you. Maybe I'll see you around campus or on another flight."

He sat now, leaning casually against the trunk of his car, legs outstretched, crossed at the ankles, watching her, his duffel at his feet on the ground. She smiled and he returned it with a slow one of his own. *What the hell,*

Reye thought. "Hand me your phone," she said. If he seemed surprised by the request, he didn't show it, as he dug into his pocket and handed it to her.

"Call me if you want to get together, to talk, or whatever," she said, proceeding to program her name and number into his cell. Stephen laughed and accepted the phone back from her when she was done.

"Thanks," he said and his look turned somewhat more serious. "I enjoyed meeting and riding back with you, too."

Taking another chance that she was reading more than casual interest from him, Reye returned his look and stepped in closer to him, her legs straddling his, which were still stretched out in front of him. She could smell his fragrance, feel his breath, and her eyes shifted away from his and moved to his mouth. He watched her move in to capture his lips in a kiss that was a soft, tentative touching. Captivated again by her boldness, he waited to see what she'd do next. As she pulled back, his teeth captured her lower lip and held it for a second. Her eyes snapped open and met his, which were dancing. He smiled, and then they both laughed.

"See you around, Stephen Stuart," she said, still chuckling while she walked to her truck.

"See you around, Reye." He continued to lean on his car as he watched her walk away. Nice body, he thought again. Nice legs that led up to a small firm backside. Her hips tapered up to a small waist. He remembered how she'd felt when she rammed into his back. Nice breasts, he added. She didn't look back.

⌇

Stephen arrived home from the airport in under an hour. He parked in his garage and entered his apartment. Leaving his duffel at the door, he headed to the refrigerator, grabbed a beer, and walked over to the couch, parking his body in front of the TV. School started on Monday, and he planned to spend the rest of this, his last free day, sitting on his couch, feet propped up. Flipping through the channels, he settled in to watch a soccer game.

After law school, his focus would shift to taking and passing the bar exam, followed by joining the family's law practice. This semester would be the last of his freedom with women, away from the watchful eyes of his parents. Dallas was large in size, but small in its social circles. At home, he'd already started to fend off women looking to get married. Coupled with his mother and her exacting daughter-in-law standards, he knew it would be a battle to stay sane and single. So far, though, he'd never been captured by the desire to settle down with anyone for any extended period of time, and he wasn't looking to start.

He still managed to keep in touch with Beth, an old high school girlfriend, who was more his parents' choice than his. Their families were good friends who had spent a lot of time together growing up and would be overjoyed by their joining. He'd see. In the meantime, he wanted to enjoy his remaining bachelorhood.

Stephen thought back to this morning, Reye and the plane ride home. She'd been funny, sexy, and entertaining, but under the surface, his radar recognized someone who would require work and maybe a commitment. He was so not going there, doing that. So kiss or no, he probably wouldn't call her.

CHAPTER 2

It was a clear, sultry fall day in Austin, and there had been enough rain this year to make the fields green, soft, and firm. Soccer fields and tracks were like second homes to Reye. She'd practiced and played on both most of her life, enrolling in her first soccer academy at age six. Standing here looking out over the fields reserved for intramural games, she grew nostalgic. The academy had introduced her to the basics skills and strategy of the game and she'd perfected them by playing with her brothers and later on select teams in and around the Austin area. Soccer had filled in the spaces schoolwork hadn't covered during the academic school year, keeping her busy after school and on week-ends. Track had taken over her summers. Her mom had made sure she'd been kept busy and free of boys—an idle mind and all that.

She was a good player, quick and fast, but not inter-ested in playing college ball. Actually she'd been more than a little burned out by the constant practices, games, and tournaments. Playing soccer could be rewarding, but it was also hell on the body, and, as her mother loved to say, "It don't pay the rent." Her parents wanted her to get an education, first, no distractions. They were old school that way. So college soccer had been discouraged.

These days she just played for fun on her brother's team, "The Graduates." Her brother Sam founded the team, which competed against other teams of graduates within the university recreational system. Sports were big at the university, especially football, but for those athletes that were good, but not great, or who wanted to pursue school full-time the university offered the chance to get involved in sports via the intramural system.

As intramural systems went, this was one of the oldest and largest among US colleges. The intramurals had different levels of play, A, B, and C, with A being the most skilled. A team's composition could be all female, male, or co-ed, as The Graduates were. The winners of each level received a t-shirt, placement of their team's picture on the intramural website, but, most importantly, bragging rights. Sam had petitioned for Reye, an undergraduate, to join his team, which consisted of eight men and four women.

Sam had been both drill sergeant and coach at practice today. Their team placed second in the playoffs in Division A last year and he wanted to win it all this year, driving the team nuts with his demands. They were currently tied for first with another team, The Wizards, which they would encounter soon. All of the teams met and played each other twice, and the best record won the division.

Reye remained behind after practice to perfect her shot, specifically her aim, and stood now kicking the ball into the goal. Sam walked over to stand in as goalie. He considered spending this time with Reye as fulfillment of one of his big brother duties. You know, check in with little sister, answer questions, provide guidance and wisdom to her youth. They were one year apart, so Reye found his behavior hysterical when it wasn't annoying.

"What's up baby girl? How's school?" Sam said as he caught the ball from Reye's kick, rolling it back to her.

"I'm still here," she answered, kicking again. "What about you, still resolving the world's problems?"

"You know me, no problem too big or too small." He caught the ball and held it. "You need to visit your parents," he said. "You haven't been in a while."

"Yeah, I know, and I will. I haven't been in a mom mood lately." Sam liked to pretend that their parents belonged to her solely; that way he could also pretend that they weren't related. He'd started this pretending in high school, and it was now a long-standing joke between them. Reye, however, did tend to avoid her mother, visiting when she knew her dad would be around, to act as a buffer.

She loved her mother, but she was a pusher. She pushed them to play sports; for the boys it was football, baseball, soccer, and track, and for her, basketball, volleyball, soccer, and track. She pushed them all to be the best in academics, a worthy goal for parents born with talented children. It worked for her brothers as they met and exceeded their mother's expectations. She was the ugly duckling in the sea of swans, excelling at sports only. Reye stood in front of the ball Sam had rolled to her. "I met a guy coming home from Dallas about a week and a half ago. We were both running late and he helped me make the flight. I gave him my number, but he hasn't called," she said.

"I bet you put the old bum rush on him," he said, holding his hands up in front of his face to block the ball Reye had just kicked at him. "You do realize that some guys like to pursue the female," he added.

"Whatever, Sam. You know I don't play by any rulebook. It's too much trouble, and the rules don't make sense to me anyway. Why isn't being me enough? Why do women have to pretend to get a man? What's wrong with going for what you want, if you've determined what that is? And anyways, life is short." Sam watched her and waited until she stopped ranting. He rolled the ball back to her.

"If he's interested, he'll call you," he said.

"Maybe," she said, gathering up her ball and ending the discussion. "Do you think we're ready for the next game?"

"Of course we're ready. I'm in charge here, right?"

Reye rolled her eyes heavenward. "And humble, too." She walked over to her truck and Sam followed, watching as she exchanged her cleats for flip-flops and hopped in.

"Take care, baby girl. I'll see you next game."

"Yeah. You, too."

Later on that week, Reye walked into the East River Community Center located east of town, a more economically challenged part of the city. She was here at the request of one of her professors. Professor Wallace had suggested strongly that she volunteer her time in a program offered here that allowed kids with learning problems to get help after school. Since she served as Reye's advisor and played a major role in Reye's ability to graduate, she took her professor's advice and made an appointment with the director of the program, Dr. Susan Houston.

She approached the main information desk, where a young girl sat talking on the telephone. A striking pink hairpiece was interwoven into long black twists that hung down the girl's waist and lay against light brown skin. Small in stature, she sat behind the desk manning the receptionist station while talking on the telephone. Reye walked over, stood next to the desk, and waited for the young lady to complete her call. She appeared to be in her mid teens, but who knew these days. Young girls grew up so fast. Eleven-year-olds could pass for early twenties nowadays. Reye took a moment to look around the interior of the center. The area next to the desk contained small couches and tables; standard city issued furniture, where children sat slouched and huddled talking together. One brave child sat alone reading a book. On the other side of the entry was a room that held computers and more children. The walls were made of glass so she you could see in. All ages sat around the computers, playing games or, for the more studious ones, completing homework.

Reye turned at the sound of the phone being hung up. The receptionist looked up. "May I help you?"

What was it with women? thought Reye. From little girls to full grown adults, regardless of race, they could run an eye over another woman and sum her up faster than you could blink. Add another second and they could recite your dress and shoe size, the cost of your attire, and if said attire worked for you or not. Reye was treated to such an assessment from the young woman, and, judging by the sour turn of her lips, Reye hadn't measured up.

"My name is Reye Jackson, and I have an appointment with Dr. Susan Houston."

"Let me call her." She picked up the phone, dialed, and sat in silence for a few seconds. "Dr. Houston there is a . . ." She paused and looked at Reye. "What did you say your name was?"

"Reye Jackson."

"A Reye Jackson is here to see you. Okay," she said, and placed the receiver back in its place.

"Have a seat, she'll come and get you when she's ready," the girl said to Reye as she picked up her telephone, hand moving swiftly on the keys, texting. *Dissed by a teenager, how sad,* Reye thought. She found a seat next to the door to sit her disappointing ass down.

Ten minutes later, a woman in her early fifties appeared. A neatly trimmed afro sat atop a handsome face covered in dark brown skin. She was neatly dressed in a cream-colored business suit with matching three-inch pumps. Gold jewelry adorned her hands and ears. She walked over to Reye with both of her hands extended.

"Well, hello, Reye, I'm Dr. Susan Houston. You may call me either Doctor or Susan. Professor Wallace has told me so much about you."

About me, Reye thought to herself as she returned Susan's smile.

"Yes, you," she said as if she'd reached into Reye's brain and plucked that thought out. "Did you have any trouble finding us?"

"No, no trouble at all. I grew up in Austin, so I know my way around."

"Great. Let me show you the center while I tell you about our program," she said and turned away after indicating that Reye should follow her. "Children come to our center after school for assistance with homework. Most of the children require some type of assistance in the three R's, and we do our best to help. But, like most non-profits, we always fall short of recruiting volunteers. Professor Wallace told me that she felt that you had a particular talent, a gift, even, and, more importantly, a heart for those children who had difficulties learning."

"Professor Wallace told you that? About me?" She voiced her thoughts out loud this time.

Dr. Houston laughed, a small sound, like little bells.

"She probably had me confused with someone else," Reye said jokingly. "I would think you would need the best and the brightest to teach kids with learning issues, and that is *so* not me."

"I think you underestimate yourself," Dr Houston said. "Professor Wallace told me that you dedicate yourself ardently to those tasks set before you. We need volunteers who have that passion, and it's a bonus if they come with an insiders view into our student's struggles."

Dr. Houston stepped into a room Reye hadn't seen earlier. Five children, four boys and one girl, sat around those little tables and chairs that she'd outgrown by kindergarten. Pencils, scattered papers, and books littered the tables. A tall, slender Hispanic young man leaned over the back of a student's chair, talking. They all turned at the sound of the door opening.

"Hello, children," Dr. Houston said as she moved to stand in the middle of the room. "I have someone I would like you to meet." She turned and pointed to Reye. "This is Ms. Reye, and she is visiting the center. She may work with some of you after school, like Javier." The young man smiled while five pair of eyes stared at Reye. Dr. Houston introduced Javier, also a volunteer, who had been with the program for two years.

They spent time observing him work with the children. He moved between the children answering questions and redirecting them when they became distracted. After about ten minutes, Dr. Houston stood up to leave, and Reye followed.

"Thank you, Javier and children, for your time," Dr. Houston said. She led Reye from the room. Outside the door, she turned to Reye and asked, "Well, what do you think?"

Reye paused for a second to look around the center again. "If you and Professor Wallace think this is a good idea, I'll do my best to help you."

"Great," Dr. Houston said and beamed.

"When do you want me to start, and how many days would I be here?" Reye asked.

"Well, I was hoping you would be available to work at least three days a week. Monday, Wednesday, and Friday would be preferable, but we are flexible. Do you think that would work?"

"Yes, I do."

"Could you start Monday?"

Yikes, so soon, she thought. "Yes, I think so, but let me double-check my schedule and call you," Reye said. By this time they had walked back to the front entrance of the center.

"Thank you so much for your time, Reye, and I look forward to working with you," Dr. Houston said, moving to engulf Reye in a hug.

"Thank you." Surprised by the hug and the easy camaraderie between them, Reye returned the embrace and left.

Finally, the weekend had arrived, ending a very long and demanding week for Stephen. His fraternity, Phi Beta Nu, was preparing to host an end of the week party and he had been toying with the idea of inviting Reye. He hadn't called her at all, but she'd been in his thoughts. He remembered her smile and her laughing after her fall, but mostly he thought about that parting kiss and contemplated the potential for more. Maybe he just needed to get laid.

He should invite her tonight and see if taking that kiss to its natural conclusion would loosen the hold it had on his interest. What the hell, he thought, and, locating her number in his cell, he called. She answered on the first ring.

"Reye here."

"Hey, stranger, it's Stephen. Remember me?"

"Sure," she said. Her voice sounded cool. "I had given up hearing from you."

"School has been crazy busy, but I'm taking a break tonight and I thought you might want to come over to the frat house for a party. Sorry for the short notice, but I just decided to go myself," he said.

"What time?"

"We don't really have an official start time, but most people get here by about 10:30."

"Okay."

"Do you know how to get here?"

"I think so. Are you near all the other frat houses on College Avenue? There's a Starbucks nearby?"

"Yep, we are about three houses down from that Starbucks. There is a sign in the yard, Phi Beta Nu," he said.

"Okay, I think I can find it."

"I'll be at the house, just ask for me and someone will find me. Okay?"

"Sure. See ya."

Surprise, surprise, she'd given up on hearing from him. She'd been kicking herself for kissing him and maybe being a little too bold. How often had Sam told her that she could be too aggressive? She'd never learned how to play the demure, coy, pretending non-interest game, refusing to relinquish the notion that she couldn't just be herself. Honestly, it seemed deceitful somehow to hide, to pretend to be someone other than you. Although sitting home alone on Friday and Saturday nights hadn't been her goal, either. She was excited about his call, and she refused to consider the reasons behind it, late at night, out of the blue. She really wanted to see him again. She'd been attracted to him from the start and she'd been very much afraid she'd blown it.

Around seven that evening, Stephen pulled into the driveway behind the fraternity house. He spotted his roommate and best friend. "Henri, come give me a hand," he shouted, calling him over to help. He and Henri had been friends since elementary school. They grew up in the same neighborhood, their parents hung out together. He trusted him.

"Dude," Henri said by way of greeting. "You sure you've got enough beer? Don't we usually get kegs?" he asked.

"I'm just the delivery guy, I didn't order anything." Each grabbing a case of beer, he and Henri walked to the back porch and set the first of several cases near the back door.

"I've invited a friend over to the party tonight, and since you've been assigned to the door, I thought you could be on the lookout for her, point her in my direction when she arrives. Her name is Reye," Stephen said, walking back to his car to grab more cases.

"Sure, what does she look like?"

"She's a couple of inches shorter than me, African-American, slim, long legs, nice smile, and short hair."

"Oh," Henri said, eyebrows shooting up. "Where did you meet her?"

"On the trip back from Dallas two weekends ago, remember? We sat next to each other on the plane ride back."

Interesting, Henri thought, picking up another case and following Stephen back to the porch. "Sure, I'll bring her to you." He couldn't remember Stephen ever inviting a girl to a party. Most women came by themselves and they plucked one from the multitude, no strings and no commitments.

"That's unusual for you, isn't it?"

"Not really. She's just a girl I wanted to see again, nothing more."

"If you say so." They made their last trip to the back porch, depositing the last of the beer.

"I'll see you later," Stephen said, walking back to his car.

"No problem," Henri said, watching him leave.

What to wear, Reye wondered as she stood in the bedroom closet of her home trying to choose. Jeans and t-shirts comprised her usual attire, but the desire to feel soft and sexy tonight had her rummaging through her closet and dresser for something more. After about ten minutes, she decided on a dress, simple in form, white, and great against her skin. It cinched underneath her breasts and flared out, resting mid-thigh. She added a pair of matching flat sandals to her outfit and began scrounging around for earrings. She'd showered and dressed, adding perfume, and now stood looking at herself in her mirror. Pleased with her appearance she grabbed her keys, locked her door, and headed for her truck.

Most of the fraternity houses were located near the university and she'd driven by them often, never going in. Old money and legacies lived in those houses. The university was where old money sent its best and brightest to be educated. Reye used to hold a minor grudge against the school, as it was the last school in the school's athletic conference to play African-American football players. She always pulled for the other side, her personal form of protest.

The fraternity was located on a street that ran parallel to the main drag, and it was not known for its parking availability. She ended up parking at a lot about two blocks over and walking the remaining distance. The fraternity houses sat next to each other, covering the next two blocks. Most were two stories high, with old-school porches arranged around them. She passed two homes belonging to other fraternities before spotting the Phi Beta Nu sign in the yard. Lots of people were hanging out on the steps, mostly tanned and white with a few brown spots of Asian, Indian, and African-American sprinkled in. A couple of heads turned her way. With her height, she was usually not hard to miss and received more than her share of second glances. Taking the stairs, she approached the front door where a young man appeared to be the ticket agent or keeper of the door. He was tall, tanned, and even in his careless style of dress, gorgeous. Apparently only the good looking needed to apply to this fraternity. A head full of thick, wavy blond hair graced his head and he gave her the once-over. He was slick about it, but she still caught him looking.

"May I help you?"

"Sure. I am looking for a guy named Stephen, do you know him?"

"Sure, I know Stephen. He was in the kitchen the last I saw him. It's in the back of the house. Lucky for you, he asked me to look out for you. You're Reye, right?"

"Yes," she said.

"I'm Henri. Stephen and I are old friends, we grew up together in Dallas and went to elementary, middle, and high school together. Follow me, and I'll take you to him," he said, turning to lead her through the living room, which was currently serving as the dance floor, to the back of the house. They entered a small kitchen jammed with men and women sitting and standing. Stephen stood with his back leaning against the counter surrounded by males and females who were listening intently to something he said. He was dressed in worn jeans that hugged him in all the right places and a t-shirt, his feet in flip-flops.

The golden one, her nickname for him was an apt description. He appeared to have it all, golden in wealth, looks, brains, and brawn. He held a beer in his hand and talked to the group. Several heads turned as she and Henri entered. His eyes found hers and he smiled.

"Reye, glad you could make it," he said, all smooth and relaxed. The sound of his voice seeped into her skin, traveling straight to her insides, turning them to syrup. It was frightening, this reaction to him. He waved the arm holding the beer to encompass all who were in the kitchen, and said, "Everybody, this is Reye. Reye, everybody." Reye took note of the look of surprise found on some of the women's faces, certainly understanding their reactions. She was surprised, too.

Stephen then proceeded to tell the story of their meeting, hilariously describing her run through the airport and subsequent fall. Everyone laughed and Reye walked over to stand next to his side. He turned his head to her. "Glad you could make it," he said again, more intimately this time. "Want anything to drink?" His eyelids were lowered, a sure sign that the beer he'd been drinking was working its magic. He seemed looser, more relaxed than on the airplane.

"I'll take a beer," she said.

He pulled one from the sink, which had been turned into a makeshift cooler. He handed her the beer and, grabbing her hand, pulled her behind him, walking them through the back door and out into the night. A few couples sat deep in conversation. They didn't look up.

He led her toward two lounge chairs located at the far end of the porch away from the others, in the shadows. He sat in the first lounger, stretching his feet out before him, and she did the same in its twin. It was quieter here and starting to get dark out. They sat quietly for a while, drinking their beer. He had yet to release her hand, and it felt nice being here with him like this. She glanced over at him and he was exactly as she remembered, strong, lean, muscular, but not overly so, beautiful in a very masculine way, with lips that were just the right size and shape. He seemed so sure of himself, like he was used to getting his way in life. He caught her looking at him and smiled. His eyes and mouth were a study in smooth and sensuous. "I'm really glad you came," he said, not breaking the connection of their hands.

"I'm glad I came, too. I've driven by here a thousand times, but this is my first trip inside. I like the architecture of these old houses."

"Me, too."

Reye offered to him what she'd been thinking privately. "It took you a while to call me. I didn't expect to hear from you again," she said.

"I didn't expect to call you, either, to be honest." He paused for a second, taking a deep breath. "Truthfully, you're not my type."

"Ouch," she said, trying to hide her shock. "Then what am I doing here?"

"Don't get mad. I can tell that you're one of those women who require a lot of work. More than I'm willing to give right now."

"You got all that from one ride home on a plane?"

"Yes. It's in the way you carry yourself." He looked over her face, taking in its shape and smoothness. Her lips had been imprinted in his mind, full and soft. That was why he'd called her. "Law school is really demanding, and the last thing I need is a distraction. You have the potential to be a major one. I'd only end up disappointing you," he added.

"Okay," Reye replied. "So why *did* you call?"

"I couldn't forget these," he said, and he softly touched her lips with his finger.

Silence.

Stephen sat down his beer, one hand still holding hers. Removing the beer from her hand, he sat it down next to his. His arms snaked around her waist as he pulled her to him for a kiss. It was soft, his lips barely touching hers, testing her response. She moved her arms to surround his neck and the kiss changed, became more passionate. She opened her mouth for him, both of them tasting beer as their tongues touched tentatively.

Reye pulled back and looked at him, although she wasn't sure what she'd expected to see. A part of her knew she needed to slow down. What did she really know about him? He called and she came, not a good move on her part, and now he'd just told her he wasn't looking for a serious relationship. She ignored that voice, seeing in his gaze a desire equal to her own. Lifting her in his arms, he pulled her from her chair and placed her in his lap. She sat facing him, legs straddling his. His hands moved to her waist and slid upwards towards her breasts. He was glad that she had chosen to wear a dress. It was soft, and she looked very pretty in it. The feel of her body softly encased in it was sexy as hell. Her breath hitched at the touch of his hands on her breasts and he watched her give in to the pleasure, slowly pulling her in for another kiss.

This is what he'd been wanting since the parking lot, and he'd felt an equal yearning in her. Continuing the soft, open-mouth kisses, he played with her tongue, learning the texture of her mouth. They spent seconds, minutes maybe, exploring each other's mouth. He started to pull away, and Reye snagged his lower lip, gently pulling him back to her, and the intensity of the moment changed, becoming more charged. His hands roamed over her body, not landing on a spot long before they moved on to another place. They traveled over her breasts, her shoulders, her face, and downward, to stop at the curve of her ass. Here they glided over until they trapped her in each hand.

He wanted her closer and pulled her hips to his, spreading her legs wide so that she sat in a position that could stimulate them both. She felt him through his jeans, hard and strong. Shifting and rocking her hips forward and backward, he rubbed her against him. His jeans were rough against her, so her hands worked their way to the button at his waist. She opened it and lowered the zipper of his jeans, pulling back the sides to get even closer. *Much better*, she thought as she pushed herself closer to him. She could feel him through the cloth of his boxers, the hardness of him underneath her. Forward and backward he moved her, as close to him as she could be with clothes on.

Tuning out his surroundings, Stephen focused on the movement of her hips as they slid over him, unable to sense anything but this. Jesus! He was going to come, outside, fully clothed, and he couldn't, or wouldn't, stop. He kissed her harder, and his hands turned forceful as they pushed and pulled her over him. Reye moaned long and low into his mouth as she came. His breathing increased as he continued to move her, up and back, his grip on her ass firm. Seconds later, his body grew stiff and he growled into her mouth.

Reye had no idea what to say, to herself or to him. She lay on his chest for a second to regroup. Did she just do what she thought she'd just done, outside for anyone and everyone to see? His hand moved to her waist to steady her as she lifted herself off of him. She stood and straightened her dress and he moved to zip up his jeans.

"Is there a bathroom around here?" she asked, feeling awkward and needing to gain control.

"What?" he asked as he stood up beside her.

"Bathroom," she repeated.

"Oh, yeah, there is one by the pool over there in the cabana." He looked as unsettled as she felt, pointing his arm toward the back of the yard.

"I'll be back." She turned and walked toward the back of the house. She could see a small cabana in the distance, at the end of a large pool.

Stephen sat down, elbows on his knees. He ran his hand over his face and through his hair. When was the last time that had happened? He hadn't dry humped anyone since middle school. He continued to sit, staring out at the cabana, waiting for Reye.

"Hey, dude, out here enjoying the night air?" he heard someone ask. Jumping at the intrusion, he looked up sharply to see Joe standing several steps away. How long had he been standing there? Joe was another frat brother, one that he didn't care for much. "I saw your friend leave, what's her name?" he asked, pretending to remember. "What I wouldn't do for a piece of ass like that. I can see you've been partaking in the delights of Reye. That's her name, I remember now."

"Go away, Joe."

"Dude, is that the way to treat a fellow frat brother? What do you think, Stephen, any truth to that saying that once you go black, you never go back?" he said, laughing at his own joke.

"It's not like that," Stephen said.

"You know what I'm talking about, dude, don't pretend that you weren't out here with her just now. I saw you. Hey, I understand, dude. I'm totally feeling you with the black girl booty call thing. I hear they can be really freaky in bed, and, if tonight is any indication, you have your hands full."

They both looked up as Reye cleared her throat. She'd been standing there listening to them, her face now etched in stone.

They turned to her, Joe with a smirk on his face, Stephen's face apologetic.

"I'd better get going," she said as she stepped up on the porch.

"Hello," Joe said, walking toward her with his hand outstretched. "I'm Joe. We met earlier in the house. Glad you could make it to our party."

Reye didn't respond to his greeting, nor did she shake his hand. His face hardened. "Well, I guess I'll be going so you and Stephen can finish up here. You know if Stephen is not up to meeting your needs, feel free to call me, anytime."

Stephen moved to stand in front of Reye, blocking her from Joe's view. "Leave now, Joe!"

"No worries, man, I'm gone," replied Joe, walking away.

"I'm sorry, Reye, he's an asshole." Looking over her face he asked, "Are you okay?"

"Sure, I'm fine, but I do need to get home," she said curtly.

"Where did you park? I'll walk you out."

"No need, I'm good."

"I'm walking you to your truck, Reye, end of discussion."

"Fine," she said sharply.

Sensing anger and resistance in her stance, he reached for her hand. She pulled it away. He turned to leave and she followed him. She was angry, it was evident in the stiffness of her posture and the briskness of her walk.

They walked through the backyard, around the side of the house, and out toward the street.

"Where did you park?" he asked again.

"Just down the block at the parking lot, and you really don't need to walk me. I can make it by myself," she said.

He ignored her and continued down the street toward her truck. The crowd of students that had been there earlier had moved inside. It was now quiet. You could see them through the windows, dancing and drinking. Neither of them spoke during the walk to her truck.

"This is it," she said, walking to stand next to the driver's side of her truck. Stephen put his hand on the truck's door, preventing her from opening it. Boxing her in, using his arms, body, and the door, he waited until she raised her face to his. She stood, arms folded and crossed, silent. He read hurt and anger in those beautiful brown eyes and felt awful.

"I'm glad you came tonight, and I wish I had called sooner. I'm sorry for the things Joe said back there. They are offensive to me. His views aren't mine," he said.

"Have you ever dated anyone who isn't white before?" she asked sharply, eyes on his face.

"No."

"So why now? Experimenting?" Not waiting for a response, she continued, "You know what, let's put this one on me, my mistake, my bad," she said, in full tirade mode. "I don't want to be anyone's experiment, booty call, or whatever. It was my fault I came. What did I expect? I like you, thought you liked me, but I can see that this was not a good idea!"

Stephen let her rant, and when he'd heard enough he leaned in and put his lips to hers.

"Shhhh," he said against them. "I want to see you again."

"Don't think so," she said, leaning back.

For a moment neither moved nor spoke. Reye looked everywhere but at him and eventually he backed up. She opened her door, slammed it closed, started her truck, and left.

The next day, Stephen called her. "Hi, Reye, what's up?" He tried going for casual and friendly in his tone.

"Nothing much."

"I wanted to tell you that I had a good time last night."

"Great," she responded, her tone flat.

"Would you like to see a movie this weekend?"

"No thanks. I've got a lot of studying to do. You know how things can be at the beginning of a semester, right?" she said.

"Sure." Dismissed, he thought to himself, but he'd give her a little more time and try again.

CHAPTER 3

Reye was slowly getting used to working with the children at the center. There were seven of them who attended every day. Anthony, Eric, and Jésus were Hispanic. Shondra, Tyson, and Deetric, D for short, were African-American. Shane was the lone Caucasian. They all needed varying degrees of tutoring in reading, writing, and math. They all had distinct personalities.

Anthony was the youngest and shortest of the group and all energy, like a tornado. He was funny, a happy kid, already working on his playa status. She imagined him growing up to be a heartbreaking, multi-tasking adult.

Shondra was the only girl in the group and had rapidly reformed Reye's understanding of divas. She now understood that divas were born, not made over time, as she'd originally believed. Ms. Shondra was a little African-American princess with long hair, usually worn in multiple pigtails. She was all sass and ruled the world with an iron hand, or at least the boys in the class.

Shane was the student she'd worried over the most. He'd fallen way behind in his classes at school, requiring a big portion of her attention. He was a sweet kid, painfully shy, and one who could get easily lost in school. She'd hoped to talk to his parents so they could coordinate their efforts. Reye had called his mother at the only number listed on his application. She hadn't received a response yet. Reye knew from experience that being the only anything, anywhere was tough. She'd attended private schools where, with few exceptions, she'd been the 'only one', so she felt a specific kinship with Shane.

Before now she'd never considered working with elementary-age children. She'd thought she was better suited to teach middle and high school, but her time spent at the center so far had her revising her opinions, rethinking old assumptions about herself.

Today had been special. She'd witnessed the implementation of a lesson she'd taught the kids a couple of days ago. She'd overheard one of the kids last week give voice to some pretty hurtful things about another child in the program. In response, she'd sat down with them and discussed how hurtful insults could be, the damage they could cause. To demonstrate, she'd located darts and a picture of a dart gun, explaining the purpose and use of them by vets to calm animals to prepare them for capture. "When you're hit with a dart you feel a sting, like getting a shot," she explained. "A tiny pain at first, but the damage comes later, when the poison or medicine gets under your skin, knocking you unconscious. Our hurtful words can be darts that sting each other at first, but as you remember the hurtful words later, those words can hurt more and for a long time afterward." She sat waiting for her words to sink in, before continuing. "We are going to make our room a dart-free zone." Enthralled, the children watched her as she demonstrated the procedure for dart removals if any were to make their way into their room.

Today was Friday, the end of a long week for the kids. Tempers and nerves were frayed. Reye was supervising the room's cleanup when she heard Shondra shout out in frustration, "Shane, you're so stupid!" Reye looked up to see Shondra walking towards her dragging a tearful Shane along behind her. Before Reye could intervene, Anthony, D, and Eric shouted "incoming" at the top of their lungs, startling Reye with their intensity. All three ran over to Shane, grabbed his arms from Shondra and proceeded to remove a make-believe dart from it. "It's a dart, right, Ms. Reye, when someone tells you that you're stupid," Anthony said, looking grave.

"That's right," she said, getting into the game. "Are we ready to remove it, guys?"

All three heads gazed up at her with too serious expressions on their faces that had her pinching herself to keep from laughing. At this moment they were not children in an after-school program, but had morphed into surgeons prepping for a major life saving operation. "Shondra has to perform the surgery," Reye said, looking over at Shondra, who by now had recognized her error. "Let me get my doctor's bag," she said, demonstrating her superb acting skills as she pretended to remove a dart and cleanse the wound.

"What do we do now?" Reye asked.

Shondra looked at Shane. "I'm sorry for the dart."

"What do you say, Shane?" Reye asked encouragingly.

"It's okay," he said, smiling in pleasure at all of the attention.

"Thank you, skilled surgeons, your work here is done," Reye said, also smiling, ushering them back to the cleanup, beyond pleased with their understanding.

Stephen looked around The Garden, the restaurant and bar where most of his friends from school hung out. It was also the place where the soccer teams came after their weekend games. The Garden had been an old hole in the wall that had been refurbished about ten years ago. Wood floors and wood walls gave it the appearance of an old down-on-its-luck hunting lodge with a college-themed décor. National college and university banners dangled from the ceiling, most worn out years ago. The university's banner was the only relatively clean one, displayed prominently above the front door, religiously replaced every year. Wooden picnic tables sat close to each other to achieve maximum occupancy. The food, standard American fare, was inexpensive, a necessity for college students.

Stephen sat at one of the tables waiting for a waitress to take his order. He was tired and restless. With the demands of law school, soccer, and monster study sessions, he should have been exhausted, but instead he was fidgety. It has been almost two weeks since he'd met Reye at his fraternity's party. He'd call her relentlessly at first to reconsider going out with him, but to no avail. The answer was always the same. No. So getting a yes now had moved from more that just a desire to a personal mission.

Reye was always friendly when he called. Annoyingly polite, she even thanked him for calling and asked about school, but her answer was always the same: no. No, I won't meet you for coffee. No, I won't meet you at the library. No, I wouldn't like to go to a movie. Hey, he didn't have time for any of the above anyway, but it irritated him that she'd not given him another chance, wouldn't even consider it. It wasn't even his fault. He hadn't said any of those things to her.

Who needed this kind of aggravation? He knew plenty of women who would welcome his attention, and why he was still pursuing this one he'd yet to understand. It was the possibility of sex with her that was making him twitch. It was sex, plain and simple. He'd created this super fantasy in his mind of what it would be like with her. And it was this unusual desire that had been created from that one night at the party. He'd sampled enough to drive him crazy. He was sure that if he could only follow through, take it to its natural conclusion, he could exorcise her from his mind. Take tonight, for example. He'd just played a hard, competitive game against the Cobras, a fairly good soccer team in the A division of the intramural league. Not the best, but not recreational league, either. He should be exhausted, but not so. He labeled Reye as the source of his unusual moodiness.

He sat waiting for Henri to arrive for their usual routine following a game, rehashing and celebrating their win and planning strategy for the next match. He'd looked up to find Henri and Joe approaching. What the hell was he doing here? He hadn't spoken to Joe since the night of the party. Both Henri and Joe played on his team. They sauntered over to the table, plopping down next to him. The waitress, a perky blonde who seemed available for more than taking orders, came over.

"What would you like?"

"I'll have a cheeseburger," said Henri.

"Make that two," Joe said, giving his menu to the waitress.

"Three," said Stephen, "and could you bring over a pitcher of beer for us?"

"Sure. Anything else?"

"Nope, that's all for now. Thanks," Stephen said, giving her a quick smile.

"I've got to take a leak," Henri said, excusing himself, and walked to the back of the restaurant where the restrooms were located. The Garden also offered take-out to its patrons with a separate entrance in the back to avoid overcrowding. The Garden was a popular place. Henri passed by the take-out line on his way to the bathroom, scanning the room as he went. He spotted Stephen's Reye in line. Taking a detour, he walked over to her, calling out her name.

She looked up. "Reye?" he asked. "Phi Beta Nu party, remember?"

Stephen's handsome friend, the keeper of the door at the party, she remembered. He'd been nice to her.

"Hi. Henri, right?"

"Yes, you've got a good memory."

"You were at Stephen's party?"

"Yes, that was me. How are you?"

"Fine," she said. "You?"

"I'm okay. Hey, Stephen is here with me, sitting towards the front, we've just finished a soccer game." He pointed toward his jersey. "You could bring your order over and join us."

"No, that's okay. I've got to get home," she said.

"You sure?"

"Yeah, I'm sure, but thanks. It was nice seeing you again."

"Yeah. You, too," Henri said, turning to continue on to the bathroom. He waved to Reye a final time as he returned to his table, itching to watch Stephen's reaction to this newsflash. He'd listened to him bitch and moan for the last two weeks. By now Henri was unapologetic about finding humor in his friend's predicament.

"You'll never guess who's here." Henri looked directly at Stephen as he sat down at the table.

"Who?"

"Reye. She is in the take-out line in back," Henri said.

"Reye's here?"

"Yeah, didn't I just say that? She is in the take-out line in back," Henri repeated, slowly enunciating every word.

"I'll be back in a minute." Stephen stood and walked away.

"Sure," Henri said to his retreating back. Joe shook his head in disgust.

Stephen entered the back portion of the restaurant and found Reye leaning against the wall, her back to him. She looked great and extremely fit in a pair of form-fitting jean shorts, t-shirt, and sandals, typical college student attire. She wore a baseball cap pulled low over her eyes. Surely she wasn't trying to hide from him, he thought. He walked over and stood behind her, close enough that he could smell her scent. Leaning in, he whispered in her ear, "Hello stranger."

"Stephen," she said, her voice neutral.

"Come here often?"

"Sometimes," she said, although she still faced forward.

"Come eat with me?"

"Nope."

"I'm here with Henri. You like him. Come eat with us, then?"

"Nope. Nice guy, that Henri, not like some of your other friends," she said.

"Can't give that a rest, can you? I'm not responsible for all the idiotic things people say."

Reye turned her head to face him, lifting her hand up, palm outward. "Been there, done that, please don't explain again." Before Stephen could respond, her order was called. She walked over to the counter to pay. "Thank you," she said to the boy behind the counter as he handed her order over. Swinging her book bag over her shoulder, she walked to the back exit and out through the back door. Stephen rushed out to follow her.

"Wait," he said, catching up to her just outside the door. It was starting to get dark. "Where are you going?" He stepped in front of her, halting her progress.

"Not that it is any of your business, but home," she answered.

"Where is your truck?"

"Again, not your business, but I didn't drive it today. I took the bus to school."

"So does that mean that you live around here?"

"Good bye, Stephen."

"How about I give you a ride home?"

"Nope." She started walking away from The Garden.

"Wait, I'll walk with you." Frustrated, he started after her. "You can be incredibly difficult, do you know that?" he said, catching up to her.

"Don't you have somewhere to be, someone to be with?"

"Apparently, I'm trying to be with you."

Reye lifted an eyebrow, pretending indifference, but warmed by his attention.

"Well, come on if you're coming," she said, stepping around him.

Stephen grabbed her book bag from her shoulder. They walked for a while in silence until he spoke.

"It wasn't me that said those things about you, you know?"

"Yeah, well, I don't need the hassles, and you are who you hang out with, right?"

"I don't hang out with him," he said, striving not to get angry.

"So you say."

They walked about two blocks through Reye's neighborhood. Funky, colorful homes owned by young families mixed with the old-fashioned neatly kept homes of its senior citizens. Homes here boasted color, swings and toys in the yard, neatly trimmed flower beds, yard art, all characteristic of this part of town, where homes were reflections of the owner's personality. The neighborhood was built before deed restrictions and home owner's associations that traded individual freedom and personality for uniformity and order.

They turned at the next corner and Stephen spotted Reye's truck. It sat next to a small brick house painted grey, trimmed in white with a very red front door. Plantation shutters covered the windows and the yard was neatly trimmed with flowerbeds holding a profusion of yellow, blue, and pink flowers.

"Nice house," Stephen said, looking at the huge tree sitting in the middle of the yard, surrounded by flowers.

"It's home," Reye said, walking down the sidewalk leading to the front door. "My dad preached financial freedom to us beginning when I was in diapers. Save, own your own home, yadda, yadda, yadda, be self-sufficient, take care of what belongs to you. He purchased a fixer-upper for each of us and taught us how to do the fixing up. If my brothers could do something, I had to learn to do it, too." Reye reached the front door and took her book bag from Stephen. She gave him her food order to hold so that she could search for her key. Finding it, she unlocked the door and pushed it open enough for her to drop her book bag on the floor inside. She reached to take her meal from Stephen's hands. "Thanks for walking me home."

"You're welcome." He moved his hand holding her food out of her reach and looked into her eyes. "This is the last time I'm going to ask you, Reye. Hang out with me again?"

"Last time I'll have to say it, then. No."

"Bye," he said tersely, handing her food over to her.

CHAPTER 4

Another Saturday night found Reye at home alone watching a movie she'd rented. Her cell phone rang. It was Sam, calling to remind her of the game tomorrow. As if she could forget it, her team would play Stephen's for the first time. Surprise. He'd worn his jersey that day at The Garden, the last time she'd seen him. The Wizards logo was clearly displayed on the front of he and Henri's shirts.

"Hey, don't forget the game tomorrow. I need you to play forward for the whole game. I've done some scouting, and I think you can beat at least one of their defenders."

Sam took this soccer business way too seriously. Scouting an intramural game was taking things a bit far, as far as she was concerned. "Sure, no worries, I'll be there."

"See you tomorrow."

"Sam," she said, "I know you've dated girls of other races before. What was that like?"

"That was random, why do you ask?"

"I'm just curious."

"I don't date girls because of their color, and women are basically the same, give or take some cultural differences. You know how you women can be sometimes.

Irritating comes in every color. What matters is that you like the person and have something in common with them."

"I know, but did you ever encounter other people's hostility?"

"Sometimes, but that's why you have to be sure you like the person, because in the end it has to be about the two of you. Why, you meet someone?"

"Maybe, not sure if I like him enough, scratch that, I do like him, but I'm not sure he likes me. I don't want to be something different and new for him, you know, another notch on his belt," she said.

"Well, what do you want to do?"

"I'm trying to figure that out."

"Well, sometimes you have to step out on faith, you know. Nothing ventured, nothing gained. I'm starting to sound like your mother. So, on that note, let me know if you need me. I could meet him, you know, use that big-brother-checking-out-little-sister's-boyfriend routine."

"No, thanks, and anyway, enough about me. I'll see you tomorrow at the game."

Sitting here in the dark, alone she could be honest with herself. She was anxious about seeing Stephen tomorrow. He didn't know that she played intramural soccer at the university or that their two teams would play each other. She hadn't mentioned that to him on the plane ride home, and, true to his word, he hadn't called since he'd walked her home. Why was she being such a hard ass? Because she'd gotten her feelings hurt. But so what? Actually Joe was the one responsible for hurting her feelings, not Stephen. Stephen had seemed sincere in his apologies and efforts to see her again. What other guy had ever been that persistent?

The hard truth was that she was afraid. She was feeling plain old simple fear of the unknown. Intuitively she sensed that he could hurt her, really hurt her. She wanted him more than anyone she'd met or gone out with. What made him so different? Who knew? He represented the standard definition of success that most women wanted in their men. He was wealthy, great looking, smart, and athletic, and that was just the fundamental tally. Throw in his talented hands and mouth attached to *that* body and he was *mind altering*.

She was confident in herself and her abilities, on most days, anyway. Other days, though, she suffered doubts. One part of her, the part she called her half empty self, didn't believe she would be of interest to a guy like Stephen, and couldn't understand why he had been so persistent. His kind usually went for his beautiful counterparts. Why was he interested in her? Was she some game? The other self, the half glass full self, said girl, what are you waiting for? GO FOR IT! So what if he only wanted sex, when was the last time she had some? She could handle just sex. She was a big girl and crazy to throw an opportunity like this away. And since when had she become a quitter?

Enough already, she thought, she needed to get some sleep, needed to be rested for tomorrow's game. She wanted to play really, really well.

Sunday was the perfect day of the week for Stephen. Usually this day remained free from scheduled obligations, and most times he slept in. Saturday nights could last until the next morning if he found a willing woman, but that rarely occurred at his apartment. If he met someone the night before, they went back to her place. If she didn't have a place, he moved on. Hassle free was the goal, didn't want the worry of having to relocate Saturday night's leftovers from his place Sunday morning. They almost always didn't want to leave.

He shared an apartment with Henri, who had similar standards. Although Henri was much more circumspect regarding potential bed partners, but they both respected each other's privacy.

As Stephen lay in bed this Sunday morning, as usual his thoughts turned to Reye. He promised himself he wouldn't call her, and he hadn't. It didn't make sense to work that hard when there were willing women available. The problem was he didn't want others, at least for now. For some reason he had yet to wrap his head around, it had to be her. He had always been able to move on from a girl. Yet, here he was. The mere thought of Reye had him getting hard. He could remember vividly how her body had felt and how it had fit so snugly on his. If they could generate that amount of heat with clothes on, he couldn't bear to imagine the heat that they would create with her naked skin touching his.

Up, he had to get up and get some lunch and then head over to the fields. The game started at three. He stood up, grabbed his t-shirt, and walked to the kitchen. His mother's monthly food service delivery kept the kitchen stocked with minimal help from Stephen and Henri. Having an overindulgent mother worked for him most times. The food service delivered staples—bacon, eggs, and bread, as well as things he and Henri could cook in between eating out or ordering take out—once a month. Usually, his school schedule was way too hectic for culinary treats, but today he would treat himself to a home-cooked breakfast, or brunch, whatever it was called.

He was one of the last of his team to arrive at the fields. The day was perfect for a game. He loved the fall, clear crisp days, lots of sun. Baseball, basketball, and tennis were some of the sports he sampled in high school, but soccer would always be his love. All over the world, people regardless of race, sex, wealth, or age played. No pads, no helmets, just your body and skills pitted against another. Defender was his position of choice and he gloried in his ability to shut down the other team's offense. Most dudes wanted to play the forward position, achieving status by scoring, but not him. He wanted to stop those guys, send them back home crying to their mamas. He loved the chance to match abilities with anyone who thought to run by or over him.

He was looking forward to this game. This was supposed to be a fairly good team with a record that was identical to his team's. They had to play each team twice during the regular season, and it would be nice to beat this team today. If they could win both times, they would be the outright winners of this division, avoiding a playoff game. They'd come in first in this division last year, second the year before that.

Most of his team members were already on the field warming up. Standing near his sideline bench, he took the opportunity to size up the opponent. Hard to tell anything from looking at them, he had learned long ago that outward appearances were deceiving. There were four girls, the requirement that allowed a team to be considered co-ed, the same number as his team. It is difficult to recruit women, most preferring to play against other women. He observed the women as they stood in a small circle passing the ball between them. A blonde, somewhat attractive, athletic looking; so was the brunette standing next to her. An African-American girl with short locks stood with her back to him. He knew that hair, that body, she was tall. "Turn around," he whispered to no one. She did, leaving the circle to retrieve a ball. His eyes roamed her face. Reye. Racking his brain, he tried to remember their prior conversations. Did she tell him she played soccer? He would have remembered that. Yep, it was her all right. Long legs he would recognize anywhere, encased in shorts that weren't designed for soccer, or at least not when playing against men. His eyes traveled over breasts tucked into a snug t-shirt, remembering the feel of those, too, and up to her face. She stood staring back at him.

He was surprised, pleased, and slightly turned on. His body was particularly pleased at seeing her in shorts. She peeled away from the circle of girls and walked slowly toward him, hips swinging slowly from side to side. He watched her walk to him, not moving to meet her. It was nice to have her come to him for a change, and pure pleasure to watch those hips sway.

"You play soccer for this team?"

"Yeah. I'm surprised to see you, too. You didn't tell me you played."

"I play with my brother Sam, actually this is his team."

"You must be good if you're playing in this division."

"Not really, he just needed another female."

"What position do you play?"

"Forward. You?"

"I usually play halfback."

"Well, good luck," she said, turning to walk back to her side of the field.

"Yeah. You, too."

The referees had arrived and had taken their positions on the field. Reye lined up against the left defender on Stephen's team. She overheard someone mention that the defender's name was Frank. Stephen would play right defender. Scoring against Frank was like taking candy from a baby. She was much more skilled than he, and faster, quickly scoring two goals for her team.

Sam's strategy was different for each game, depending on the information garnered from his scouting expeditions. Today he wanted Reye to play forward against the weaker defender and score. In most games, this was an effective strategy as most men usually underestimated her, to their misfortune, of course. She would get one or two goals before they recognized the mismatch and changed their line-up. Today wasn't any different. She scored for the second time a minute before the first half ended. They were up by two at the half and it was now time for Sam's usual halftime speech.

Changes and adjustments were made for the second half of the game. Sam expected Stephen's team to correct the mismatch and play their better defender against Reye. To counter this, Sam would move up to the front to play in the forward position opposite Reye. He and Reye played well together. They'd been playing together since grade school. They'd played against their older brothers, who'd picked on them. Learning to play together had been a matter of survival.

The second half started. As predicted, Stephen moved to play defender against Reye.

"Think you can keep up?" she asked as she stood in position.

"I won't need to. You seem the type who quits when things get tough."

"What is that supposed to mean?" she asked him. He shrugged, and the whistle blew starting the second half. The ball was passed to Reye, who received it and began to move down the field. Stephen stood away from her, taking time and space to watch her commit to a direction. She ran towards him and he stepped up to block the ball, stopping her momentum, kicking the ball out of bounds.

"What, you can't get by me?"

"Watch me," she said.

She received the ball again and moved it downfield. Stephen stepped to her and she switched the ball to her other foot and ran by him. He was quick and able to catch her, but not before she passed it off to Sam, who took a shot on goal. The goalie watched it fall into his hands. Reye walked back to her position and play resumed. The ball was passed to Reye again, this time Stephen leaned in with his shoulder and interrupted her drive. He swept in front of her, aligning his back to her front, taking the ball away, kicking it out of bounds again. Reye and Stephen played tough, demanding soccer, in their own world for the remainder of the game. They pushed, shoved, ran, and fell over each other, one driving to score, the other determined to prevent it. Stephen's team was able to pull out the win, because Sam's strategy had left them weak in the defender position and Stephen's team had taken advantage. They scored three times in the second half to win the game.

Both teams walked over to their benches to drink water and change out of their cleats. Sam walked over to Reye. "So what's going on between you and the defender?"

She was seated on the bench removing her cleats, and looked up sharply at his question. "Nothing. Why?"

"Just wondering, you two were all alone on the field. We all noticed," Sam said. He moved his head and hands to include the other players on her team. Reye put her socks and cleats in her bag and slipped her sandals on while continuing to talk.

"No, I just really wanted to win. You know how I dislike being underestimated."

"Sure, Reye, whatever you say," Sam said, preparing to walk away.

"Whatever, Sam," she returned. "Are you coming to The Garden?"

"Sure. I'll be there," he said, and left the field.

Reye walked over to her truck, meeting both Stephen and Henri en route. "Good game, Reye, didn't know you played, let alone so well," said a smiling Henri.

"Thanks," she replied.

She looked over at Stephen, who stood covered in a thin layer of dirt and sweat. She felt his body calling out to her as she looked him over. His clothing clung to his body, reminding her of her time spent draped over him. She moved her eyes from his body to his face and she could tell from the smug smirk of his lips that he'd caught her staring.

He had been wiggling his fingers in front of her trying to get her attention, and laughed outright at the look of chagrin on her face. "We are going over to The Garden for some beer, would you like to join us?" he asked, trying to contain his laughter.

She smiled at being caught, laughing in spite of her embarrassment. "Our team is going over, too," she said.

"Seriously," Stephen said. "You're a really strong player. I had to work hard to keep up with you."

"Thank you. You're no slouch, either," she said, moving to open her truck door. "See you two later."

Reye walked into The Garden to find that Sam had already secured a table for their team. The Graduates were well into their beers as they looked over their menus. Everyone had arrived. It was as always, lively at The Garden after a game, win or lose. It was loud, filled with the grunts, shouts, and friendly trash-talking that was found between teams after a game. Saturdays at The Garden were reserved for festivities surrounding the other football game, American football. Sundays at The Garden were reserved for the real "futbal", soccer. Reye enjoyed hanging here reliving the game, where she usually accepted praise from her fellow teammates for her exceptional play. She slyly looked around The Garden searching for Stephen, who hadn't arrived yet. So she sat, both nervous and excited, surrounded by her brother and her teammates, but only concerned about the appearance of one person. As much as she would wish those feeling away, they didn't seem to want to go. So why not give into them? She had always taken pride in her ability to push past her fears. Why stop now? So, she decided tonight that if Stephen seemed interested still, she would go for it. Having reached this conclusion, she sat back, more than ready for him to arrive.

Stephen pulled into the parking lot with Henri riding shotgun. He cut the engine and stared out the window for a second, lost in thought. He had been quiet on the drive over, his mind occupied with Reye. What to do with her? He hadn't called her, but he'd felt his connection to her reignite today on the field. He didn't want any more rejection, but he wasn't ready to let it go, either. He decided that if he detected any interest from her, he'd try again.

"So what's up?" Stephen turned at Henri's question, a little surprised. He been wrapped up in his thoughts and had forgotten Henri was there.

"What do you mean?"

"You know what I mean. You still like her?"

"Yeah, so what?"

"You haven't asked for my opinion, but for what it's worth, I think it's mutual. I watched her scoping you when you were playing," he said with a smirk. "Here's another question for you. Why her?"

"Damned if I know," Stephen said. With that said, they headed into The Garden.

Reye noticed him immediately as he entered with Henri. He spotted her and gave her a nod in acknowledgement. He didn't come over, but headed instead to his team's table. Her stomach dropped. What had she expected? She looked around her table. She'd been half listening to the conversation going on around her. It had moved on from the soccer game to graduate school stuff, which didn't interest her. She hadn't wanted to talk anyway; her mind was occupied elsewhere. Now that Stephen had arrived, she spent her time glancing covertly at his table. Unfortunately, he seemed engrossed in the conversation surrounding him. Okay, enough of this! She was going home. In a last ditch effort, she would stop by his table and congratulate his team on her way out. She wouldn't continue to sit here doing nothing, watching and waiting. Sam laughed at Reye as she stood up to leave. "You're leaving?"

"Yeah, I think so. School tomorrow."

"Sure," he responded sarcastically. She looked down at him, giving him the evil eye.

"What does that mean?" Reye asked as Sam looked at her, pretending innocence.

"You can't keep your eyes off Mr. Defender is more like it."

"Whatever. I'm out of here." Taking a deep breath she walked over to Stephen's table. All eyes turned to her.

"I just wanted to stop by to congratulate you all again for your win. We look forward to playing you again, and we won't take it so easy on you next time." She smiled and they laughed. Most looked at her through bright and shining eyes. Beer made people very friendly. Stephen sat watching her. She couldn't read his expression, but after she finished, he introduced her to the team members as his friend. Some of them she'd recognized from the fraternity party. Henri she knew and Joe she refused to look at. Stephen retold the story of how they'd met at the airport and that he'd been surprised to see her on the field. His face as he told the story was unguarded, open, with that slightly wicked smile of his that left her feeling all liquid inside. She loved that smile. His eyes were clear, filled with humor.

At this moment, she wanted him beyond anything she'd ever felt before. "Well, good night," she said, moving away from the table. His teammates resumed their talking and he stood up to follow her, reaching her at the door.

"I'll walk you to your truck," he said.

"Okay," she said, walking through the door and out into the night. It was dark out, the lights from the garden providing very little illumination. She took the lead with Stephen following closely, his hand in the small of her back as they walked, both of them quiet. Reaching her truck she turned to face him. He stood closer to her than she'd thought.

"Thanks for walking me out." Before she could lose her nerve she blurted out an invitation. "Would you like to come over for dinner Saturday night?" He didn't answer, just stepped in closer to her, so close that she could see the new growth of hair on his chin. He placed both of his hands at her waist and slid them upward to rest just under her breasts. His eyes remained locked with hers and his thumbs begin to graze the undersides of them, a slow movement back and forth. Slowly he moved in and tugged her lower lip in between his teeth before settling his lips on hers, kissing her softly. She opened for him and his tongue marched in. She felt like one of those cartoons that turned into a pool of liquid and slid into a puddle on the floor. Slowly he relinquished her mouth, but he still held her.

"I would love to come to your house for dinner."

Reye gazed into his eyes, her mind a blank canvas as she tried to gather her thoughts. They'd packed a bag, destination unknown.

"What time?" he asked, as she continued to stare back at him. Stephen gave her a small shake and asked her again, now grinning, "What time Saturday evening?"

"Seven? Do you remember where I live?"

"I remember where you live, and I have your number that you programmed into my phone in case I get lost." He removed his hands from her body and backed away so she could get into her truck.

"See you soon," he said as she backed her truck out and drove away.

He shook his head and smiled to himself as he watched her truck go down the road. Some of his parts needed time to cool before he went back into the restaurant. He wanted her badly. Bare, his skin touching hers, laid out before him, on top and under him, in all the ways that were possible. He would have to throw himself into his studies this week if he wanted to hold on to his sanity until Saturday. Perhaps afterwards, he could finally put her into perspective. He would scratch an itch that had plagued him since the party. Who was he kidding? His obsession with Reye had begun at the airport, when she fell on her butt and then sat there, smiling and laughing at herself. He couldn't wait.

CHAPTER 5

Reye arrived home just as her cell phone rang. It was Sam. "Hey, it's my annoying big brother Sam calling," she said by way of greeting.

"I saw you leave with Mr. Defender. Is he the one you were talking about the other night?"

"Yes, nosey, his name is Stephen. Remember when I spent the week in Dallas taking care of Jack's rug rats?"

"Yeah."

"Well, we met at the airport on the way back and got to know each other a little on the plane ride home."

"You like him?"

"Yep, he invited me to a party that didn't end too well. One of his fraternity brothers said some things about African-American women that I found offensive. I guess I needed to make sure Stephen didn't feel the same way."

"Are you sure now?"

"I think so. I want to try, anyway. What do you think?"

"It's your call, your consequences. Just be careful."

"I will."

"You know I'm always around if you need to talk."

"Look at you, being nice to your little sister. Thanks, Sam, that means a lot to me." Reye hung up and her cell phone rang again. It was Stephen this time. Her heart did a little dance. *Please don't be calling to cancel,* she thought.

"Hello."

"Hey, it's Stephen. Just making sure you hadn't changed your mind about Saturday."

"Nope, it's still on, and I'm looking forward to it."

"Yeah, that makes two of us. Do I need to bring anything?"

"Nope, just you."

"I will. Take care and I'll see you Saturday."

Reye's after-school class was growing. She looked around the room at the three additional children that had joined the program since she'd started. Her group now totaled ten. She had learned a lot about the kids, and a lot about herself, since joining the center. As part of the university's degree course work, she'd been introduced to the concept of teaching children based on the way in which they received and processed information. Luckily she'd paid attention, not realizing she'd have to put her knowledge to use so soon.

Tutoring the kids at the center had challenged her perceptions about how kids learned. Her involvement with them, her need to see them succeed, drove her to find out as much as she could to help them. Her free time was now spent reading, researching, practicing, and testing theories learned on and with the kids during the program. The belief that one could identify the way in which a particular child learned opened a door for her.

She began to understand her own issues with learning, finding answers to questions that had plagued her growing up. She now understood why she'd done better with some teachers and less so with others. Her favorite teacher had been her third grade teacher, Mrs. Sanchez, an older Hispanic lady. She'd sat with Reye, continuously reviewing the sounds that letters made, over and over until Reye understood. Reye had fallen behind her other classmates in school, and she needed the extra attention. Mrs. Sanchez had also used pictures to help Reye remember. But it had been the repetition that made the information stick with her. Mrs. Sanchez had shown so much patience, along with her mother's help at home. Their efforts resulted in a tenfold improvement in her reading that year. Now she recognized how much Mrs. Sanchez and her mom had done for her. Armed with the knowledge regarding learning styles and with a new level of self awareness, she felt compelled to come up with the means to incorporate what she'd learned every day. She observed her kids, worked with them, seeking to identify each of their styles. More importantly, she sought a way to explain these concepts to them, hoping to arm them with tools to use to help themselves once they'd moved on from the program.

Reye settled on several funny phrases to describe the differing styles. "Seeing is Believing", "Shake, shake, shake your body", "Talk to me, baby", and "Order is Among Us" were the names she created.

"Seeing is believing" was the name for the kids who learned visually, by seeing images. They typically enjoyed art and drawing and were interested in how machines worked and with inventing. They were often accused of being daydreamers in class.

"Shake, shake, shake your body" referred to the kids who processed information using physical sensations. They were highly active, not able to sit still for long periods of time, and they showed you rather than told you. They needed to touch and feel the world. They were naturally athletic and loved sports, and were quick to be labeled with attention deficient disorder.

"Talk to me, baby" described her talkers. They were joke-tellers, and language came easy to them.

"Order is among us" referred to the kids that were logical and orderly thinkers. They were the easiest to teach. They were good at figuring how things worked.

She was proud of her kids and how much they'd improved. Michael, a shy African-American boy, had joined their group a few days ago. He'd walked in the class with his head down, where it remained while he suffered though introductions to the other children. Shane, usually shy, approached him. "What are you?"

Michael lifted his head, giving Shane a puzzled look. "I'm Michael," he answered, his voice high pitched.

Shane, not receiving the answer he needed, but not giving up yet, asked again. "I know that, but what are you?" Again, Michael looked puzzled. Shane continued, "Are you a shake, shake, shake your body?" He demonstrated by moving his hips. Reye hadn't been able to resist adding movement to accompany that phrase, not really expecting any of the children to perform it. "Or are you a seeing is believing kid?" Not waiting for an answer, he said, "I'm a seeing is believing kid."

Now Michael really was confused. Reye walked over to him and explained what that meant. "What Shane is trying to ask you is how you learn. He knows that we all learn differently." She looked at Shane with a smile.

"We'll find your learning style as we get to know you, and that will help us and you with your homework. For now, how about we finish introducing you to the other kids and show you around the center."

It was Saturday evening and Reye was going through her pre-dinner checklist. She'd gone grocery shopping earlier in the day and purchased wine, spaghetti, salad ingredients, and bread. The meal she had planned was one of the few things she could cook decently. Who couldn't boil spaghetti and add sauce to it? But in light of this special occasion she splurged, purchasing a more expensive brand of sauce instead of her usual Ragu.

Dessert tonight would be her if she were lucky, but just in case, she'd also purchased fruit tarts from a bakery down the street. Reye had gotten to know the family that owned it, a husband and wife with two school-age kids. She'd stop in on her way to catch the bus if she hadn't been able to eat breakfast at home. She admired the way this family managed to incorporate the whole work-life balance thing. They owned a home in the neighborhood, owned the bakery nearby, and rode bicycles instead of driving to work. Not driving a car in Texas was saying something. She didn't know if they owned one or not. She'd only seen them with bikes. In the morning, she'd catch a glimpse of them, the dad and the two children, helmets on everyone's heads, backpacks secured on the backs of all three, as they rode toward school. Dad was the leader of this motley caravan, stopping to make sure they kept up and helping them to navigate around and through busy intersections. It was so cool to see them, and she loved watching them.

She'd picked up some condoms and put them in the drawer next to her bed. She'd also put some in the couch seat cushions, under the couch, in the kitchen and other strategic places around her house. Safety first, and she was a safety girl.

She'd heated the spaghetti sauce earlier and added a few of her secret ingredients. All that was left to do was to boil the noodles and brown the bread. The salad sat prepared and waiting in the refrigerator.

She'd spent considerable time on her body today, too. She soaked herself in a tub filled with her favorite scent and conditioned her skin until it was as soft as a baby's bottom. Well, maybe not that soft. She donned her favorite khaki shorts that hugged her curves and came to just above her knees. She added a top in white that looked great against her skin. Next came a pair of flats and some dangling earrings, and she was done. It was casual at-home wear, but it showed off her body to perfection. She'd remembered that they both liked John Mayer, so she added his most recent CD to the mix. She was ready. The house was usually kept clean, she'd given it extra attention last night.

Stephen had stopped by the market and picked up some flowers. He couldn't remember ever doing that before, not since prom, and even then his mother had picked those up. The Garden had been his starting point as he followed the path he'd taken walking Reye home. He parked his car behind her truck in the drive and walked up to her door. Again, he was impressed with her home. You could tell that someone took time with it. There were attractive flowers in a neat bed, the yard was cut and the hedges trimmed. Did she take care of that herself? He knocked on the door and waited. It opened almost immediately. He stood there for a second, taking in her eyes and her wide smile. She was so open sometimes that he felt afraid for her.

"Come in," she said. He tracked her eyes as they moved to his hand and took in the flowers he held.

"These are for you," he said, handing them over to her.

"Thank you, they are beautiful. Make yourself at home while I put these in something." God, she thought, what was she, the hostess with the mostest straight out of a scene from a family sitcom. It was annoying sometimes, but she couldn't help herself. Her mom had relentlessly drilled manners into her and her brothers.

Stephen watched her walk away, his body responding to the picture she presented. Her clothes fit her like a second skin. To take his mind off that part of his anatomy, he looked around her home. It was cozy. Light green, light blue, and yellow covered different walls in the room, and the molding and trim were white. Tiled floors were covered by equally colorful rugs, matching the colors on the walls. There were lots of framed posters anchored to the walls. Pictures covered most surfaces, her with her family, and he guessed with friends, all with faces smiling into the camera.

In the kitchen, Reye located a pitcher to put the flowers in. F.I.N.E described that man, fanning herself with her hand as she set about putting the flowers in a vase. He'd kept his attire casual, too— cargo shorts topped off with a blue polo that matched his eyes. He was her "Mr. Golden" all tall, lean, and sexy. She went back to join him in the living room.

"I like your home. You like *color*," he said as she re-entered the living room. He put heavy emphasis on the word color.

She laughed. "Is that a good or bad thing?" She smiled as she looked around her. "I do like color. It cheers me up, gives me energy. My Dad and I did most of the work on the house ourselves, including painting the walls with color. He gave me a hard time about it, too. You wouldn't know it to look at me, but I'm mean with a hammer and nails." She paused. "I've got to finish some things up in the kitchen. Do you want to sit here or come with me? I'm almost done. I just need to finish cooking the noodles for the spaghetti," she said.

"I'll come with you, maybe I could help."

The kitchen was like the rest of her home, neat, cozy, and, oddly enough, limited to one color, white. He looked around taking in the table which had been set with a white table cloth and white dinnerware. "Would you open the wine and pour a glass for us?" she asked as he stood looking over her space. She gave him the bottle, two glasses, and opener. She put the bread in the oven and took noodles out to drain and added the sauce. Stephen handed her a glass and she took a large gulp. "A little fortification," she said. He laughed.

Reye placed the food on the table and they sat. She had gone out of her way to make this night special. She'd set the table with a table cloth and linen napkins her mother had given her when she moved in. She'd used her best and only china, more like Target-ware, but it worked. She added some candles on the table and throughout the house.

They ate in silence for a while.

"This is great, I'd thought pizza and beer, but this is so much better," he said jokingly. "Really, thanks for inviting me."

"Can you cook?"

"A few things. Breakfast is my best course. Maybe I'll cook for you some time," he said.

"Maybe," she responded, not sure what to do with that statement. "Law school keeping you busy?"

"The last year is not as bad as the first two. The first year was mostly core courses. You get some choices in your second year, and, by the third year, you are pretty much primarily studying your area."

"What is your area again?"

"My dad and gramps, and his dad before him, specialized in tax, personal trust, and estate law."

"I remember you telling me that on the plane ride back. It sounds lucrative."

"It can be, but sometimes it can be dull."

"So why study it?"

"I like it. It's easy and established. I'll join the firm and continue in the family business. It does have its ancillary benefits, long lunches, schmoozing clients, and golfing expeditions."

"Is that enough for you?"

"For now, anyway. I'm a simple man. I don't have any major desire to work in any other field. Not looking to save anyone from lethal injections, plus it's easy for me." He looked over at her speculatively. "Why is it that we always end up talking about me? How about you? How are your classes?"

"School is school, but I've started working at one of the community centers here in town, and I'm starting to really like it."

"You had some doubt?"

"Maybe," she said a little pensively. "It's working out better than I'd expected. As I've said before, school was always a struggle for me growing up. Out of the five of us kids, I had the most difficulty. Sam, the brother closest to me in age, also attends the university in the graduate school. He is in the psychiatry department. He, along with tutors, helped me get through a lot of the work as I grew up. You saw him at the game, remember?"

"Sure, the other forward?"

"Yep. Anyway, to make a long story short, I feel like I can make a difference at the center with the kids." She paused. "Too altruistic sounding, huh?" She twirled the wine in her glass.

"Nothing wrong with altruism." He placed his napkin on the table and leaned back in his chair. "That was good, better than some of the finer restaurants I've been to."

"Yeah, right, very funny," she said, the wine making her more relaxed. She gave him a slow, wide smile, her eyes lowering as she looked him over.

"No, no kidding, it was great," Stephen said. She looked very relaxed sitting there, and way too sexy. They'd gone through a bottle of wine and were halfway through their second. "Before you get too relaxed, would you like me to help you clean up?"

"I don't have much to do, just load the dishes into the dishwasher, put the food in the refrigerator."

"Okay, how about you sit and continue to drink your wine, and I'll put the dishes in the dishwasher for you."

"I appreciate your looking out for me, but I'll help. Maybe I can work off some of the effects of the wine."

He smiled at that. "Is that really a good idea?"

She laughed. Feeling playful, she grabbed a towel from the holder and attempted to swat him with it. They worked together for a while. They talked as they worked. The conversation eventually turned to a recap of their previous soccer game. "You do know we are going to win the next game," she continued, leaning back against the sink watching him load the last few dishes. "I was just taking it easy on you during the first game, you know that, right? I didn't show you all my best moves."

"Oh, yeah?" Stephen said with a smile in his voice. He stopped loading the dishwasher and turned to her. "You holding out on me? Other moves, huh? Show me?"

"Nope, I don't want to strip away all of your confidence, leave you with no hope of winning."

"You think you're that capable?" He moved slowly toward her, a tiger stalking its prey, until he stood directly in front of her. Her eyes opened wide at his movement and he moved in closer still, so close that her breasts lightly touched his chest. "Show me what you've got," he repeated, and all the laughter had disappeared.

He was serious; she could see it in his eyes. She also read hunger, a hunger that matched what must be visible in hers.

"I've been waiting since the party to be able to hold you again," he said and put his hands on her hips and gripped them loosely. "I felt something that night that I need to figure out. I think you need to figure it out, too."

"Maybe."

He moved in for a kiss, which she met with an open mouth. This was not your garden-variety kiss, this one meant business. No more games. It turned hot fast. Both Reye and Stephen moved closer to each other. Her hands roamed his body, going under his shirt so she could feel his skin; she wanted badly to feel skin. He was equally hot. One of his hands moved to her breast while the other cupped her ass. He squeezed both at the same time, pushing his hips into hers so that she could feel him, could answer his silent question. She pushed her hips against his in answer.

"Where is your bedroom?" He asked the question with his lips against hers. She grabbed his hand and pulled him behind her. Inside the door of her bedroom, she turned and grabbed him for another kiss. They pulled and tugged at each other's clothes. Shirts were discarded, and she reached for his shorts, stopping long enough to rub her hand along his penis. She couldn't resist. He groaned into her mouth. He helped her get rid of her clothes and she returned the favor. They now stood naked before each other, and he stopped to look his fill, marveling at the beauty of her body. He pulled her in close so that his body was flush against hers, and his hands could touch. God, he loved the way she felt, soft, smooth, and firm. He lowered his head for another open-mouthed kiss while his hands moved to her breasts and he squeezed. He backed her to the bed until the back of her knees hit and they fell. He landed on her, but flipped them.

"There are condoms in my pocket," he said. "I need to get them?"

"No, I've got some here." She reached into the end table next to her bed and located her stash. She retrieved one, opened it, and rolled it on him. He watched her, his breathing heavy, as she then straddled him and slowly lowered herself, her eyes never leaving his. Impatient, his hips shot upward, meeting her. She could feel him shudder and she started to move. He pulled her forward for a kiss that was forceful. His arms locked around her waist, transforming into bands holding her as he moved her up and down to meet his thrusts.

He dictated the pace, and it was hard and fast at first. Holding her tight he flipped them over so that she was below him and he slowed, setting a determined, slow rhythm where he would pull completely out of her only to push back in, equally slow. He closed his eyes to fully concentrate on the slow glide in and out of her body. Reye loved the feel of him against her, the slide in and out, so full, so hard.

"Please," she moaned against his mouth. He looked down at her.

"Please what, Reye?" His lips captured hers again and he kissed her to the rhythm of his thrust, slow and sure. He could feel her start to come and he slowed down even more.

"Please what, Reye?" he asked again. "What do you want?" he whispered to her as he glided in again, hard this time, and picked up his pace as she met him thrust for thrust as they both raced toward completion. They climaxed together, moaning into each other's mouth at the intensity of their joining.

They lay afterward, him on top and inside her, finding their breath. He didn't move, just lifted his head to stare down into her face. He knew it would be good, but the episode at the party had not prepared him for this. It was more than he'd imagined it could be. He pulled out, stood up, and removed and discarded the condom. He came back to bed, pulling Reye into his arms so she faced him as he lay on his side. He captured her face and kissed her lips softly, continuing to hold her.

They both fell asleep. Reye woke up much later and checked her clock on the nightstand. It was midnight and the lights were still on in the house. Stephen was asleep and she didn't want to wake him. She moved away from him carefully. No worries there, as he hadn't moved. She stood at the end of the bed looking at him. He was a beautiful naked male, sprawled on her bed, facedown, satisfied, and apparently dead to the world. This could be dangerous for her she thought. She didn't want him to leave, and that scared her, too. *Girl, just one time and you have lost your mind, ready to turn over yourself gladly for more.* How many other women had felt this way about him? He told her he only wanted casual, he told her that at the party, but could she handle casual? What would she do to keep him, and what if that wasn't enough? They were from different worlds, and not just in skin tone.

She grabbed his polo from the floor and pulled it over her head. It covered most of the important body parts. She walked through the kitchen and the living room, turning lights off as she went, making sure that the front door was locked. In the kitchen, she finished loading the dishwasher and started it. They'd gotten all but a few dishes loaded before they'd gotten sidetracked.

After her tasks were accomplished she went to the refrigerator for something to drink. She opened the door and stared inside, not really seeing the contents. She heard a small noise and felt Stephen's naked body at her back. He put his arms around her waist and rubbed his slightly rough cheek against hers. "What are we looking for?" he asked.

"Something to drink, I thought, but maybe not." She turned into his arms, her own snaking around his waist. She just held him.

"You okay?" He pulled back to look into her face. "Don't get serious on me, Reye," he said, bringing her back in to his body.

"I'm okay, and I won't," she said. He grabbed her hand with one of his, pushing the refrigerator door closed with the other. He walked back to the bedroom, she trailing along behind him. Once inside, he reached for his shirt and lifted it up and over her head. His hands moved to cup her breasts, and he looked into her eyes, while his hand began to slowly circle the tips, causing her to gasp. Those wonderful hands slid up to cup her face and he kissed her, slowly at first and then more demanding, moving her back to bed. How was he able to just take over? Her body had a mind of its own, and apparently it now answered to his. All she wanted to do was just feel him, in her, touching her. He proceeded to make his claim on her in a way that no other before him had.

CHAPTER 6

Stephen awoke to the smell of coffee, taking a moment to get his bearings. He knew exactly where he was, Reye's house, Reye's bedroom, and, last night, Reye's body. He allowed himself a few minutes to reflect on the events of the previous night. Somehow parts of his psyche knew what it would feel like with her. That was the part that had driven him to get here, and it had not disappointed. Sex with her had been incredible. After he'd found her in the kitchen with a too-serious expression on her face, he returned to her bedroom and he'd pushed and drove her relentlessly the remainder of the night. He hadn't known that you could have sex with such intensity and abandon.

He sat up and looked around for his clothes. They were neatly stacked on a chair next to the door. He stood up, picked out his boxers from the stack, and put them on. He needed to find the bathroom fast. After using it, he finished getting dressed and took the new, unwrapped toothbrush and toothpaste that had been neatly laid out for him and brushed his teeth. He threw some water on his face and took a moment to look at himself. He was a little unnerved and unsure of his next move. Last night had turned more serious than he'd intended and he wasn't anywhere near ready for that. Taking a deep breath, he headed to the kitchen.

Stephen entered the kitchen to find Reye leaning against the counter, a cup of coffee in her hand. He paused just inside the doorway and she looked up to see him.

I am not going to cling, I am going to be composed, Reye reminded herself. They'd agreed to keep things casual, although it now felt more than casual to her. She slept with him once, and, although it was incredible for her, it didn't mean he was ready to meet the preacher. She needed to play it cool.

"Morning," she said somewhat tentatively. "You must have been tired. I usually make breakfast for myself before I head out to class. This being Sunday, however, I usually go over to my parents for breakfast before going to church, but I overslept and missed it. So I'm going to stick around here all day. That was not an invitation, by the way," she said quickly. Way too much information, she said to herself.

"Thanks, but if you don't mind, I need to get home."

"Sure, not a problem." Reye moved through the kitchen to the living room to stand next to the front door with Stephen trailing her. At the door he paused. "I really had a great time last night. I'll call you soon. Okay?"

"Sure."

He leaned in and gave her a quick kiss goodbye.

Later on that afternoon, Stephen sat on the couch in his apartment, books spread out around him. The TV was on with the sound turned off while the Sunday football game played in the background. He stared at the game, but he was really watching last night's events replay in his head. That had been all he'd been able to do since leaving Reye's. Should he call? What would he say? He couldn't explain to her what he wouldn't admit to himself, that this could be about more than sex. His instincts regarding her being serious were spot on. He'd recognized that look, and so he'd played it cool and left.

Reye had dozed off and on throughout the morning, and who could blame her after last night? She sat in front of her TV, sprawled on the floor, totally not studying. She'd showered earlier after Stephen's departure, putting on hand-me-down sweats from Sam and a t-shirt. She'd thought she could make use of her day by studying, but she'd ending up staring into space and reliving last night over and over again, examining every action for gold nuggets to tuck away in her mind for later. The ringing of the doorbell startled her and she went to see who it was. Looking through the peephole, she was surprised to find Stephen standing there.

"Can I come in?" His book bag was slung over his shoulder. "Since I knew you were studying and I also needed to, I thought I could join you." He hadn't been getting much done on his own, so maybe if he was here next to her, he could focus on school or on something else.

"Sure," she said. "Come in, make yourself at home." He took a seat on the couch. Looking around, he could see her books were scattered around an empty space on the floor. She smiled. "I'm glad you came by. Do you want anything to drink? I ordered pizza for myself earlier and have some left if you're hungry."

"Nope, I'm good," he said.

She resumed her seat on the floor, picked up her textbook and pretended to read. Five minutes later she gave up and looked over at Stephen, who was looking back at her. She smiled again. "What?"

"Nothing." he replied, also smiling. He turned back to his book, thinking that he was glad he'd come. He liked being around her.

She continued to watch him, admiring how good he looked in sweats and a t-shirt. His hair stood in tufts on his head, probably from being finger combed, and the stubble from last night was a good look for him. After a few seconds, he looked up. She smiled again. She didn't seem capable of doing much more when he was around. She stopped pretending to study.

"You are a good looking guy, but you know that already, don't you?" she said.

"Me?" he said smiling that wicked smile of his. "What about me looks good to you?"

Where to start, she thought. "I really like your eyes, but your smile gives them a run for their money. It's slightly wicked, cocky even, and after last night, I now know why." She grinned back at him.

"Is that so?" he replied slowly.

"Yep, that's so."

"What else do you like about me?" he asked, slowing drawing out his words again. His mood had changed from playful to sexy. He stood up from the couch and looked over at her lying on her side on the floor, her head resting in the palm of her hand. He stretched his hand above his head, and then lowered them to move to the bottom of his shirt. Reye watched, transfixed. He smiled at her again and began to peel his shirt over his head. He was dangerous, from the top of his black, curly head to the bottom of his feet, and who knew feet could be so stimulating? She turned over on her back to really get a good look at him, unabashed in her admiration, as he walked over to stand at her feet, shirtless, and looked down at her lying on the floor. Long, lean, smooth, sexy, and so open was the way he saw her. They stared at each other for a second and then he bent down, his arms outstretched as he reached toward the floor and placed his hands on either side of her face. He was now posed in the classic push-up position. He held that position for a second, taking his time to examine her body from head to toe. She squirmed under his gaze, her body lifting on its own volition toward his. He slowly lowered himself until he completely covered her.

"Want me to tell you what I like about you?"

"What?"

"Well, I really like your body. It's sleek, firm, and smooth," he said. His body rested on her, his weight now on his elbows. He moved his hand to her breast. "I like that you are close to my height, and that all my parts fit yours perfectly. I like that you run off at the mouth when you get nervous, and I like how you challenge me on the soccer fields and in other places. I especially like your sense of humor." He paused, dragging out each work like it was candy to be savored.

"However, my two most favorite things about you are, one, your smile, and following in a close second is the way you moan and say please when I touch certain parts of your body. I like how you beg, Reye," he said softly about a hairsbreadth away from her lips, his eyes hooded now. They both moved in to kiss, a kiss that was tender at first and then became more. Her hands roamed over his back and then lower to cup his ass, firm and strong in her hands. He lifted himself up and pulled her t-shirt over her head. He began to kiss his way down her neck to her breast, capturing one in his mouth. She started to moan and he lifted his head from her breast to catch her eyes and he smiled. "See what I mean," he said and dipped his head to retake a nipple into his mouth.

Her hands pulled at the waist of his sweats and he stopped, rolled over, and pushed them and his boxers down his legs and off. She took advantage of the break to rid herself of her remaining clothes. He settled back down on her body and gave her a scorching kiss. Both their hands began to move relentlessly over each other.

"I need a condom," he murmured into her mouth. She reached under the couch and pulled out one, a souvenir from last night. He looked up in surprise.

"I had strategically placed them around the house. You never know," she said.

He laughed out loud for a minute, and she joined him. He took the package from her hand, opened it, and put it on. She pulled his body back to hers and pulled his head down for another kiss. His hands moved to the inside of her thighs, pushing them open to settle between them. He cupped her hips to prepare her to receive him and to hold her steady. As he pushed into her, she gasped, more than ready to receive him. He was welcomed into a warm, wet place. Lifting her legs, he wrapped them around his hips and initiated a slow rhythm that she followed, lifting himself with his arms so that he could look down at her as he pushed in and out of her. She didn't disappoint, all warm, caramel smoothness. His movement forward pulled another moan and a sigh from her. He watched her react to him, and it made him harder and more forceful. His thrusts picked up speed and they both lost control.

"Please," she whimpered, but he was beyond smiling at her pleas, as they came together, hard, with mouths entwined and moans pouring forth.

They lay still while Stephen placed butterfly kisses just below her ear. He then touched his forehead to hers, laying there while their breathing returned to normal. He lifted himself, pulled out of her and pushed to his feet to dispose of the condom. He hadn't said a word. He returned to stand above her looking down at her lying on the floor. He looked serious.

"What?" she asked.

"It's nothing," he said. "I like being with you, that's all. I can't make you any promises, except that you are where I want to be right now. Can you work with that?" he asked.

"Yes."

He smiled and so did she. Their smiles turned to grins and then they both started to laugh.

Over the next several weeks, Reye and Stephen spent most of their time together at Reye's house. They'd meet after school to study followed by long nightly sessions of lovemaking. The Saturday morning before the second scheduled soccer game between their teams, Reye and Stephen awoke after having spent the night together. Her back was snuggled next to his front. He said into her ear, "I am going to spend tonight at my apartment. I need the rest. Between you and school, I can barely keep my eyes open. I especially need my rest if I am going to beat your team's butt tomorrow."

"We'll see, but I'll agree to give you the night off. I do realize that I've been using you too much, wearing you out." She turned to face him, putting her arms around his neck as she pushed her body against the front of his. "Be back and ready after Sunday's loss."

He smiled at her and gave her a long tender kiss. "Will do," he said.

Stephen arrived at his apartment Saturday evening after a long day spent at the library. Henri was sitting on the couch watching a soccer game on TV and turned at the sound of the door opening. He was more than a little surprised to see Stephen.

"Dude, you look like a guy I knew once. My roommate, in fact, but I'm not sure he lives here anymore," he said jokingly. "I haven't seen you in what, two weeks. Where've you been?"

Stephen dropped his book bag by the door and sat down on the chair next to Henri. "Reye," he said. "You remember her?"

Henri laughed. "Sure I do."

"I've been over at her place off and on for the last couple of weeks," he said.

"Man, she must be something special, 'cause that is not your style. Must be love, huh?"

"Nope, just a serious case of lust."

"You think so?"

"Know so."

"Whatever you say, dude."

"No, believe me, you know me better than anyone. She is compelling, I'll give her that, and the sex is amazing. We just connect on that level. Anyway, we've agreed to keep it casual."

"She agreed, too?"

"Yes."

"Dude, be careful, women are always thinking long term."

"I hear you, and I will."

"Are you ready for the game tomorrow?" Stephen asked the question to change the subject to something other than his love life. Henri had caught him off guard and he wasn't ready to discuss something he hadn't figured out.

"Be careful around Joe, dude. You know how he feels about people of color. He's been talking trash about you around the frat house, so keep your eyes open."

"Always."

Stephen had mostly ignored Joe since the frat party. He played with him on the team, but he didn't trust him and tried to avoid him.

The second game between The Wizards and The Graduates arrived on another perfect Sunday afternoon. Fall in Austin could be brutally hot or freezing cold, and those changes could happen in the span of a few hours. Today, however, was perfect, the grass green, the air crisp, the sky clear. Stephen arrived late, making him the last person to take the field. Reye and her teammates were already on the field warming up. He scanned the players and quickly located Reye among the other women. She gave him a wink and a smile. He hadn't seen her since yesterday morning, and he was looking forward to going by her home after the game. Just looking at her pushed his adrenaline in gear as he remembered the many nights spent wrapped in her embrace. She was kicking the ball around with another team member, wearing the shorts she worn to the last game and her team's t-shirt. He liked seeing her in her gear and he liked playing against her. It was a little bit sexy the way she would push and shove him around in her quest for a goal. It also gave him a kick to match wits and skill against her; he could take her, of course, but she didn't cut him any slack. She held her own against him and he respected and admired her for it.

The referees had arrived, both teams were lined up and in position, and the game started. Reye was once again lined up in the forward position against Stephen as defender. They spent most of the first half pushing and shoving each other, laughing and smiling as she would get by him or he'd stop her. Stephen was able to contain Reye and she wasn't able to score. But who cared, Reye thought, as she smiled to herself. It was worth it just to have all six feet, two inches of golden male focused on her. That was heady stuff. Oblivious to the stares of those around them, they played like they were the only ones on the field. At the end of the first half, the scored was tied 0-0. In the huddle, Sam thanked Reye for all the special attention she was giving to Stephen, and because of it, he changed their game strategy. They would continue to play like they had in the first half, but during the last ten minutes they would change their alignment and allow him to play as a third forward instead of midfielder. The two forwards, Reye and Jose, would move the ball forward and after both Stephen and the other defender committed to Reye and Jose, they would pass the ball to Sam to score.

Sam's strategy for the second half of the game worked like magic. They were able to score not once, but twice, while simultaneously using up the clock. The Graduates won. Because both teams had identical records, including a head-to-head split, they now had to play a final game to determine the division winner. The game would be scheduled for the following weekend.

Reye's team began their celebration as soon as the referee blew the whistle to end the game. Her team-high fived each other, patted themselves on the back, and shook hands with Stephen's team, making jokes and talking trash. The real party would take place at The Garden, where the tasty beer would act as a lubricant to encourage a much more relaxed and boisterous celebration. Reye walked over to Stephen. "We are going over to The Garden for beers, you coming?" she asked as she looked him over from head to toe, taking in his sweaty body.

He smiled at her boldness. "Sure," he said. "You know you didn't play fair during the game today. I'm going to make sure you are properly punished for the bad sportsmanship you displayed." He winked slyly.

"Promise?" she asked sassily in response. They started to laugh and he watched her as she sauntered away, exaggerating the swing of her hips as she walked. He laughed again and shook his head.

Henri and Joe walked over to a grinning Stephen. "Hey, dude, thanks for losing the game for us," said Joe heatedly.

"What? What are you talking about? I didn't lose the game," Stephen said, taken aback by both the words and the heat with which they were delivered.

"Who are you kidding? You couldn't keep your eyes or your hands off of your little girl," Joe said as he stepped closer to Stephen. "Man, she must have some pretty powerful pussy for you to lose your brain like that."

Stephen took a step toward Joe until they were within an inch of each other's faces.

"Fuck you, Joe. I played my position, I'm the best one out there. I can't play the whole damn field. Your sorry-ass game didn't help!"

"Well at least I'm not stuck in the jungle with a fever that has fried my brain," Joe shouted.

"Come on, calm down," said Henri as he stepped in between them.

"Dude, he's just mad because we really wanted to win today to avoid a playoff. Let it go," Henri said, turning to Joe.

"You think I didn't want to win?" Stephen shouted, pointing his finger into Joe's chest.

"You don't need to speak for me," Joe said to Henri. "I meant what I said!" Turning to Stephen, he asked, "What got into you, dude? As self-centered as you are, you'd never put winning over some girl!"

Stephen turned away abruptly and walked to his car to avoid punching Joe in his mouth. "I'm out of here!" *Who is he to tell me I didn't play well,* Stephen thought to himself. *Asshole! He wouldn't know what to do with pussy if it hit him in the face.* He arrived at his car and stopped. He took a deep breath and tried to calm down. He looked up to find that Reye had approached him.

"You okay?" She could read anger in the tense stance of his body and the hard look on his face. She had witnessed the confrontation with Joe.

"I'm fine." He was quiet for a second. "Look, I'm not going to The Garden. I'll see you later. I don't think you'd appreciate being near me now." He didn't wait for a response, but opened his car door and got in. He drove off, leaving Reye standing there.

Joe walked over to his car. He really didn't like Stephen, never had. He was too good looking, too smart, and, as far as Joe was concerned, he had too easy of a life. Unlike Joe, who had to work above and beyond everyone else to support not just himself, but his family. His sorry-assed dad had walked, followed not soon after by his equally sorry-assed mother, leaving him with a sister and a nephew. He was left to take care of them both while trying to get through school. So he resented that Stephen was given so much and didn't seem to value his good fortune. If he had the looks, money, connections, and smarts that Stephen had, he would be head and shoulders above everyone else in life. Stephen was such a waste. Take today, for example. They could have easily beaten that team. Reye's team was an average team as far as he was concerned, but Stephen was so busy chasing tail that he couldn't see straight. It was disgusting! Stephen could have anyone he wanted, probably had, and who did he choose, a black girl. Joe had yet to get his head around that.

The desertion of his parents had forced him to grow up early, in foster care. He and his sister had always lived in the poorer parts of town, surrounded by blacks and Hispanics. There were a few who had been kind to him, but most hadn't. It had been a dog-eat-dog world.

Stephen had lost the game for them today with his laughing and playing around. It really pissed him off. Joe liked pussy as much as the next guy, but it never stood in the way of winning. So, when he and Henri had walked over to Stephen and he was laughing and smiling with that girl, he hadn't been able to rein in his temper or his mouth. So what the fuck? It had needed to be said.

CHAPTER 7

She didn't hear from him that evening, much to her discomfort and dismay. She remained at home on the off chance that he would come by, trying to distract herself by pretending to study. She couldn't focus, so instead she grabbed her work gloves and headed out into her yard. Working in the yard was a more productive use of her time, killing two birds with one stone, reducing her anxiety while getting her yard winter ready. Beds were cleared of leaves and dead flowers, leaves were raked, the grass cut and fertilized for the last time this year. She checked her cell; still no word from Stephen. What had she expected? They had a good time for two weeks, and so what if this casual whatever they had was ending sooner than later. She'd enjoyed it, right? Joe was persona non grata in her book, that was for damn sure!

Looking around at her yard, she felt satisfied at what she'd accomplished today. Time for a shower maybe she could study. No such luck, she was tired, not enough to sleep. Instead she laid down on the couch and watched TV. Eventually she dozed off.

Stephen sat in his apartment and nursed a beer while he stared blankly at the soccer game, a rerun on TV. He'd left the game and gone home immediately, not being much company for anyone. What had he done? He'd allowed this infatuation with Reye to come before the game. That had never happened before. Reflecting back, he realized that he'd spent most of the time trying to touch her, to feed a desire for her that he couldn't shake after two weeks in her bed. He had enjoyed the challenge of keeping her from scoring with the side benefit of being close. He'd forgotten that he was there to help his team win. His teammates depended on him, and he'd let them down.

This semester was coming to an end. Thanksgiving was two weeks away, and then Christmas. One more semester and he was done. Next, his focus would shift to studying and passing the bar exam. Although he had been raised to pursue law, he really did love it and had aspirations of surpassing his father and grandfather in his law career.

His cell rang and he reached for it, hoping it was and wasn't Reye. It was his mother. "Hi, Mom."

"Hello, Stephen, how are you?"

"I'm fine."

"You don't sound fine." She could always judge his mood by his voice.

"I'm just a little tired, that's all. I had a game today."

"Oh," she said. "How is school?"

"It's good," he answered. "How's Dad?"

"He's fine. What are your plans for Thanksgiving? Do you know when you'll be coming home?"

"No, not yet." That was his mom, no fawning stuff for her. It wasn't that she was cold, she just had her own agenda and marched forward with it.

"Well, let me know soon. I wanted to finalize our plans. I had hoped to invite Beth and her family over sometime during the holidays. Check your schedule and call me back soon."

"Will do, Mom. Bye."

He hung up and went back to staring at the TV. He checked his watch again; eight o'clock. His thoughts again turned to Reye. Wonder what she was doing? He'd looked forward to spending the evening with her after the game. The play between them earlier had been foreplay for him, and he'd planned to finish by making love to her this evening. He should call her. He was equal parts sexually frustrated and angry at himself. He was also angry at Joe, who'd reminded him why dating Reye would be difficult.

Reye woke up, stretched out on the couch. It had to be around eleven, judging by what was on TV. She needed to go to bed or she wouldn't be able to get up in the morning. She checked her telephone, no calls from Stephen. She missed him. He'd somehow gotten under her skin in a relatively short amount of time. She wondered what he was doing, and, before she could talk herself out of it, she picked up the phone and called him. He answered on the second ring.

"Hey, it's me. I was just calling to see how you were. I hadn't heard from you."

"Yeah, I'm fine, I didn't feel like company after the game, so I came home. I started in on some homework and got a bit sidetracked."

"No worries, then. I won't keep you," she said trying to keep the disappointment out of her voice. "Well, call me if you have some time this week and you want to get together."

"Okay, I will," he said.

"Bye."

"See ya."

Reye hung up and continued to lie on the couch, trying not to feel sorry for her lovesick self.

She left the center midweek and got into her truck and sat there. She needed someone to talk to. Sam was always a good listener when she needed to talk, so she called him.

"Hey, baby girl." The sound of his voice was a comfort to her. He had always been there, would be there for her, warts and all. Sure, he got on her nerves sometimes, but today she was glad he was her brother.

She couldn't get any words past the lump in her throat.

"Is something on your mind?" he asked. He knew Reye, and he could tell by the sound of her voice when something was up.

"You remember me talking about Stephen?"

"Mr. Defender?"

"Yes. After our last game he had an argument with one of his teammates about me, the same frat brother from the party. I don't think it went well, and, anyway, I haven't heard from him since."

"I thought you two were going at it pretty heavy."

"That was before his anti-race-mixing friend gave him a hard time about me again. I think he blames himself for their team losing the game to us." She paused. "Why do you think he's interested in me?"

Sam could hear sadness and maybe the onset of tears in her voice. "Ah, Reye, take it easy on yourself. Stephen is a big boy and I can't believe he let little ol' you take him off his game if he didn't want you to. You are a beautiful, kind girl. Any guy would be lucky to have you. Come on, now, don't worry."

"Why haven't I heard from him, then?"

"Have you called him?"

"Yes, later on that night. He said he was tired and so I didn't push. I guess I'll see him at the game on Saturday if he doesn't call before then."

"Try not to worry about it. You know I can knock him down at the game and you can accidentally run him over."

"Thanks, Sam," she said, laughing a little at his comments. "See you Saturday."

It was two in the morning Thursday night, or rather Friday morning, and Stephen had been stuck in the library conference room with three of his fellow law class-mates, preparing a case study for a presentation before his professor tomorrow. It was grueling work, and he wanted to be anywhere but here. Taking a break, he went in search of a soda, locating one in the vending machine located on another floor. He wondered what Reye was up to, remembering the past couple of weeks spent in her bed. He'd missed her and should have called her on Monday, or Tuesday, or Wednesday. The longer he waited the more like a jerk he felt. Maybe he could talk to her on Saturday at the game.

It had taken forever for this day to come, Reye thought, as she pulled up to the field for the final game between her team and Stephen's. She hadn't seen or spoken to him for a week. She was beyond hurt now; really, who was she kidding? She was still hurt, but now she was really, really angry. He could have called her, could have at least had the balls to tell her it was over.

She had come to the game prepared to bring it, and she hoped he would be the one to defend against her. All of the players from her team had arrived. She didn't know if Stephen or his team were here, because she refused to look over to the other side of the field. Sam had discussed the team's strategy with them yesterday and she knew she would play in the midfield instead of as a striker or forward. He felt that Stephen's team would expect them to employ the same strategy they had for the previous two games, but she thought Sam was just looking out for her, keeping her away from Stephen. They would move her to the forward position only if they needed her, and only in the second half.

Today Reye would play midfield at least during the first half, far away from Stephen. He was in his usual position as defender, and he was a really good one. She'd hoped to avoid him for the entire game and leave immediately after it ended.

Stephen was one of the first to arrive at the field, ready to play. This had been a long week for him, long in school and long in guilt. He wanted, needed, to apologize to Reye. Maybe he could talk her into hanging out with him after the game. He'd missed her more this week than he thought he would. He'd seen her arrive, but he hadn't been able to get her attention. She hadn't so much as glanced over at his side. He and his teammates were warming up on one half of the field while Reye's team took the other half. Maybe he could talk to her during warm-ups, before the game began. The opportunity came as a ball was kicked to Reye and it went over her head and rolled toward him.

"Reye."

She looked up, eyes unreadable. No smile, no emotion. She just scooped up the loose ball, turned, and walked away from him.

Stephen was surprised. He'd expected her to be angry, but he'd thought she'd at least talk to him. Henri, who had watched the exchange, walked over to him.

"Ouch," he said with a chuckle.

"What did I do?" Stephen asked, turning to Henri.

"Dude, you don't know? Really?" Henri shook his head sadly. "Well, you two were going at it pretty strong, and then you stopped. Did you ever call her?" Watching Stephen shake his head no, he continued. "Well, it's been my experience that women usually take exception to that sort of behavior."

Stephen shot him an evil look.

"I'm just saying," said Henri, backing up with his hands raised. "Don't forget we've got a game to play today," he added.

Stephen shot him the middle finger and strode over to get into position on the field.

The referees had arrived and both teams were lined up on the field, ready to play. The whistle blew and the game began. It was evident as both teams attacked the ball that they had come ready to play. Both sides ran fast, determined to be first to the ball. In one play, the ball was kicked to the space in front of Reye. She ran to gain control of the ball, and so did the opposing player. They collided, a solid hit that had both falling to the ground. They were up and on their feet immediately, running toward the ball again. Reye got there first, gained control of the ball and passed it off to the forward in front of her. Stephen met the forward, and not only took the ball from her, but began to move it down the field toward the goal, intent on scoring. As a midfielder, Reye stood between him and her defender. Running forward to meet him, her eyes on the ball, she kicked it away from him and sent it over to Sam. Her momentum carried her and she crashed hard into Stephen. They fell. He gave her a sharp look as they both stood up, but neither of them spoke.

Today she played harder than usual. When Stephen came near her, she did her best to prevent him from moving the ball, either by leaning into him hard or running to position herself in front of him, stopping his momentum. He was fast, but so was she. In an all-out foot race, she probably couldn't beat him, but it was easier for her to keep up when he had to both maneuver the ball and run. He began to respond to her physical play and she noticed a marked increase in his intensity. The intensity of both teams increased. Both teams played tough, physical ball. The first half came to a close with the score tied at zero.

Both teams huddled to re-evaluate strategy. Stephen would continue to defend, and take any opportunity to score. Henri turned to him and laughed.

"I have to give her credit, she is one tough soccer player. You must have really pissed her off," Henri said. Stephen didn't respond, he just walked away to sit on the bench for a while by himself. He needed to rehydrate before the second half, and he also needed some time alone. Henri was right, of course, she was a very good soccer player, and he hadn't seen this level of play from her during their previous matches. He loved watching her play and playing against her.

On the other side of the field, Sam had decided to move Reye to the forward position. Their team wasn't getting anywhere near close to scoring with her in the midfield. She would be once again paired against Stephen. *Keep focus, Reye*, she thought. Her anger at the beginning of the game had dimmed somewhat. It had dissipated as she continued to glance over at him. Always the golden one, with a body and face that could make her melt. *Get a grip, Reye, we've got a game to win*, she thought to herself. *Remember, he dissed you.*

The second half started with Reye receiving the ball several times, resulting in two shots on goal, both misses. She was trying to shoot from ten yards back, reducing her ability to take a good shot, but she hadn't wanted to get any closer, didn't want to directly encounter Stephen. But in order to get off a more direct shot, avoiding Stephen would have to end. So, during the next play she received the ball and ran forward. Out of the corner of her eye, she tracked him as he approached her. She faked right and kicked the ball to her left in an attempt to get around him. It didn't work.

"Is that the best you can do?" he said as he kicked the ball out of bounds. She ignored him and waited to receive the ball again. This time, she ran with the ball right towards him, a full-out sprint, hoping at the last minute to pass the ball off to the other forward. Stephen didn't move and neither did she, so again, they collided and both fell hard to the ground, she landing on top.

"Are you okay?" she asked sarcastically, lifting herself off of him as she extended her hand to help him up.

"No problem," he said back, as he accepted her help. The game remained tied at zero until the end, with neither she nor Stephen surrendering any ground.

The final game required a winner, so foregoing overtime, they moved straight to a penalty shootout to decide the outcome. A shootout usually called for five players on each side to take alternating kicks at the opposing team's goalie. Reye hated penalty shootouts. It had never seemed fair to her that this part of the game should rest on the goalie's shoulders alone.

Five members of both teams lined up to take their shots. Stephen's team selected all men, while she was the only woman included with Sam and three of her other teammates. Stephen's team did not miss on shot, while Matt missed for their team. They lost, and you could hear Stephen's team's jubilation in their shouts and screams.

Sweaty from a tough and tightly played game, both teams shook hands and congratulated each other. Henri walked over to Reye.

"You are a really good soccer player. I enjoyed watching you play. I'm surprised you aren't playing college ball," he said.

"Thanks," she said as she shrugged her shoulders. "Too big of a commitment for me. You were good, too."

"Thanks. Are you going to The Garden for drinks?" Henri asked.

"Don't know." She felt rather than saw Stephen approach to stand at her shoulder.

Henri looked between the both of them. "I was just telling Reye what a good player she is," Henri said to his teammate.

"I agree. I hadn't seen you play like that before," he said to Reye.

"Thanks, Henri. Good seeing you again," Reye said. She ignored Stephen as she turned and walked over to her team's bench.

Henri looked over at Stephen, fighting not to laugh but falling short. "Dude, that is one pissed off woman." He turned and walked away, his shoulders still shaking with laughter. "Good luck," he called over his shoulder. "See you at The Garden."

Stephen turned toward Reye's team's bench and watched her as she changed out of her soccer shoes. His eye caught hers, but again, she gave nothing away. No smile, no nothing. Talk about stubborn. Disappointed at her response, he turned and walked to his car. Hopefully she would be at The Garden; if not, he would drive by her house later. He would see her again.

Reye hadn't planned on going to The Garden after the game, but somehow here she sat outside the building, trying to talk herself out of going in. She gave up, opened the truck door, and got out. Both teams were there, but they sat in different sections of the restaurant, Stephen's toward the front and Reye's in the back. She took a seat next to Sam. Taking a menu from the stack, she searched intently for something to eat, although she always ate the same entrée, grilled chicken sandwich with a side of fries. Sam turned to her. "Are you all right?"

"Why wouldn't I be?" she replied.

"You tell me. And, by the way, you played a really great game today. I haven't seen you play that well since high school."

"Well, thank you, big brother," she said with a smile.

"You know, someone else noticed your play today, too." Reye just stared at him and he continued. "I saw him watching you when you weren't looking."

"Yeah? What's your point?"

"Hey, don't pretend with me. I listened to you on the other night on the phone, remember?"

"Yeah, I do, but I'm over it. Why would I bother with him again?"

"Because you like him, maybe," Sam replied. Reye gave him a hard look.

"How about we change the subject?" Sam said.

Reye had consumed three beers and needed to find the ladies' room fast. The beers had helped her relax and she was feeling loose. She stood up and excused herself to go the restroom. Stephen had been watching for an opportunity to talk with her alone. This looked like his chance, so, excusing himself under the guise of going to the bathroom, he followed her down the hall.

The bathrooms were located in the back of the building, past the takeout window and down a short hallway, women on the right, and men to the left. Next to the men's room was a small door that Stephen opened. He was looking for somewhere private to talk to her. This would do; it was a small storage closet, more like a pantry, as it was filled ceiling to floor with paper products. He stood next to the ladies' bathroom door and waited for her.

Why are you still here, she asked herself in the mirror. *What were you expecting?* She threw the paper towels into the trash and opened the restroom door, stopping in her tracks as Stephen stood before her. Her mouth opened and closed as he continued to look at her.

"Hey, will you give me a second?"

"Maybe another time, okay?" she said. She tried to move past him, but he blocked her path.

"Look, I'd rather not share my business in the middle of the hallway, if that's okay with you," she spat out. *Talk about nerve,* she thought. Stephen grabbed her hand and hauled her into the storage closet, locking the door behind him.

"What are you doing? Let go of me."

"Wait, Reye, listen to me. I just want to apologize."

"Okay, is that it? Apology accepted, now can I go?"

"No, I want to see you again."

"People in hell want ice water."

"I missed you."

"Yeah? I could really tell. All those phone calls I received from you this week. Is that how much you missed me?" Her tone held both bite and hurt.

Not wanting her to leave, but not wanting to argue with her anymore, either, he slowly pulled her to him, giving her time to stop him if she wanted. She pulled in the other direction at first, but he persisted and she ended up standing in front of him. He lowered his face and touched his lips to hers, softly at first.

"I'm sorry," he said and kissed her again. She opened her mouth for him and it was all the consent he needed. He had been hungry for her all week, and only one thought remained in his head, the one pressing him to be inside of her, now. Breaking the kiss, he walked her backward across the small space until her back hit the wall. His lips returned to hers for another open-mouthed kiss, delighting in its warmth and wetness. Pulling at her shirt, he lifted it up to allow his hands entry underneath. They moved over and up her flat stomach to capture each of her breasts in a strong grip. She moaned loudly into his mouth making him harder. He was all need, continuing to feast on her mouth before lifting her shirt and her bra to feast on her breasts. Gone was gentleness, replaced by aggression and immediate need. He found her mouth again, accepting her moans and pleas, his favorite sound, kissing her again and again. He stopped abruptly and pushed her shorts and underwear down, only taking the time to remove them from one leg. He was impatient to gain access. He wrapped one of her legs around his hip and pulled the front of his shorts down enough to free himself. He lifted Reye's other leg and put it around his other hip, leaning into her so he could feel her skin next to his.

He returned to kissing her mouth, his hands traveling around his back to make sure her legs were anchored to him. She would need to be as he pushed up and into her, hard, whispering her name reverently. She felt so good surrounding him. He started to fuck her, hard strokes in and out of her body, aware of only two spots on her body, two openings from which he fed. Holding on to her tightly, he began to lift her up and down, coordinating with his thrusts, pressing harder and harder into her. He couldn't get close enough. Feeling her climax building, he swallowed the sounds that spilled from her mouth and moved his hips into another gear, pumping faster, furiously seeking his climax. Capturing her breasts tightly, he continued to pump hard and steadily into her. Her orgasm hit her, threatening to push him over. *Please, not yet,* he thought. "Fuck," he said over and over again, in time with the thrust of his hips.

He came, and this climax was beyond any in his experience. His hands moved to her ass to capture her cheeks, to tilt her hips upward, and hold her in place while he finished. He would apologize later for the marks that he was sure would be on her body and lowered his head into the curve of her neck, working through the last of his spasms. He slowly regained a sense of himself, as if waking from a dream, recognizing the position he had Reye in, backed up against the wall in a storage closet. He lowered her legs to the floor but remained embedded in her, not quite ready to leave. He moved his mouth to hers and kissed her again, gently this time, capturing her tongue and entwining it with his.

"I am really sorry for this week. Can we get past this?"

"I think we just did."

She leaned in for another kiss, which he gladly gave. "You make me crazy," she said, her head resting against his.

"Yeah?" he said. He moved his lips to her neck.

"Yeah," she responded, loving the feel of him.

"Can I come by tonight?" he asked, his lips continuing their movement up her neck, now leaving small kisses below her chin.

She sighed, but nodded. "Give me about a hour," he said, helping her with her clothing. "I need to run by my apartment first."

"Okay."

He tugged her into his arms again. "I'll see you later, and again I really am sorry about this week," he said, kissing her one last time.

Opening the door, looking both ways, he left. Reye waited for a minute, then followed on legs filled with jelly. Her body tingled. She remembered a line from *Ghost,* her favorite movie. "You're in danger, girl." It was her favorite line from that movie, one that she repeated occasionally, and it seemed appropriate for this moment. Yep, she was in danger.

Reye arrived home thirty minutes later and took a shower, washed her hair, and changed into some sweats and a t-shirt. She put on a CD and turned off the lights except for the table lamp next to the sofa in the living room. She located several fat candles that she kept around and lit them, placing them in the living room. She then turned off the remaining lamp and sat back on the couch to wait for Stephen. She didn't have to wait long. She went to the door when he knocked and let him in. He dropped his books by the door and followed her back to the couch, taking a seat next to her. They were both quiet as they listened to music.

She took a moment to look at him. He'd changed into some much-worn jeans and a yellow polo-style shirt that clung to his upper body. He was beautiful to her, filling her with both joy and dread. She knew she was attractive, but not as much as he. She wondered how she matched up to the other women he had been with. He also had that whole arrogant, confident, I'm-used-to-wealth thing working for him.

Stephen was glad to be here. He sat on the couch and pulled Reye over to him to rest her head on his chest. He kicked off his sandals and put his feet up on the table in front of him. He hadn't felt this relaxed all week. He looked down at her, and he was touched by how beautiful she was. He'd missed her this week. He loved her soft skin, wide smile, and sparkling eyes. He moved his hand through her hair and down to trace over her lips.

It was quiet except for the John Mayer CD playing in the background.

"Reye, you know I didn't use a condom earlier."

"Really?" she said, thinking to tease him. As she looked up to his face, she changed her mind. He was serious.

"Relax, I've used birth control for a while now for reasons other than sex. You don't have to worry, no babies for me. I'm clean, too, if that's what you're afraid of. I know I came on strong to you in the beginning, but I've never been really sexually active."

"I'm not worried, just making sure. I'm clean, too. You were my first. Really," he said, acknowledging the look of disbelief on her face. "My dad and mom drilled condom use into me from sixth grade onward. Taking instruction from my dad, that I could handle, but my mother was something altogether different. I've always used a condom."

"Feel free to continue, if you want. I'm okay, either way."

He didn't want to go back to protection, or at least not with her. What they did earlier had been unbelievable; she'd felt incredible wrapped around him.

"I am glad you came over," Reye said.

"I am, too." He paused. "Joe and his comments about you after the game last week and from the frat party before hit me unexpectedly. When people say things like that it always comes as a surprise to me. In this day and age, I wouldn't expect to hear those things. I'm sorry again that I let them get the best of me. Just be patient with me, Reye. This is uncharted territory for me, too."

"I know," she said, "but your task is easier. I make it easier, you know, with me being beautiful, smart, and sexy." They both laughed.

She turned in his arms and kissed him.

"Ready for bed?" he whispered in her ear as his hand moved to capture her breast.

She laughed again. "Did anyone tell you that you have a one-track mind?"

"It's a guy thing," he replied, smiling back at her. She stood up, blew out the candles, reached for his hand, and led him to her bedroom.

CHAPTER 8

I'm beat, Reye thought, walking towards the center's main entry, heading home and looking forward to some major face time with her couch. Stephen had called earlier, telling her that he would be spending the night at the law library. Poor guy, she'd miss him, but she could definitely use the sleep.

"Reye." She turned at the sound of her name to find Dr. Houston walking towards her. She was impeccably attired in a pretty black and pink floral skirt paired with a sleek black top and, of course, there were the matching three-inch heels on her feet. She'd bet good money that Dr. Houston had a personal clothing fairy tucked away at her home somewhere.

"Do you need to get home or can you take a minute to talk with me?" She'd stopped walking and was now looking up at Reye for an answer.

"Sure, I've got a minute."

"Let's go to my office," Dr. Houston said as she turned and led the way with Reye trailing along behind her. When they entered the office, Dr. Houston moved to sit behind her desk. Reye took the seat immediately in front, facing her.

Always direct, Dr. Houston started. "Reye, first I want to thank you for the amazing job you've done with the children and the after-school program. You have gone above and beyond what's been asked of you. I really appreciate the hard work and dedication you've shown our children. You have a gift for working with kids."

"Thank you," Reye said, feeling a little overwhelmed by the praise. "I'm learning as much as I'm teaching, and it's been great volunteering."

"I'm glad. So, as to why I've asked you here. I would like you to consider taking a more permanent position with us instead of a volunteer. I would like to offer you a paid position. You would continue to work with the children in the after-care program. The only major change would be that I need you to be here every day. Your schedule would remain the same otherwise. Is that something you'd be interested in?"

"Yes, I'm interested, but why the change?"

"The board, parents, and the children love the work that you've done here so far, and we've gotten more than a few request from parents wanting you to spend even more time with their kids. Do you think it'll interfere with your studies? I realize this is your last year at the university, and I wouldn't want it to jeopardize you graduating."

"No, I could manage the extra days and I could certainly use the money," she said, looking into Dr. Houston's smiling face.

"Great!"

"Now, I have a question for you," Reye said.

"Shoot."

"I've given some thought to coaching the kids, you know, helping them learn the game of soccer. I could work with them following the aftercare program in the evenings and maybe some on the weekends if there is interest. Who knows, maybe we could eventually play as a team in the spring league. I know of several recreational leagues in the city."

She rushed on, leaning forward in her chair enthusiastically. "I think it would be helpful for the kids to have another outlet. One that would keep them fit while helping them gain confidence in other areas of their lives. I've always been involved in sports, and it helped me when school was difficult. I think it would be good for them, too."

"Okay, I haven't said no. What are the costs?"

"Let me put something more formal together for you. Off-hand, there are uniform costs, but those can be kept to a minimum. There are rec. league fees, but I could look for sponsorship for parents who can't afford to pay."

"Well, you do your research. We would need to get the parents' permission, but if they're willing to let their children play, I don't see why we can't make it work," Dr. Houston offered.

"Yes!" Reye shouted, beyond excited.

Reye sat down at her kitchen table to study for school, thrilled with the progression of her life so far. She was excelling in her classes at the university, the after-school program had grown, and she would get to coach a soccer team, having received approval from the parents.

The first practice was scheduled for next Monday. And, finally, there was Stephen, her first relationship in a very long time. Well, technically it wasn't a relationship, but he did spend most evenings and nights at her house and that had to count for something, didn't it? It had been four weeks since the last game, but when she added the two before that it came to a total of six weeks. It was her longest non-relationship so far. She'd steered clear of probing his prior dating history, and he hadn't voluntarily offered any information about it. She avoided discussing anything that had to do with the future or the past with Stephen. She wasn't going to press him. Right now she was happy with her life.

Reye sat in the passenger side of Stephen's car as he drove them home from a movie. It was their first and only venture outside of her home so far. They were now driving over to his apartment. He needed to pick up some additional clothes and books. He drove into the gate of what she knew were townhouses for the up-and-coming in Austin. This neighborhood was clearly out of her price range.

"You live here?"

"Yes." She was surprised and impressed, at least with what she'd seen so far.

He pulled up to a garage that apparently belonged to his town home and, on cue, the garage door opened. After parking inside, he preceded her up a set of steps that led into a small room equipped with a washer and dryer. He continued on into a kitchen that was large and beautiful. Maple cabinets and stainless steel appliances gleamed and converged with beautiful hardwood floors. She couldn't name the wood, but she knew it was not your standard local hardware store laminate. *Wow,* she thought, taking it all in. A bar separated the kitchen from the living room and the dining room. The breakfast area stood off to the side of the kitchen. Stephen walked on toward his bedroom down the hall while she wandered into the living room, trying not to gawk. Floor to ceiling windows let in the sun and looked out to the unit's shared swimming pool. Nice view. Framed artwork graced the walls, sitting alongside a lovely flat screen TV. What student lived liked this? A large sectional leather sofa sat on hardwood floors that continued from the kitchen. "Wow," she said again, out loud this time, recognizing quality and its cost from having renovated houses with her dad. A hallway led to two bedrooms, Henri's on the right and Stephen's on the left. She walked into Stephen's room, which was also spotless and beautifully decorated.

"How do you keep this place so clean?"

"My mother hired a bi-weekly cleaning service for us."

"Oh."

"What do you mean, oh?"

"Nothing. That's really generous of her."

"Generous, my ass. It's just a way for her to keep tabs on what's going on in my life. She employed the cleaning service, and I'm sure she is informed of any out-of-the-ordinary occurrence around here."

"I see," she said, standing in the middle of his room, which also possessed floor-to-ceiling windows and a sliding door that opened out to a small patio. The wood floor continued throughout the house, accompanied by walls painted a light brick color. In Stephen's bedroom, a king-size bed covered with a beautiful white duvet was positioned along the non-windowed wall. Matching nightstands flanked the bed with books scattered and stacked on them. Reye knew very few students with coordinated furniture. This wasn't your regular student housing; not for anyone in her crowd, anyway. Framed pictures also adorned the walls in here. Impressive; she bet good money that a designer had decorated this place.

She followed Stephen into a large walk-in closet and stood watching him. He stood in the middle of his closet looking through his clothes. He really had a lot of clothes. Funny, she could only recall seeing him in jeans, shorts, or t-shirts. She continued to stand and watch him, admiring the way he moved. He always seemed at ease in his skin, something she'd envied sometimes. He'd also proven to be a very sexual being, and he was comfortable with those thirsts, too. She closed the closet door and walked over to stand behind him, putting her arms around his waist. She loved that she was close to him in height. She loved, absolutely loved, his body. She'd grown accustomed to their unexplainable sexual connection and his endless supply of sexual energy.

She leaned over his shoulder and planted a kiss on his neck as he continued to look forward, pretending indifference. She knew better. She moved one of her hands to the front of his jeans and followed the hard length that seemed to grow in size under her hand. She loved that part of him, too. He remained still, but she could hear his desire by the change in his breathing. She unbuttoned and lowered the zipper of his jeans slowly while she moved to kiss the space just under his ear, another favorite. She closed her eyes and gave herself over to the feel of him. One of her hands moved under his shirt to touch his skin. Grabbing the end of his t-shirt, she pulled it up and over his head and moved to stand in front of him, looking into his eyes, finding them simmering with desire. That was a look she'd also come to love. It made her feel extremely sexy, and could take her from zero to sixty in two seconds flat. She kissed him, mouth open and hungry. She loved his mouth, his tongue, and his intensity. She loved that he took control of her body, moving into a zone that had him making love to her each time like it would be his last and he had to make it count. Lowering herself on her knees in front of him, she pulled her shirt over her head and released her bra. She opened his jeans, pulling them down his legs and off, running her hands over his hard length, smiling at his sharp intake of air. She looked up at him, all golden, and all hers, at least for now. Removing his underwear, she leaned over him, taking him in her mouth. They both moaned. His hands found purchase in her hair, positioning her head to his liking. She loved the feel of him and allowed him to set the pace, finding a rhythm that she could accommodate and groaning at the rightness of her mouth on him. Moving his hips faster, he held her head steady and pumped into her mouth. Not soon after, a steady stream of words escaped his mouth, a sure sign that he was close.

"God, Reye," he whispered. Grabbing his butt, she pulled him closer. He whimpered but continued to pump. "Reye," he moaned again as he came. She continued to hold him to her until she felt his body relax, and then she sat back on her heels and looked up at him. He stared back at her, his eyes unreadable.

He didn't say a word, pulling her up to him for a kiss, lifting her arms, placing them to circle his neck while his hands moved on, seeking her breasts. *Perfect*, he thought and rubbed circles around them. He was getting hard again, but this time he would be inside of her. He leaned back away from her. "Take off your pants," he said with quiet authority. That worked for her; she was more than ready and would have done just about anything he'd asked of her. When all of her clothes were gone, he pulled her back to him, loving the feel of his body next to hers, skin on skin, smooth and firm. He backed her up to the closet door, turned her so that she faced it, lifted and placed her arms high on the door and took a moment to admire her as she stood.

"Oh, Reye," he said at the picture she made. He moved his hands in front of her to capture her breasts, squeezing them gently, hearing her moan. One of his hands made the trek down the front of her body to the opening between her legs. He found her wet, always wet, his finger playing with her until her panting became fast and erratic.

"Please," she begged him.

He moved in closer to her, touching the front of his body to her back. Leaning over her shoulder he whispered in her ear, "What do you want, Reye?" His hands continued to play her body, eliciting another moan from her. He moved them to her waist, pulling her ass outward, away from the door. With one of his legs he spread hers, moving in close, and, without warning, he plunged into her. She couldn't think, could only feel. His hands found her breasts again, and, leaning over her back, he sucked her neck while he fucked her hard. He didn't stop, couldn't stop, relentless in his stokes as his mouth feasted on her neck. His hands moved, frenzied, at her breast. She came, quick, strong, and sharp, rendered incapable of speech.

"Reye, Reye," he growled, her name a mantra, his chant, as he came into her, holding her hips tightly to him. They didn't move. He stood leaning over her, with her slightly bent towards the floor taking in gulps of air. Straightening, he turned her in his arms, walking her until her back touched the closet door, rubbing his thumb over the mark now at her neck. Cupping her face in his hands, he kissed her again and again, content to have her skin next to his. He would get past this need for her. He just needed more time. What was it about her that left him shaken and craving for more?

Practice soccer fields in the city were hard to find. The center didn't have land of its own, just an area out back that held a swing and a slide for the kids' use during its operating hours. Reye needed land, not a full-scale soccer field, just enough for her kids. Most of the fields in this city belonged to soccer clubs that had negotiated large contracts for their usage for the entire year. Although she'd grown up playing in the clubs, it still annoyed her that children had to pay to play.

Lucky for her and her team, Dr. Susan had connections. A friend of the director had given her the hook-up on a field located within walking distance to the center. Practice was scheduled for six, immediately following the after-school program. Reye had arrived at 5:30 to set up cones and her other equipment. She needed more balls and more training gear, but she was learning to be inventive with her equipment requests. Dissipating rapidly was her fear of approaching businesses, or anyone, for that matter, to ask for money. Amazing, that when you felt passionate about something, it could drive you out of your comfort zone. Coaching her team had done it for her, making her fearless on the kids' behalf.

Sam walked over to her. She'd asked him to help her out today, a little nervous her first time coaching.

"Thanks for coming," she said.

"Hey, you owe me, and I'll collect, don't worry. What do you need me to do?"

"Nothing much. Help me when you think it's necessary. Let's see if I can manage by myself first."

Reye looked over the children and their parents who were here waiting for her to start. Nine kids so far: her six regulars from the program, all with their parents' permission, plus the new children who'd recently joined the aftercare group. Seeing Shane standing among them was a surprise, having not yet received permission from his parents. They'd not responded to any of her calls, ever. She'd have to deal with that later.

She called the kids over to her. "Today we are going to learn how to pass the ball to each other. I need you to line up side by side," she said and waited as they moved to follow her instructions. "Nice line!" she said. "This is how we pass the ball." Placing the ball at her feet, she demonstrated while she talked. "When you pass the ball to each other, you can use different parts of your feet, the inside, the outside, or the front, not with your toe, but with your laces." Reye demonstrated, touching the ball using all parts of her feet. "Okay, let me try with one of you. Shondra, come here, please?" She waited while Shondra, who was dressed from head to toe in pink, walked over to her. "I'll pass the ball to you, and I want you to pass it back to me. Okay?" Shondra nodded. Reye passed the ball and Shondra kicked it back to her, striking it with her laces. "Great, now again, using another part of your foot. Great! Now kick one more time with the other side of your foot. Awesome! Thanks, Shondra. Now let's form two circles and practice kicking the ball back and forth to each other. Remember to use the three sides of your feet." She and Sam walked to each child, helping them to practice the new skill, providing encouragement and correcting if necessary. "Okay, great work! Let's take a break and get some water."

After the break, Reye spoke again, the kids surrounding her. "In soccer, you have to run and run, and run, and then run some more. So, in order for us to get used to running, we have to practice running, right? So every day after our drills, we are going to form a line and run. I'll be the running leader this time and you all can follow me, but after this, one of you will be the running leader. This will be our way of getting in shape and getting used to running. Are we ready?"

"Yes," the kids said in unison. She took off and they all followed behind her. If any one fell behind, she would either slow down or fall back to help. At the end of practice Reye demonstrated several drills to help their bodies cool down. Before they left, she said, "We need a name for our team, so by next week, I want to hear some of your suggestions."

After all of the children had gone, Sam helped Reye pack up her cones and other equipment.

"You are great with those kids, Reye. I do believe you have found your calling. Who would have thought it was possible?"

"If that's your version of a compliment, I'll take it. Thanks for helping me today."

"You know, you could ask that boyfriend of yours to help you. He's not as good as me, but he would do in a pinch."

"He's not my boyfriend, and anyways, he's busy with law school right now."

Stephen sped through the night after having spent an exhausting day at school. He needed to go home and get some sleep, but instead he was once again headed to Reye's. This attraction was troublesome, and exorcising her from his system wasn't working like he'd expected. In fact, quite the opposite, it had began to mean more, encompassing more than just sex. The more he had gotten to know her, the more he liked her. She was compassionate, loving, spunky, and supportive. She excited him, moved him, and sated him like no other so far. Could he see a future for them? Was he even ready to settle down? He admitted she was the first that'd held his attention for this long, but that didn't mean she would be the last.

Dallas was different from Austin, more old school, more inflexible. As much as he disliked Joe, he suspected his parents' reaction to Reye would be similar. He didn't think he'd have to worry with the consequences of that; the likelihood of them meeting Reye was slim to none. She'd be long gone before that could potentially happen. Thanksgiving break was approaching, three days off, away from Reye. Maybe time spent at home would re-acquaint him with his old life and help to clear his head.

Claire hung up the phone, hearing Stephen Sr.'s car pull into their drive. Her home office resided next to the kitchen, strategically placed to keep an eye on the kitchen staff and an eye on the landscapers. One had to trust, but verify; that held true for staff and children. She'd just finished the final details of her latest charitable committee assignment. It had taken up most of the morning.

Stephen Jr. would arrive home tomorrow. He'd finally called her yesterday. Nothing like giving his mother advance notice. He knew she'd wanted to entertain Beth and her family, she'd told him so. How could anyone make plans with only a day's notice? Thankfully, she knew her son well, and had already tentatively scheduled coffee and dessert with Beth's family for Thanksgiving evening.

She had this sixth sense when it came to Stephen, and had kept tabs on him by any means possible. That meant the cleaning people, who'd reported his place clean, barely used for the last month or so. This bit of knowledge was confirmed by Henri, via his mother. Unlike Stephen, Henri had always been close to his mother, dutifully keeping in touch weekly. In contrast Stephen kept in touch with his dad weekly; two peas in a pod those two were, speaking in their own language. Stephen Sr. was always telling her about a conversation he'd had with her son.

Mothers weren't always close to their children; more than a few pushed their parents away. It was her job to protect him, and she did it in her own way. Having grown up with nothing, the baby of six children, she'd had parents who worked tirelessly and never had enough. She knew what it meant to rise to her current position in society, something both father and son took for granted.

She figured out early that she needed to find her own way in the world. She assumed the reins for her future in eighth grade. She'd talked her parents into applying for a private high school scholarship, which she'd received. An innate sense of style had helped her get the most out of her limited wardrobe, and she picked up the essential social graces and skills by watching others. She made friends with those who could help her. She would never be on the outside again. After high school another scholarship and a few small student loans helped to finance college; she was the only one in her family to attend.

Some considered her cool to the touch and unfriendly. Not so; she chose carefully who to befriend. Friendships were not to be squandered on those with no future. She joined the right sorority and went to the right parties, hosted and attended by the up and coming in Dallas. She'd met Stephen's father at just such a party.

She wanted the best for her son, only the best, and Stephen needed to be reminded of what that was. She was slightly worried. This staying with some girl was highly unusual for him. She knew and understood men and their needs, having grown up around her brothers. She was sure that he just needed a reminder of their standards and all would be well. He'd see Beth again, and she would be a big reminder.

CHAPTER 9

"I am going to miss you," Reye whispered into Stephen's ear. He was quiet, his breathing deep and even. She lifted her head from his chest and turned to look at him. He'd fallen asleep; they were both tired, both looking forward to the Thanksgiving break and the three days off from school. He would be in Dallas, she would remain in Austin. She didn't even want to contemplate how much she would miss him, so she turned, laid her head down, and snuggled into his chest.

It didn't happen much, but from time to time she'd persuade him to lie down. She'd switch off the lights, turn on music, and light a few candles. They would lie there, she on top, and discuss the events of their days. Mostly she did the talking and he'd listen, occasionally commenting. The center's after school program and coaching supplied her with more than enough stories and anecdotes to tell him, and it helped her work through issues. She felt really close to him on nights like these, dodging the reality that he didn't share much about himself. Sure, he talked of his days at school, but he never mentioned anything personal. He hadn't shared anything on the subject of his family or friends. Starting to feel anxious, she pushed those thoughts from her mind.

He would leave for Dallas tomorrow, so she'd just enjoy now. She gave some thought to waking him but decided against it. He needed the rest. So she took this time to admire him, pretending that he would be hers forever. She didn't really believe that's how this would end, but she was way past the point of no return in her feelings for him.

"Mom, I'm home," Stephen shouted as he entered the front door of his parents' home. The drive down I-35 had been uneventful, but tiring. Driving between Dallas and Austin offered little in the way of sights, just small cities packed with fast food and outlet malls, sandwiched between flat, wide-open spaces.

He wanted a shower and a bed, in that order. He walked in through the garage, toward the kitchen located in the back of the house. His parents had lived here forever. The décor had changed frequently during his childhood, every five years or so, making it feel new. Decorating, along with volunteer work and gardening, was a hobby of his mother's. He was her single most important hobby, making sure his life marched according to plan; his or hers, he hadn't decided yet.

"Mom," he called out again, walking into the kitchen. Finding her sitting at the table, casually but faultlessly dressed, supervising the cooking staff. As far back as he could remember, there had always been staff in their home. It was too large for one person to manage, and, even if it had not been, his mother was not up to such a task.

He'd tried to be lenient in his regard for his mother; he knew she had grown up poor, a fact that she reminded him of frequently—especially when she'd thought he wasn't living up to his potential.

"Hello, Stephen," she said, lifting her face to him for his kiss. "I am glad you made it home safely. Did you stay within the speed limit?"

"Yes, of course I did," he said, smiling at her.

"Are you hungry? Sonia made some soup and fresh bread for dinner tonight, but you can have some now if you like." Sonia, an older African-American woman, looked up and smiled. He returned her greeting.

"No, I'm okay. I ate something before I left."

"Then we will have dinner when your dad gets home. He said he would be here earlier than usual. Oh, and I invited Beth and her parents over later for drinks and dessert. I'm sure you'll want to see her."

"I'm going to go up and catch up on some sleep. I'm exhausted," he said. "Wake me for dinner if you don't hear me moving around."

"Of course."

Stephen sat down on the bed in his old room and answered his cell. It was Reye. "Hey," he said.

"Are you there? I was just checking to make sure you'd made it."

"I'm here. I was just about to get in some sleep. My mother has dinner plans for this evening."

"I didn't mean to interrupt you. You do sound tired, so I'll let you go."

"It's okay." He paused. "Look, Reye, I might not have a chance to call you much. I'm sure my mother has a thousand things planned, she usually does."

"No worries. I'll see you when you get back, then. I'll be busy with my family, too. Take care."

"I will. You, too," he said, hanging up.

Thanksgiving at the Jackson family's home was big, loud, and loving. "What else do you need help with, Mom?" Reye asked. So far they had prepared enough dessert and food to feed the Fifth Army, which was a close description of her family when all were present. Her three oldest brothers were married, with three children each. There seemed to be a competition to see who could reproduce the fastest, and each and every one of them was coming for dinner.

"Let's see, we've got two potato pies, one pecan pie, chocolate cake, your father's favorite, peach cobbler, and a coconut cake that I've not prepared yet. That should be enough, don't you think? We still need to make the corn-bread dressing, and you need to wash and cook the greens," her mother said.

"Okay," she said, smiling at her mom. She was the only girl, so during the holidays, kitchen duty primarily fell on her shoulders. She became the head sous chef, dish washer, and errand runner. The boys had been recruited when they lived at home, but they learned how to get out of the kitchen fast, sometimes sending their girlfriends in to serve as replacements; the ones they didn't mind losing, that is. Working with her mother was demanding stuff. She had very rigorous standards and she didn't put up with foolishness, as she was known to say. Her brothers had lost many a girlfriend in the mines of her mother's kitchen. Only the strong survived.

Reye placed the stopper in the sink and allowed water to fill to begin washing the greens, her least favorite chore.

"So," her mom asked. "How is school?" Did she mention that this was also the time her mother grilled her about her life, school, and love? Anything and everything was open for discussion.

"It's going great. My professor asked me to volunteer at the community center in their after-school program."

"Is that so? Which center?"

"You know the one, the East River Community Center over off of First Street?"

"I know the one," she said, stopping in her stirring of the cake batter and looking at Reye. "Is that a safe place for you to be?"

"Is there really any unsafe place in this town?"

"No, but some are safer than others."

"I'm no longer a volunteer," Reye continued. "I'm getting paid for working there. I'm also working every day instead of three days of the week. The best part is that we've started a soccer team for the kids, and yours truly is the coach."

"Hmmm," her mother said.

"What hmmm?"

"Do you have time to work, teach soccer, and study? I don't want you to forget why you are in school."

"That's not likely, as this is my last year. I wouldn't jeopardize graduation."

"With all that going on, do you have any time to meet any young men? You realize it gets harder to meet nice men after you leave college. I bet you've not given that any thought."

"Hey, Mom," Sam said from the doorway. Thank the Lord, Reye thought, a reprieve.

"Hey, baby girl," he said to Reye, winking at her. He walked over to gather their mom into a hug.

"I am so glad you've come by early. Isn't that nice, Reye?" her mom asked as she returned Sam's hug.

Reye rolled her eyes and mouthed 'thank you' to Sam. She turned back to the sink and concentrated on the greens. Would it hurt for her mom to say "great job, Reye" just once, she wondered as she worked on the veggies. Let her grill Sam for a while, she thought, let her prod and probe him about the state of his life and loves for a while. And as far as meeting young men, she'd met one, all right. She just chose not to share that info with her mother yet. First, he wasn't serious, and second, he wasn't serious. Meeting her mom came with questions that only a man serious in his pursuit of her would be open to answering. She knew race wasn't an issue. She was secure in that knowledge. She and her brother had friends and girl-friends of every hue, of all ethnicities and backgrounds. Her parents had treated anyone who came over with warmth and friendliness. She suspected they would treat Stephen the same way. Her dad and brothers would be tough, but for reasons other than race. They would be hard on any of her beaus because she was the baby girl.

Dinner that evening at the Stuarts' was a quiet affair. His dad had arrived home earlier in response to Stephen's homecoming and they'd eaten in the main dining room, which was large enough to accommodate twenty-four of his parents' closest friends. His dad and mom hosted many dinner parties related to the family's law practice or his mom's volunteer commitments.

Stephen had gotten his height and looks from his dad, who wore his age well.

"How are your classes?" His dad didn't wait for a response. "I spoke with Professor Laycock last week. He was in Dallas for a seminar at the office and he reported that you were doing quite well in his class. He was impressed by your range of knowledge."

"Classes are fine. It's amazing how much I picked up from clerking for you in the summers."

"How is Henri?" asked his mother.

"Fine."

"Your mother tells me that Beth and her family are coming over for drinks after dinner tonight."

"So I heard."

His dad liked Beth, but knew that he couldn't press Stephen. Men needed to make their own choices concerning women. "Your mother tells me that Beth is completing her degree in the spring."

"I guess so. I haven't spoken to her much this semester. I've been tied up with classes, and I'm sure she has been, too." His mother turned the conversation to some upcoming charity event and they finished dinner to the sound of her voice, a familiar occurrence.

A young Hispanic girl walked in and began to remove their dishes from the table.

"Stephen, would you mind helping me in the kitchen? While Maria cleans up dinner, you could help me prepare dessert and coffee."

"Sure," he said as he stood and followed his mother into the kitchen. She pulled a tray containing several types of desserts from the refrigerator and set them on the counter.

"Are you looking forward to seeing Beth?"

"I guess," he responded.

Stephen gathered the dishes and utensils that had been set aside earlier and placed them on the tray his mother had set before him. He lifted it, trailing her into a smaller room reserved for more intimate gatherings.

"Are you seeing anyone in Austin?" she asked.

He was surprised by the question. "No one in particular," he said.

"Well, that's not what I hear." He didn't respond. "I hear you're rarely at home these days," she continued.

"Is that so," he said, neither confirming nor denying her comment.

The doorbell rang, ending his mother's line of questioning. "I'll get the door," he said and walked to the foyer. The Barnes family, all three of them, stood on the porch. They fit perfectly with the three members of his family, a partner for each of them, and they'd always been a part of his life. He and Beth had played together when they were young and attended the same school from elementary through high school. Henri with his girlfriend and he and Beth were a regular foursome, hanging out together most of their senior year.

"Happy Thanksgiving," said Beth's dad, extending his hand to shake.

"Hello, Mr. and Mrs. Barnes, glad you could make it," Stephen replied. Behind them trailed Beth. She was a petite girl, gorgeous, with long black hair and striking green eyes, and as always dressed to perfection, showroom ready.

"Hi, Stephen," she said, brushing against him as she entered through the door.

"Hi, Beth." He leaned forward to kiss her cheek, but she moved her head towards his and he caught the outer part of her lips. She smiled, her eyes filled with mischief.

"I've been looking forward to seeing you all day," she said, turning as his parents entered. "Hello, Mr. and Mrs. Stuart," she said, giving them a beautiful smile. His dad engulfed her in a warm hug and his mother followed suit.

"You look more gorgeous every time I see you," his mom said.

"Thank you, Mrs. Stuart, so do you. I was hoping to steal Stephen away for a while this evening, if you don't mind," Beth said before they went further into the house. "Some of our friends from school are having a party and we do have some catching up to do," she said, gazing into Stephen's eyes as she spoke.

A chorus of "no, we don't mind" came from all of the parents in the room. "Young people prefer to be with other young people," said Stephen's father.

Stephen had been manipulated. Manipulation was Beth's forte, but it had never irritated him before. He'd even found it cute and amusing at times. He'd play along this time. "Let me get my keys and a jacket," he said, leaving the room. A minute later he returned with both items in his hands. "Let's go."

"Goodbye, everyone," Beth said. She gave all of the parents a kiss and then proceeded Stephen out the front door.

"Where is this party?" he asked as he walked around to the driver's side of his car.

"I'll drive," she said, snatching the keys from his hand. "We are going to a friend's party. I met her in school, you don't know her."

Beth had driven his car before, so he changed direction and went around to the passenger side. She slid in and adjusted the seat.

"How long are you going to be in town?" she asked as she started the car and pulled onto the street.

"Until Sunday morning, I think."

"Well, you look good, as I'm sure you know," she said, giving him a thorough once-over. He wore jeans that hugged his frame, a long-sleeve t-shirt, and a leather jacket.

"Do you want to hang out Friday, maybe go see a movie?"

"Sure," he said. He was here to test out his feeling for her anyway, and what better way then to spend some time together with her. He wasn't feeling that overwhelming sexual thing that he felt with Reye, but he still found her attractive.

They pulled up to one of the more exclusive apartments in an exclusive area of Dallas and parked. The apartment they entered was huge, and there were people everywhere. Beth introduced him around to her friends. They were all well coifed and on the prowl, giving him second and third looks. He'd stick with Beth tonight, ignoring the other glances thrown his way. Beth took his jacket, and what she did with it he didn't know.

He tagged along behind her from one room to another before they entered a large room with a dance floor, or what passed for a dance floor tonight. Slow music played from a hidden sound system somewhere within the apartment. She stopped and put her arms around his waist. Her head came up to the top of his chest. He'd gotten used to Reye's height, and it was a little disconcerting to adjust to Beth's. Strange that he used to prefer short girls, imagining himself as some sort of protector, apparently another preference shot to hell by Reye.

147

Beth pushed herself closer to him and he put his arms around her. Most of the others on the makeshift dance floor seemed to be coupled up as well. All were busy in their own personal embraces. It was dark in the room, save for a lamp or two. Beth put her arms around Stephen's neck and pulled his head down for a kiss. He complied reluctantly at first. He had to remind himself that he was there to test his feelings. He lightly put his lips to hers and she opened her mouth, seeking his tongue. After a few seconds, Beth broke off the kiss and looked up at him. "Is everything okay with you?"

"No, I'm all right, I'm just getting used to being home. I'm a little distracted is all," he said.

"Okay," she said, pulling back from him, for which he was grateful. They continued to hold each other and dance. After the song ended, Beth left him alone while she went in search of something for them to drink. He stood with his back to the wall and looked at the other beautiful people in attendance. They were dancing, talking, and all having a good time. Most of the people present seemed to be his age or younger, probably home from college like him, looking to have fun. He wasn't having much fun, and he was more than ready to get back to his place in Austin.

"Here is a beer." He turned to see her holding two Fat Tires in her hand. He took one from her.

"Thanks," he said.

"Are you good here for a while? I wanted to talk to some of my girlfriends. Do you mind?"

"No, I'm good."

"I'll be back to check on you," she said, turning to leave. He nursed his beer, relaxing, listening to the music. He moved on to the next room where a pro basketball game played on TV. He noticed two men seated on a couch and joined them, managing to get through an hour's worth of the game before he checked his watch. He'd had enough and went in search of Beth, whom he found in the kitchen, surrounded by five other women, seated around a very large table. They all looked up when he entered, and, judging from the guilt and surprise he saw on their faces, they must have been talking about him.

"I'm ready to go. Are you?"

"Sure, let me get our jackets," Beth said. He stood there in the doorway as she walked by him. He looked over at the girls left in her wake. All of them returned his look with interest. Some friends, he thought, turning away. Beth returned quickly with their jackets and they walked out the door to his car.

"Do you want me to take you home or drive you back to my parents? Yours are probably still at my house," he said.

"Take me home," she answered. As they both got into the car, she gave him directions to her apartment. It was a quiet return trip. She gazed out of the window while he focused on driving, lost in thought, his mind two hundred miles away.

He pulled up to the curb of her apartment and shut off the engine. He reached for his door handle to open it, intending to walk her to her door. Beth interrupted his movement.

"Don't walk me in," she said.

"I don't mind."

"No, really, it's not necessary." She turned to face him. "Has something changed? You seem distant," she said.

"No."

"I know you see other women. We don't have any agreement. I know that."

"Okay," he responded slowly, not sure where this conversation was headed.

"Forget I said anything. I'll call you around noon on Friday to see if you're still interested in a movie." She opened the door to leave.

"Sure. I'll try and find Henri and see if he can scrounge up a date, and it'll be just like old times."

"Maybe not quite like old times," she said as she smiled, the smile not reaching her eyes. She exited the car and his eyes followed the swing of her hips as she walked to her apartment. Nice, he thought, just not the ones he'd gotten used to.

CHAPTER 10

Stephen caught up with Henri early the next morning. They'd agreed to meet to play basketball at the gym.

"Dude, get ready to get your ass kicked," said Henri.

"In your dreams," Stephen replied as they both joined in a pick-up game that was starting up. They played for a while and afterward sat drinking a sports drink and watching a new game with new players begin.

"I went to a party with Beth last night," Stephen said.

"Is that so? How is she?"

"Gorgeous, as usual," he said, his tone neutral.

"You don't sound excited about that," Henri pointed out. Stephen knew that Henri had never been that fond of Beth, because he thought her beautiful in a shallow, vain kind of way.

"No, it was good to see her," Stephen said.

"She's just not Reye, huh?"

Stephen gazed speculatively at Henri. "I thought seeing Beth might jolt me out of this obsession with Reye."

"Did it work?"

"No, not yet. I like her, just can't see bringing her home."

"I think you underestimate your parents, or at least your dad. Your mom may require more effort, but it's your life and your woman. I think they would accept her if you were serious about her," Henri said. He paused for a second. "Are you?"

"Am I what?"

"Don't play dumb."

"Don't know if I would refer to Reye as my woman. I really think my dick has an obsession with Reye, and it appears to be in control these days," Stephen said.

"You know, Stephen, Reye is a nice girl. You shouldn't play around with her if you aren't serious. She could be hurt," Henri said in a disapproving tone.

"Dude, what, you're her guardian now?" Stephen said with a chuckle. He looked over at Henri.

"Whatever. I like her, you could do worse, that's all."

"Okay, this conversation is getting way too serious for me. I'd better get home for Thanksgiving dinner. Come by tonight if you want to," he said as he stood up to leave. "Let me know if you can scrounge up a date for the movies tomorrow."

Stephen leaned back from the table. "Great dinner," he said.

"Thank you."

"You look great Stephen," his maternal grandmother said. "We don't get to see you nearly as much as we'd like. Isn't that right Frank?" Frank was Stephen's grandmother's second husband. His mother's dad had died when Stephen was in elementary school.

"Are you taking Beth out this evening?" asked his mom.

"No, I am going to stay in and enjoy my family. She and I are going out tomorrow."

"Well, that's nice. She really is a beautiful girl."

"Yes, she is," agreed Stephen.

"Dad, are you and Frank up for a game of poker?" he asked, standing up from the table.

"If you don't mind losing," replied his dad with a wink. "I don't mind taking your money."

The men moved to the study. Stephen retrieved the cards and chips while his dad poured drinks and pulled out the cigars. He knew his dad appreciated this time with him, and he loved being able to offer it. He loved his mom as well, even with her control issues, but he'd spent more time with his dad, and he'd always sought him out when he needed comfort and support. It was from his dad that he'd felt unconditional love, so it wasn't a sacrifice to spend time with him.

We are bunch of loud-mouths, Reye thought to herself fondly as she looked around the table. At the head of the table sat her dad. He was the glue that held her family together. She loved her mother, but her dad was her rock. He was as soft as her mother was demanding and hard. Tall, at six feet, five inches, and with dark, rich chocolate skin, he was big and wide, useful for playing football when he was younger and then helpful for knocking his sons' heads together as they grew up.

"Everyone, grab hands, bow your heads," he said, waiting. "Heavenly Father, thank you for allowing my family to come together this Thanksgiving. We sing your praises for all of our blessings and seek your forgiveness for our transgressions. Keep us in your heart and show us your will as we complete the remainder of the year. Amen."

"Amen!" The table was immediately filled with conversation. Reye loved her family. Her brothers had always looked after her. Sam, who sat next to her, hit her elbow to get her attention.

"Pass me the turkey platter," he said, winking at her. She held it to her left so he could select the slices he wanted. "How is Stephen, by the way? Are you two still seeing each other? You haven't called to cry on my shoulder, so I guess everything is okay." Her eagle-eyed and sharp-eared mother turned to them, looking intently at Reye.

"Tell you later," she returned. Turning to her sister-in-law, Reye asked about her nieces and nephews.

Friday afternoon found Stephen at Beth's apartment at noon as agreed. Henri hadn't been able to find a date, or he hadn't wanted to join them. She opened the door, hair wet from a shower, with one of the smallest robes he'd ever seen covering her body.

"Hi, Stephen. I'm not ready yet."

She moved to allow him entrance, managing to brush against him as he entered. In the old days, he wouldn't have minded and would have taken her up on her unsolicited offer, but not today. She seemed to sense his impatience. "Are we in a hurry?" She sauntered over to stand directly in front of him.

"Well, the movie starts in about forty minutes and if we don't hurry we're going to miss it."

She moved her finger to his lips. "Would it be so bad if we missed the movie? We could entertain ourselves here in other ways," she said coyly. She reached up and put her arms around his neck. He caught them before they were able to connect and placed them by her sides.

"Not a good idea. I've wanted to see this movie for a while." She seemed surprised by his abruptness and hurt by his rejection.

"Let me finish getting dressed, then," she said sharply. She turned to walk away from him. This was a bad idea, he thought to himself. He didn't want to go anymore. But if he could just get through the movie, he could go home.

Later on that night he lay in his room, head propped on his pillow as he watched college football games, his second round of football games today. Earlier, after dropping an angry Beth home, he'd joined his dad on the couch in the game room and they'd watched games together. He left his dad there a while ago to try and get some sleep, but it eluded him.

He missed Reye. He reached for his cell and dialed her number. She hadn't been far from his thoughts this week. She answered on the first ring.

"Hey, stranger," she said softly.

"Hey," he said, equally softly. "What are you doing?"

"Nothing much. I'm still at my parents. I think I'm going to spend the night here, get in some major family time. All of the brothers are here with their kids and I don't get to see them as much as I'd like. Auntie Reye, the favorite and only aunt, is a popular item around here. And as usual the brothers are giving me grief, especially Sam. By the way, he asked about you."

"Did he?"

"What have you been up to?"

"Nothing much, really. I've been spending time with my parents and grandparents. I met Henri for some hoops yesterday and hung out with old high school friends one night." He paused. "I was thinking about coming back early, leaving tomorrow morning, actually."

"Okay." Reye wasn't sure how to respond.

"Will you be home?"

"Not in the morning. I have a practice scheduled with the kids from the center, but after that I should be home. You could come by then if you want to," she offered quietly.

"I will," he said. "Should I call before I come?"

"No. If I'm not home, you know where to find the key, right?"

"Yes."

"Well, then, I'll see you tomorrow."

"Okay. See you."

"What drills are you going to start with today?" Sam was looking around the field, noting Reye's practice setup. During the last couple of practices they'd worked on passing, shooting, and trapping, really basic stuff, keeping it simple for those new to the game. Getting Sam to help had been a great idea whose outcome could have gone either way. Sam considered himself the guru of soccer, so she'd expected a power struggle to maintain her position as coach; twenty-four years of being the little sister was difficult to overcome. He'd surprised her though, by not interfering at all, totally assuming the role of the helpful assistant, offering suggestions which she felt free to accept or discard.

"Today I would like to introduce them to field positioning." There were enough kids now to field a team of eleven, with two left over for subs. The initial nine had grown to thirteen, most from the after-school program, others from the surrounding neighborhood, friends and siblings of her kids. They were all here for today's practice, kicking the ball between each other, waiting for practice to start. She called them over to form a half circle in front of her. "Listen up, guys, today I am going to introduce you all to your positions on the field. Then we can begin to use the skills we've learned in our other practices to play a game." Between Reye and Sam, the kids were placed in their assigned position on the field. Shondra and Eric were the last to be assigned, and, because they were fast for their ages, both would play in the forward position. "Shondra," Reye called. Shondra trotted over, her shin guards sitting on the outside of her socks. "Baby girl," Reye said. "Remember your shin guards belong on the inside of your socks."

"But I like them this way, Ms. Reye. They're too pretty to wear inside my socks where no one can see them," she said earnestly. Reye turned her head and rolled her eyes at Sam, who chuckled.

"Ms. Reye, can we take a water break? I'm thirsty," Anthony said.

"Sure," she said, signaling the other players over. They all gathered around the thermos, waiting their turn for water.

"Does everyone understand their positions?" she asked.

"Yes, Ms. Reye," the more conscientious of the group responded.

"Well, let's spend a little more time working on playing our positions and then we can stop for the day. Let's also thank Mr. Sam for helping us again today."

"Thank you, Mr. Sam," they sang out loudly, and of course Mr. Sam ate the attention up, the ham, bending at the waist like a Japanese samurai soldier.

"You're welcome," he shouted back.

As usual, Reye waited until all of the kids had been picked up by their parents. Shane stood next to her, silent, his standard operating procedure. "Where are your folks?" she asked looking down at him. He shrugged his shoulders, looking dejected. Shane's parents made her crazy. They never returned any of her calls and she'd only seen the mother pick him up, never stopping long enough to introduce herself. She just drove by and picked up Shane like you'd pick up a hamburger from the McDonald's drive-thru line.

"Is your mother coming today?" she asked. He shrugged his shoulders. "Do you know how to get home?" Shane nodded.

"Can you show me, if I drive you?" He nodded again. "Remember to use words, Shane," she said, looking down at him.

"Yes," he said. Her Shane was a man of few words.

"Okay, grab your soccer ball and I'll give you a ride home." He helped her load up her truck, and they both got in. "Seat belt on, bud," she said, and he reached for his and locked it. "Where do I go from here?" Reye followed his directions to his home. It was a small house painted white, a little run down, but clean. It was about two miles from the center. They got out and walked to the door, which Shane unlocked using a key he kept tucked in his pocket. Just as he started to walk in, they turned to see a car pull into the driveway. She and Shane stopped as Joe, of all people, Joe from Stephen's soccer team and fraternity, jumped out of his car and stormed toward them.

"What are you doing here with my nephew?" Reye took a step back. "I'm his coach, we had soccer practice today and his mother didn't pick him up on time. I couldn't just leave him there, so I gave him a ride home. I didn't mind," she said, talking quietly and looking over at Shane, smiling weakly. Joe turned away from them, looking out at the street, taking a deep breath, reigning in his temper.

"Hey, buddy, why don't you go inside and let me talk to your coach," he said to Shane.

"Okay. Bye, Ms. Reye," the child said softly.

"Bye, Shane," she said, ruffling his hair. After Shane closed the door, Joe spoke. "Look, my sister was supposed to pick him up, but she's been having a lot of problems lately. I don't live here, but I try to help them out when I can."

"No problem," she said. Reye turned and walked to her car.

"Look, I'm sorry. I was worried about Shane. My sister has had her share of problems in the past, we both have, and she's been acting strange lately. I panicked when I couldn't find him."

"No worries," she said. "Like I said, I couldn't leave him there alone."

"Thank you," he said as if saying those words to her actually caused him physical pain.

That must have hurt, she thought. "You're welcome," she said.

Reye pulled up to her home, drained. Never in her wildest dreams would she have put Shane with Joe. Small world, huh? How could someone so hateful have a hand in raising that shy, kind boy? Stephen hadn't arrived yet and she was thankful. She needed a shower and a moment to process her encounter with Joe, knowing she couldn't discuss it with Stephen. Who knew what that would do to their non-relationship again? Letting herself in, Reye surveyed her home. She was happy that she'd cleaned up before going over to her parents' for Thanksgiving. She walked toward the bathroom, stripping as she went. Standing under the spray of the shower, she let the hot water course down her body, rinsing away the last of her worries about Joe and Shane. She'd just turned off the water in the shower when the doorbell rang. Grabbing her robe, she went to answer it. She peeked through the peephole and there stood Stephen. She opened the door and stood there for a second, admiring him. He looked great, dressed casually in jeans and a plain, long-sleeved t-shirt that cuddled a beautifully shaped chest and led upward to a lean, angular face. Lips she loved and felt even in her sleep and deep blue eyes that looked back at her.

"Can I come in, or you just going to stand there and stare?" he asked, displaying that wicked smile of his. "I know you missed me, but you have to let me in to show me how much," he continued, chuckling.

"You are so full of yourself," she said with a laugh.

"That may be so, but you love it."

If you only knew, she thought. "Come in," she said, moving over to allow him entrance before asking, "How was your drive back?"

"Fine," he said, reaching for the belt that held her robe closed. His eyes locked on hers while he closed and locked the door behind him, never breaking his hold on her. He pulled her to him as he walked backward until his back touched the door. Pulling the belt apart, he opened her robe. She was naked underneath—smooth brown skin over a perfect body had him catching his breath, same as always. He moved his eyes from her face to travel down her neck to her beautiful breasts, made uniquely for his hands. He touched them softly, reverently, lightly skimming the pads of his fingers over them. He heard her breathing change, become ragged. His eyes continued their downward perusal, over her waist, which flared out to nice rounded hips, his hands followed, resting on the part of her that he wanted now, moving to touch her, opening her. Returning to look at her face, his eyes watched as hers closed and she moaned. He leaned into her lips for a kiss, so soft, lightly touching them with his, and then spearing her mouth with his tongue to seek and find hers. He moaned now, his hand continuing its play between her legs.

"I missed this," he whispered softly. His other hand moved to her waist and he pulled her flush against him. His mouth opened more, devouring hers. He walked her backwards to her bedroom, breaking the kiss as he removed his shirt first. She stood immobile as he unbuttoned his pants and chucked them, along with his boxers and shoes. She looked at his now-naked chest and leaned over to suck a nipple.

"I missed you, too," she said to him, looking into his eyes again as she removed her robe, letting it fall to the floor. He took her hand, leading her over to her bed where he sat, pulling her onto his lap as he lay back. She straddled him, leaning forward to kiss him again. Placing his hand on her hips, he lifted her and positioned her over him, pulling her downward slowly. One of his hands moved to her chin, to secure it and hold her face in place; he wanted to see her face when he entered her. He pushed his hips upward, watching her eyes lose focus as they both groaned at the pure pleasure of him in her. He began to slowly move in and out of her body. She tried to meet him, to force him to give her more, but he refused, holding her tightly as he set this pace. He would not be rushed, had waited too long for her. He watched her as she sat up and leaned back, her head rolling backward, from side to side, absorbed by the luxurious feel of him. She climaxed quickly, it hitting her before she was prepared. "Oh, Stephen," she sighed as her head fell to rest on his chest.

He stood, lifting her with him, securing her legs around his waist. Then he lowered her back to the bed, pulling out completely before pushing back into her, hard. Gone were the soft, slow thrusts from a few minutes ago, replaced by a fierce rhythm that moved her up towards the headboard. She planted her feet and pushed back, equally forceful and strong, meeting him thrust for thrust. His lips grabbed hers and didn't let go, feeling her climax begin again as she gripped him harder. He couldn't wait, frantic in his quest to reach his climax, pumping into her, feeling her shudder as he came, his body tensed over and in hers and he gave himself over to one powerful climax. He held himself in her, then fell forward on her to lay there. He knew he needed to move, but he was wiped. Reye wrapped her legs and arms around him and held on, energized by the feel of him on top of her, one heavy and thoroughly used male.

"Maybe you should go away more often," she said to him. He lifted his head, looking down at her. She read satisfaction on his face, evident in the droopy eyelids and the self-satisfied smile he gave her.

"I don't think my body could survive many home-comings like this," he said as he rolled to his side taking her along with him and folding her into his body. "But, I'm glad I came back early, too."

CHAPTER 11

The first week of December marked the end of the semester for Reye. The law school ended later than most of the other disciplines, so she was at loose ends while Stephen studied for finals. To keep occupied, she spent a lot of time at the center filling in for other volunteers that needed time off, and working with her kids in soccer. She was worried about Shane. He'd completely stopped attending both the after-school program and soccer practices. Dismayed by the prospect of him falling behind, she knew she needed to visit his home, to find out what was up, and soon. He had made such good progress, academically and socially.

"One more semester and I'm done," Stephen said to Reye. He was sitting on the floor with her positioned between his legs, her back to his chest, watching a movie. Yesterday he'd taken his last final and tomorrow he was leaving to spend the Christmas break with his family.

"You should be proud of yourself," she said.

"So should you, with your work at the center and with your soccer team."

"Thanks."

"When are you going to your parents'?"

"Sam and I are going over Christmas Eve, but I'm coming back here the day after Christmas. See that stack of books on the floor?" she asked, pointing to a mountain of about ten or so books sitting in the corner of the room. "Well, you can picture me here, snuggled up and reading them. I'm so looking forward to some alone time, to run, relax, and sleep." She turned and smiled at him. "Someone keeps me up most nights, so I'm really looking forward to having the bed to myself." She paused. "I am going to miss you, though," she added more seriously. She considered asking him to come back early, or inviting him to meet her parents, but decided against it. If she had to ask, it wouldn't be right.

"I'll be back before you know it," he said.

"Don't worry about me, I'll be busy." She turned her attention back to the movie.

Reye woke up early on Christmas morning, just like old times. What child hadn't gotten up at the crack of dawn to check out the goods Santa had left for them? She and Sam had spent the night at their parents' home. Her other brothers would be there later on in the evening, she hoped in time for dinner. She heard a knock on her door and sat up. Sam entered, attired in a t-shirt and pajamas bottoms, just like old times.

"Ready to see what Santa brought you?" he asked, sitting on the foot of her bed.

"I asked Santa for a Transformer this year," she said playfully.

"What, no GI Joes? Remember when you wanted them and you ended up with dolls instead? You were such a weird child," he said, laughing. "How is Stephen? Where is he, anyway?"

"He went home to Dallas to visit his family."

"I see. You two still spending a lot of time together?"

"Yep. He comes by the house at the end of the day most days. I like him a lot, Sam. It's kind of scary. He likes me, too."

"Are you going to bring him by to meet your mom and dad?"

"Whoa, slow down, I don't want to run him off just yet. I'm okay in this place for now," she said, placing hands palm-to-palm slightly in front of the chest, arms parallel to the floor in the classic Zen position.

"Do you want more?"

"Maybe . . . who am I kidding, sure I do. We've got one more semester, and who knows what will happen, but I'm not pushing."

"Okay." He stood up. "Let's go and see what Santa left for us."

Reye smiled. "Give me a second and I'll be there."

After Sam left Reye reached for her telephone to call Stephen. It rang several times with no answer, rolling over to his voice mail. She sent him a text instead. *Merry Christmas! Miss you, call when you can.*

Stephen woke about mid-morning on Christmas Day. He'd stayed out too late and drank too much with Henri the night before. They'd gotten invited to a party held by some of their undergraduate friends from SMU. Beth had also been there; he remembered mistletoe and kissing. He usually didn't drink, hadn't *drank* like that since his early college days. Henri had driven them home and directed him to his front door.

He got up, brushed his teeth, washed his face, and went downstairs to find his parents. They were in the kitchen drinking coffee and reading the paper, waiting for him.

"Merry Christmas," said his mom and dad in unison.

"Merry Christmas," he responded, walking over to kiss his mom's cheek.

"Late night," his dad said, more of a statement than a question. "Hope you had a good time."

"I did, saw some of my friends I hadn't seen in forever."

"Did Beth attend?" his mom asked.

"Yep. She did." He didn't offer any further details, for they were fuzzy in his mind anyway. He walked over to the cabinet and retrieved a coffee cup. Coffee, black and hot, poured from the carafe that sat on the counter and into his cup. He needed it black and strong.

"So, the grandparents are coming over this afternoon?" he asked after he'd gotten two large swallows under his belt.

"I called them when I heard you stirring around. They are on their way now," his mom said. "I thought we would open gifts this morning. They wanted to be here when you opened your gifts."

Sometimes he thought being the only child had its downside; his family's holiday plans always revolved around him.

His mom passed his cell to him. "You left your phone on the counter last night. Someone named Reye sent you a text this morning." She looked at him curiously. "Who's Reye?"

"She's a friend, mom. Someone from school."

"Reye is a she, I wasn't sure. Have you known her long?"

"I've spent some time helping her with school, it's nothing major." Couldn't get anything past dear old Mom. He knew better than to have left his cell lying around. His mom was a world-class snoop. *I must have been really wasted*, he thought.

He met Henri for basketball the following morning. "I must have gotten really hammered at that party. I can only recall patches of what happened."

"Really? Do you remember kissing under the mistletoe?"

"Kind of."

"Do you remember who you kissed?"

"Beth."

"You win the grand prize. And here I was thinking you were getting a little serious about Reye."

Stephen groaned. "Did I do anything that I would regret?"

"Kissing her and seeing Reye isn't enough? But no, not that I could tell. Beth was glued to you, however, and it didn't seem like you minded."

"Reye and I aren't serious," he replied, sounding defensive even to his own ears. "It's just for now, anyway. We wouldn't work long-term."

"Why are you so sure it can't?"

"Do you remember Justin Smith, that African-American kid from middle school?"

"He was the running back for our JV football team, right?"

Stephen nodded. "I liked him. He was cool. We were great together on the field, me handing the ball off to him, him running for touchdowns. We made a good team. Well, anyway. I invited him home to review some plays, to prep for a game. We set up shop in my room and then we went in search of food. I was always hungry at that age and so was he, so we had gone through the refrigerator really well. We had a feast spread out over the kitchen table. I left him eating, and went up to my room to get a copy of some homework he'd mentioned he needed. I returned to find my mom with the phone in her hand, in the process of dialing 911. She thought he had broken into her house and was stealing her food. You know and I know my mom can be a control freak, but I never knew her to be mean until that day. She was rude to him, and she didn't bother to hide her dislike. She asked me to let her know in the future if I had to bring home any children that she hadn't met or that were not kids of her friends. I didn't bring anyone else new over after that incident. You know, he was never the same around me."

Henri listened to Stephen's story in silence. "Well, I don't know what to say, dude, wish I did." He also knew

Stephen's mother, but he hadn't known her to be preju-
diced. Controlling and demanding, yes. But who did
anyone really know? "You may have to talk to Beth; she
may have the wrong impression about the two of you
now," he said in a complete non-sequitur.

"I know."

Stephen would have to talk to Beth sometime, just
not now. He'd finally responded to Reye's text, wishing
her Merry Christmas, but hadn't spoken with her since
he'd left. He could call. It hadn't even been a week yet and
here he sat, missing her. He needed to get a grip.

"Earth to Stephen," said Henri.

"Sorry, dude, in another world. Is our game still on
for tonight?"

"Yep." He and Henri were meeting up later on that
evening to play soccer with some of their old select team
buddies.

They played basketball the remainder of the
morning, after which Stephen went to workout with the
weights. He hit the treadmill a little later and started running. He had one more semester and he decided that he
would continue to spend it with Reye, starting now, not
worrying about the outcome until he was forced to. He
would head back to Austin in the next day or so to spend
the remainder of the Christmas break with her. He'd
rather be there anyway; why fight it? He would break it
off for good when school ended. He didn't want the
headache that would result from trying to incorporate
her long-term into his life, his friends, and his family. He
would keep his options open, but he would not get phys-

ical with anyone else but Reye now. She was more than enough for him. Honestly, she was all he wanted right now.

Stephen's cell rang. He was driving, trying to follow his soccer buddies from the fields where they'd just completed a soccer game to a new place that apparently offered cheap drinks and an overabundance of women. He wasn't interested in the women part, but didn't want to stand in the way of his buddies and their quests. He answered the phone, noting from the caller ID that it was Beth.

"Hey, Beth," he said.

"Hey, Stephen," she said, her voice a mix of enthusiasm and playfulness. "I enjoyed hanging out with you last night, and I was checking to see if you were interested and available tonight?"

"You know what, Beth, I need to apologize for giving you an impression that I wanted something more with you. I'm sorry, I don't. I had a little too much to drink last night. It not you, it's me, and I'm just not interested in starting anything right now." Silence filled the air.

"Screw you, Stephen," she said, hanging up.

"That went well," he said into the darkness of his car, relieved.

Stephen was tired, exhausted even, as he lay on his bed later on that night. It had been a blast getting together with his soccer buddies, the same crazy nuts from high school. They all played hard tonight, capping it off with beer following the game. It was late when he'd gotten home, and his parents hadn't waited up. He'd showered, put on some boxers, and gone to bed, but he couldn't sleep. He was tired from today's workout and game, but he remained restless. He reached for his cell and called Reye.

"Stephen," she said, her voice low and throaty from sleep. He must have awakened her. The sound of her voice reminded him of the many nights he'd spent in her bed, her body, soft, warm, and open to him.

"Hey, did I wake you?" he asked. He lay on his back, his head resting against the pillow, his other hand moving along his chest.

"Not really . . . kind of . . . what time is it?"

"Eleven-thirty."

"I went to bed early," she said. "Long day at the office . . . where are you?"

"Still at my parents'. I met Henri and some old buddies for a game of soccer today. We went for beer afterward."

"Beer, huh," she said, a sexy laugh in her voice.

"Yes, beer. Why's that funny?"

"It's not funny," she said. "But you do know what beer does to you, right?" Her voice dropped to a smooth, sexy whisper.

"No, what does it do to me?" His voice dropped to match hers.

"I wish you were here," she answered instead of explaining. "If you were here, and you had finished your beer, I would be laying next to you wearing nothing but smooth, brown skin."

"Are we having phone sex?" he asked her, a smile now in his voice. He ran his hand down the front of his body, noting the change brought on by the sound of her voice and words.

"No, just thinking out loud. When are you coming back?"

"Keep talking to me in that voice and I'll drive back tonight."

She laughed. "Sam signed the team up for a soccer tournament this weekend over at the university fields. Our first game is in the morning . . . So . . ." she said slowly, "as much as I like to slide my hands all over your body, wrap my legs around you as you pump hard into me, I'd better let you go. I need my sleep."

"Somehow I don't think I should let you hang up, not after that. You *will* pay when I get back," he said, laughing.

"I'll hold you to that," she said. "And hold you in my hands, my mouth, and your favorite spot," she said, drawing out her words. "Good night, Stephen. Sweet dreams."

He laughed. "Good night, Reye."

Early the next morning, Stephen found his mother sitting in her home office, drinking her coffee, the newspaper and various magazines surrounding her. She was dressed to impress, as always. One of the morning shows played on the TV. She muted it when she heard him enter.

"Morning, Mom. Where's Dad?"

"He's gone to the golf course, getting his usual early morning start," she said.

"I'm going back to Austin today. Some friends of mine are playing in a soccer tournament this weekend, and I'm going to join them." It was not quite the truth, but close enough.

Her face showed disappointment, but it was smoothed over quickly with a smile. "But you've only been here a few days. You have more than two weeks left. Can't you stay longer?"

"I would, but I can relax better at my place. I may come back later, before the semester starts up again. Anyway, my car is already packed. I'll call you when I get to Austin," he said, ending the discussion.

"It's Reye, isn't it?"

"What?" He stopped in his tracks, taking a second to recover from the shock. "No, Mom. Reye is a friend I helped out with school," he said, his voice firm.

"Let me at least walk you to the door. I see that you've made up your mind," she said. She stood and followed him out the front door and watched him get into his car.

"Bye, Mom. Tell Dad goodbye for me," he said.

"I will. Remember to call me when you arrive, or I'll just worry."

"Will do," he said. Giving her a final wave, he drove away.

"Losing sucks," Reye said to Sam. "What kind of coach are you, anyway? We should vote you off the island." Sam laughed at her antics. They'd lost the first two of three games scheduled for today, and Reye always took any opportunity to tease her brother about his failings.

"It's your fault. You're not living up to your potential," Sam replied. "Mr. Defender needs to get back and lift your spirits. When will he be back, anyway?"

Reye shrugged her shoulders. "I don't know," she said. She didn't want to talk about Stephen just then.

"When's our next game?" she asked Sam to change the subject.

"This evening at seven, so rest up. If we lose this one we are out of the tournament."

"Aye, aye, Captain," she said, and gave him a mock salute. "I'll be there."

She sat on the bench and watched him leave, not in any hurry to get home. She was lonesome. Taking her time, she removed her shoes, socks, and shin guards and replaced them with running shoes. She pulled on her sweats. She loaded up her bag and walked in the direction of the parking lot. Where had she parked? Turning to the right, she spotted her truck and stopped dead. Stephen stood there, leaning with his back against her truck's door, looking beyond good. She felt her eyes start to water and her stomach flutter. *Get a grip, Reye,* she thought to herself. But he'd traveled back earlier than she expected, or had hoped. *For me,* she thought. He looked great, jeans riding low on lean hips, a t-shirt with some type of writing on it, and baseball cap pulled low over a gorgeous face. God, she loved him. She wouldn't admit it to him, but the surprise of seeing him solidified that knowledge in her.

He was standing there, watching her, all tall, lean, golden, hers. She imagined her smile was wide enough to drive a truck through, and he returned it. She hurriedly walked over to him, stopping directly in front of him. Both of them wore huge smiles on their faces now, his wicked and full of promises, promises she knew he could and would keep. His arms went around her waist and he tugged her to him. She lifted her head, lips slightly parted, ready to meet his. She'd missed him more than she could say, so she tried to convey her feelings with her kiss. She opened for him and he marched in, like always, owning her. She loved his command. She didn't know how long they stood there and kissed; she was only aware of him.

He shifted away from her lips, pulling her to him for a hug, wrapping her tightly in his arms. "Did you guys win?" he asked in her ear.

"No, we lost both games. One more game left to play, and I don't want to play anymore now that you're here. When did you get back?"

"Mid-morning, but I stopped by my apartment to check in before I came here."

She moved in to kiss him again, feeling like an addict. She loved the feel of his mouth, warm as her tongue met his. She felt herself melting more, and felt his answering response against her stomach. "Where are you going now?"

"With you. Where else?"

"Are you hungry?"

"Not for food," he said.

"I'll meet you at my house?"

He released her and moved so that she could get into her truck. She let down her window. "Where did you park?"

"About two cars over. You go ahead. I'll be right behind you." He stepped back to let her drive away.

Reye rushed home, hitting the door at a run. She wanted to take a shower before Stephen arrived. Who would have thought he would come back early for her? This had to mean something, right? She meant something to him? It was more than just sex? She turned on the shower and stripped out of her soccer gear. She hopped in and cleaned up, probably breaking some kind of record for the world's fastest shower. She stepped out, dried off as she walked into her bedroom, and grabbed shorts and a t-shirt. She wouldn't have anything on for long, so it really didn't matter.

She decided to change the sheets on her bed, taking time to spray a little of her favorite perfume on them. Picking up loose clothes that were lying around her house, she put them in the hamper. Passing through the living room she glanced at the books she wouldn't get around to reading, but she was more than okay with that. Her kitchen was clean, but what to do about food? She opened the door, looking at the leftovers from her mother's Christmas dinner. It would do in a pinch, and there was always delivery. As she stood there, she heard her doorbell. Beyond happy, she turned to go and let him in.

After Stephen watched Reye drive off, he'd driven to a restaurant and picked up dinner, dessert, and pastries for breakfast. He stopped by the store to grab a bottle of wine and champagne. For some reason he felt like celebrating. He arrived at Reye's about twenty minutes later. He hadn't unpacked from his trip home, so he grabbed the food, drinks, and his duffel bag and carried it all to her door. He rang the doorbell. As if she had been waiting by the door, it opened quickly. She stood there with a smile that could light up the night, her eyes twinkling. "I was beginning to wonder what happened to you," she said.

He lifted his arms showing his purchases. "I went for sustenance . . . for later."

She took the bags from him and walked into the kitchen. He followed, eyes trained on her fine backside. She'd changed into a t-shirt, no shoes, and her old track shorts that looked like underwear to him. He just loved her in them.

Placing the bags on the table, she began to pull items from them. He walked in, standing close behind her, taking in her scent. Placing his hands low on her hips, he bent his head to the curve of her shoulder. "You smell good," he murmured, placing small kisses on her neck and ear. She stopped removing the food and twined her arms up and around his neck, anchoring him to her from the back. His hands slowly found their way to the hem of her shirt, and lifting it, they moved slowly over her stomach, sliding over her ribs, upwards to her breasts. Her body was satin to his touch. His breath caught as his hands found her breasts. *No bra, good girl,* he thought. They fit perfectly in his hands and he gave them a tug, drawing a moan from Reye. He took his time touching her. She needed to touch too, and turned to face him, her arms remaining in their position around his neck. He found her mouth and plundered it, pulling her even more tightly to him, both lost in each other.

He broke off the kiss leaned his forehead to hers. "I missed you," he said. He pulled her shirt over her head and began to feast at her breast. She held on to his head as if her life depended on it. He paused to tug her shorts down, and, finding no underwear, his hands strolled along her ass, smooth and round. He spun her around to face the table, placing her hands on to the edge to hold her steady. Looking at her, his mouth watered. She was all lean, brown muscle. He pulled her body outward from the table and unzipped his jeans while spreading her legs. He grabbed on to her hips and pushed in, totally embedded in her with one thrust. Could she be any more welcoming, any more wet and snug?

"Give me a second," he said. Leaning his chest on her back, he planted kisses on her neck. She pushed back into him, impatient, and he responded with a growl, his rhythm starting out slow and gradually increasing in speed. One of his hands traveled to the front of her body and wandered between her breasts and her sex, trying to accommodate both, turning Reye into a pool of liquid. She moaned continuously; it all felt so damn good.

"Please don't stop," she said.

"Are you kidding?" he groaned out, increasing his tempo, pushing harder into her body. She met him thrust for thrust.

"Oh, babe, you feel so good." He was barely aware of the words that emptied from his mouth. Conscious only of how she felt, surrounding him, hugging him tightly, and coming. They both moaned as orgasms hit them simultaneously. Stephen gritted his teeth and held Reye as his climax washed through him. He laid his head on her back, trying to breathe, still needing somehow to touch, his mouth kissing her neck and back. His hands had somehow found their way around to her breasts, and he now released his hold on them.

"Are you okay?" he asked.

"I think so," she said as he lifted her arms from the table and turned her to face him.

"I really missed you," he said, capturing her face in his hand, kissing her softly over and over. "Hungry?" he asked, and they both laughed.

Reye talked Stephen into going with her to the next game. She was sitting in his car as he drove them both to the last game of the tournament after they'd both showered and changed into shorts and soccer gear. She would have to talk to Sam about him playing once they arrived at the fields. As they pulled into the parking lot, Reye spotted Sam. "Let me off here and I'll go talk to him," she said, grabbing her bag. "We're on field number five. I'll meet you there after you park." She leaned over for a quick kiss and hopped out.

"Sam," she shouted, running to catch up to him. He turned at the sound of her voice and waited.

"Guess what?"

"What?"

"Stephen is here, and I talked him into coming to the game. Maybe he could play?"

"Maybe. I need to meet him first," Sam said as he and Reye walked over to their field. About five minutes later, Stephen walked up. Reye turned to make the introductions. "Stephen, this is my brother Sam. Sam, Stephen."

Reye watched them take each other's measure. Sam extended his hand for Stephen to shake. Stephen accepted. Stephen could tell that Sam and Reye were related, same height, same coloring.

"Reye tells me you came ready to play," Sam said.

"If you need me, sure, but don't make any changes to your line-up on my account."

"Don't worry, we lost two games already and we're out of the tournament for all practical purposes. So you can play if you want."

Reye stood there smiling. "Reye," Sam said to her. "Would you go to the main tent and grab the game card for me, I forgot to pick it up."

"Sure," said Reye, looking anxious. She turned to leave, but not before giving her brother a warning look. They both watched her walk away.

"So, Stephen, Reye tells me that this is your last year in law school?"

"Yep, that's true."

"What are your plans after you finish? Are you going to remain in Austin, or will you be going back to Dallas?"

"Dallas is home. My family's law practice is there, so if I want to work with them I'll need to be there."

"Hmm. Let me just cut through the bullshit. You seem like a nice enough guy, so don't take this the wrong way. My sister likes you, and I wouldn't want to see her hurt, so if this is a game to you, you need to move on to someone else," Sam said, all business.

Stephen was equally serious and not at all intimidated. "I appreciate your advice, but Reye and I are both adults and what happens to us is between us," Stephen said.

"Just a warning, that's all. Just be careful. I wouldn't want to see her hurt," Sam said.

"So you've said and I've heard. I wouldn't want to hurt her, so I guess we're in agreement."

Both men stared at each other for a minute, neither blinking. Sam turned and walked off to warm up and Stephen stood there and waited for Reye to return.

━━✐

Later on that night, Stephen lay next to Reye in bed, watching her while she slept. She was funny and a bit quirky even in her sleep. When he spent the night, she'd draw her body into a tight ball and root around until she found her spot just underneath his arm, tucking herself into his chest. He didn't know of anyone besides her who could sleep in one position all night. He looked down at her again and ran his hand along her side to rest on her hip. He understood her brother's need to warn him. He was almost certain that Reye loved him. He was a jerk to remain here when he knew he would ultimately leave her. But not yet; she was his for the remainder of this semester. He leaned over and trailed kisses down the side of her face. She moaned; even in her sleep, she was responsive to him. It gave him such a kick. She turned onto her back and stretched her arms up and placed them around his neck, pulling him to her, not really asleep after all. He felt her legs stretch out under him, positioning her body so it lined up with his, squirming under him further to align herself until she was completely covered by his body. She opened her legs and secured them around the backs of his thighs, shifting her lower body until she felt him aligned with her. She lifted her hips, taking him in, kissing him as he slid into her warmth. He groaned as he pushed slowly into her, his rhythm not veering from that pace until they came together, quiet this time. He kissed her again and sought her hands to hold in his. Sated and now sleepy, he laid his head next to hers and closed his eyes, content to stay here with her, in her.

CHAPTER 12

Dr. Houston sat in her office reviewing the changes that would be made to the center's staff next year. She'd just completed a discussion with Reye where she'd offered her a full time job at the center, and Reye had tentatively agreed to accept the offer. They would talk further about Reye's role beyond the aftercare program, but for now she'd been content knowing Reye would continue to be involved with the center.

Being a mother to kids had been Susan's desire since college. She wanted to nurture and give opportunities to those kids who were born without much. She'd wanted children of her own to mother, had married the love of her life with that goal in mind, but life had a different plan, and after years of probing and testing by doctors, children were ruled out. When life gives you lemons, and all that, so she'd become a mother to the many here at the center, including Reye. She recognized a gift and talent in Reye, along with a huge heart for kids. She couldn't have been more proud had Reye been hers by birth, watching her grow in confidence as she encouraged her kids, kids who now felt safe showing Reye their deficiencies, knowing that she would treat them with care. The soccer team was a big hit, the kids and their parents were all hooked, now diligently creating a team name, and determined to locate a sponsor to buy uniforms.

She was a little worried about Reye and that boyfriend of hers, although she hadn't met him yet. As far as Reye was concerned, he could walk on water. Did Reye have plans to follow him after school? Would she put her career on hold to be with him? Reye, with all of her talents and achievements, was far from confident, unable to see how capable she was. Having grown up focused solely on her difficulties with learning, which she perceived as deficiencies, had left her unable to view her accomplishments.

Reye opened the door and walked into her home. She was excited because she'd just finished a great soccer practice. The kids were improving, not yet ready for prime time, but well on their way to being equipped for the first game in a couple of weeks. She needed to talk to Joe about Shane, and she needed to do it soon. She hadn't seen him in two weeks.

Reye stepped through the door to find Stephen on his back, stretched out on her couch, his head bent over a book, studying. He looked up and smiled when she entered. That smile always made her catch her breath.

"Hey, babe," he said, putting his book down. She walked over to him and bent down, placing a quick kiss on his mouth. "How was practice?"

"You wouldn't believe how the kids are improving." She discarded her bag and kicked off her shoes, toed her socks off, and pulled her t-shirt over her head, continuing to talk. "They have graduated finally from kicking each other's ankles to kicking shins. Do you remember when you first learned soccer?" She stood before him wearing a pair of his high school gym shorts and a sports bra. She could wear a paper sack and his body would respond to the sight of her.

"Who, me? I was born playing at the pro level. It's you regular people who had to work at soccer. I was always good."

"You have such an ego," she said, laughing and punching him in the stomach. He grabbed her hand and pulled her to sit on his lap, putting his arms around her to hold her there. "Did I tell you that Sam is helping me with the center's soccer team as an assistant coach?" she asked, testing to see if he would offer to help. She was well aware of the constraints on his time, but she wanted him to at least offer anyway.

"Yep, how is that working out?" he said, not the response she was looking for.

"It's good." She watched as his eyes moved to her lips, a clear sign that he wanted to do something other than talk. He pulled her to him, snagging her lower lip with his teeth. Undeterred and still in testing mode, she drew back and continued talking. "I was invited to dinner at my parents' house tonight. My brother Jack and his wife are down from Ft. Worth, and I was thinking that if you weren't busy tonight you could come with me." His arms loosened their hold on her, not immediately, but quicker than she would have liked.

"I can't," he said, looking at her. "I am seriously behind in this class and I need to put some more time in." He watched the disappointment form on her face, regretful that he'd put it there, but not wanting to get tangled up in her family. He captured her face in his hands, making her look at him. "I'm sorry. I would if I could." He leaned in and kissed her. She tasted like mint and Reye, his favorite flavor. He pulled back and rested his forehead against hers. "You're not too disappointed, are you?"

"No, I'm good," she said, not meeting his eyes. He lifted her chin, forcing her to look at him.

"I'm fine," she said, looking into his eyes. "Really. Will you be here later on, after I get back?"

"I'll come by tomorrow. I haven't been to my apartment in so long, I've forgotten what it looks like. I'll just work from there tonight and see you tomorrow, okay?"

"Okay." She leaned into him for another kiss, opening her mouth, seeking some proof that he wanted her in the face of his small rejections.

Later that evening Henri entered his apartment expecting the usual quiet, since Stephen had abandoned it for Reye's. He'd seen him only occasionally since Christmas, and he was surprised to find him sitting on the couch watching TV.

"Dude, what's up? When did you get here?"

"A couple of hours ago."

"What, Reye give you a free day pass?" he asked jokingly.

"She's at her parents' for some family get-together and I didn't go."

"But you were invited?"

"Yes."

"I feel you. Meeting the parents means commitment, and you aren't that serious."

"Nope," he said.

"So what are you going to do? Are we still on for spring break in Cancun?"

"Yep."

"Is Reye okay with you going?" Henri asked.

"I haven't told her yet."

"Okay. Don't you think she'll mind? You do spend most of your time together."

"I'll be just hanging with the guys, right? I've never promised her more than casual, and I've got to start backing off sooner or later. The sex is still amazing, though. Can you believe that? It's not like anything I've had with anyone else, and it's one of the things I am going to really miss."

"She's more than sex to you, dude? I know you."

"So what if it is? Okay. It is more, there, I'll admit it, I like her, a lot, but I'm putting an end to it anyway at the end of the semester. I am going home to Dallas. Period. End of story. Will I miss her? Yes. But I'll get over it, I'm sure. Okay."

"Whatever you say, dude," Henri said and left the room.

Reye pulled up to the front of Shane's house. A lone car sat parked in the drive; it belonged to Joe, she remembered. The lights were on in the house, a good sign that someone was home. Shane hadn't been at practice today and she was through with putting this off. She'd decided to go by later rather than early, figuring that later would offer her a better chance of finding someone at home. She'd stopped by a local coffee shop to grab a cup of her favorite brew, killing time while she waited.

Reye took the step leading up to the front porch of Shane's home. It was located near the center, in one of the older neighborhoods in the city. The condition of the homes on this street ran between 'don't give up the ship' to 'this ship has sunk'. Shane's home fell into the first category, needing a new coat of paint and a few minor repairs, but overall it was in fairly good condition.

Reye knocked and waited. Shane answered, a smile lighting up his face, its twin in place on Reye's. She'd missed him.

"Hey, Ms. Reye," he said.

"Hey back at you."

"Who is it?" a voice from somewhere within the house called out.

"It's Ms. Reye," Shane responded. "Do you want to come in?" he asked her.

"No, I'd better stay here," she said, looking over his shoulder to see Joe enter the room, a kitchen towel slung over his shoulder. He was dressed in shorts and a t-shirt and he walked up to stand at Shane's back, his expression blank.

"Can I talk to you a moment, Joe?" she asked.

"Shane, go and finish drying the dishes and I'll be there in a second. If I take longer, get ready for bed, okay?"

"Sure, Uncle Joe." The boy walked back into the house. "See you later, Ms. Reye," he said as he went.

"See you, Shane."

They waited until he was gone. Then Joe stepped out on to the porch with Reye, closing the door behind him.

She spoke after a few moments of awkward silence. "I stopped by to check on Shane. I don't know if you know this, but in addition to soccer, I also work with him in the after-school program at the center. He's hasn't been there in a while, so I wanted to check on him. Will he be returning?"

"I don't know."

Reye observed Joe, reading frustration in his body language as he began to pace. He stopped and spoke. His tone was defensive. "Look, my sister, Shane's mother, took off about the last time you were here. She's has emotional problems because of our parents, and they sometimes get the best of her." He must have read the unasked question on her face. "Long story, and one that I'm not sharing. Anyway, she has a problem with alcohol," Joe said and stopped pacing, walking over to sit on the step leading up to the front porch. "Sit," he said, and Reye fought back the need to voice her indignity at his command. She stood there, giving him a 'I know you didn't just say that to me' look. He looked up and revised his statement. "Please sit," he said. She did and he continued. "This isn't the first time she's left. Shane called me one morning about two weeks ago after he woke up alone in the house. So I moved in here, hoping it would be temporary, because I've got school and work. But it doesn't look like she's returning. We haven't heard a peep from her." He was quiet for a minute. "I refuse to let him go into foster care. I know what that feels like."

"Can I help?" she asked, taken in by his story and his commitment to Shane.

"You would help us?" he asked in disbelief.

"It's not you. I'd be helping Shane. I can bring him home from the center or soccer practice until school ends. What? We have two more months left, right?" she continued. "Can he get to school in the mornings?" Joe nodded yes. "And the bus can bring him and the other kids from school to the center. You just need someone to bring him home and I can do that. I hate to see him stop. He's come so far in his studies. I don't want him to lose that."

"You would do that? After all the things I said to you and about you?"

"I'd do it for Shane."

He sat quiet for a second. "Okay." There was a long pause. "Thank you," he said.

"I'll start tomorrow."

Sunday, the week before spring break, found Reye and Stephen at her house again. They were always at her house. This day they were both sitting on the floor studying. Stephen was actually studying, but she was mostly daydreaming.

"Did I tell you that I was offered a permanent job at the community center after graduation? That would mean that I would be here in Austin. What do you think about that?" she asked.

"Sounds good, if that's what you want to do," he responded somewhat distractedly. "You seem to enjoy the time you spend there."

"Okay." She'd hoped for a different answer, one encouraging her to look for work in Dallas, perhaps, where he would be.

"What are your plans? Still going to work with your family's law firm?"

"I think so. Why wouldn't I? I like Dallas, it's home."

"Have you thought about practicing anywhere else?" she asked.

"No," he answered firmly and succinctly.

Leave it alone, Reye, she thought. She'd been anxious lately about them, about how this would end. She loved him very much, and was very much afraid of the damage it would do to her if he left. And her instincts were telling her that he would.

"Are you going home for spring break?" she asked.

"Actually, Henri and I, along with some other frat brothers, are going to Cancun, this being my last time and all. We're leaving this Saturday."

"Oh," she choked out, more than a little hurt. His plans hadn't included her. She added the trip to Cancun to her growing list of slights. One, he never mentioned her meeting his parents; two, he didn't want to meet hers; three, they were always at her house; four, they never went anywhere else; five, he didn't want to help with her team; and six, he'd been distracted lately, mentally elsewhere. Could he be seeing someone else? The only constant between them seemed to be their sexual compatibility. That was the one area where she felt she had his complete and undivided attention, an unbelievable connection to him. But was that all this was for him?

Reye looked into the expectant and scared faces of her soccer team. This was their first game of the season. She'd started out with thirteen players, eleven boys and two girls. Most hadn't played soccer before and here they were now, standing in a circle waiting for her to give her first pre-game pep talk. The team's name, Lightning, had been Anthony's recommendation. Almost everyone preferred it to Ladybugs, which was Shondra's suggestion. They were all dressed in their hot pink and sky blue uniforms courtesy of Barbara's House of Braids. Blue soccer shorts with matching blue shirts timed with pink piping around the neck and sleeves. The socks were a matching blue; the girls pleaded and were granted the option of wearing pink socks. The boys refused, mutiny evident in their faces at the suggestion. Sam and Reye were dressed in matching blue shorts, with pink polo-style shirts that had LIGHTNING COACHING STAFF engraved on the left top side. Between the parents and sponsors, they'd been able to round up soccer balls, shoes, and shin guards for those kids who couldn't afford them. They were a family now.

All but a few of the parents had taken off to watch their child's first game of the season. It was being held at one of the local high schools' soccer fields, which was usually kept in fairly good condition. It was typical Texas weather for March, totally unpredictable, ranging from the high seventies at the beginning of the day to freezing two hours later. Today, however, was perfect; low seventies, with the sun shining brightly down on them, the trees starting to bud, even.

Looking down into the faces she'd grown to know and love this year, she felt a rightness and gratitude for the opportunity to help shape and be a part of their lives. She stood quietly waiting for their chatter to stop.

"Okay, guys, this is our chance to put all those skills we've worked on in practice to use. You've worked so hard in preparation for this game, so let's continue that effort. We can do this! We can win! Eric and Shondra, you'll be the team captains today." Eric was athletic, with a strong grasp of the game gained from playing at home with his older brothers and father. The other less experienced boys on the team admired him. Reye took in the kids' smiles, asking, "Are we ready?"

Thirteen mouths screamed, "Yes!" Blowing her back with their enthusiasm.

"Arms in, everybody. Lightning on three. One, two, three, Lightning! Take your places on the field. Jésus and

D, you two will be the subs today." Reye looked over at the opposing team, all shiny in their red, white, and blue uniforms, remembering herself at this age, nervous, excited, and filled with energy. One thing could make this day more special for her, Stephen's presence. He was busy with school, of course, and then he was leaving for spring break tomorrow, he needed to pack, yadda, yadda, yadda. She understood, but she also knew, but didn't voice, that you showed up for what was important to you. She was hurt.

Reye looked out at the field and saw her kids in their places, waiting for the game to begin. The referees had arrived, the center referee reminding her of Stephen; they looked to be the same age. She pegged the two linemen as middle school age. The ref blew the whistle and the game began.

The other team won the toss, giving them the ball first. Both teams played similar lineups, two forwards up front, four players in the middle, and four players in the back. Reye's strategy was basic, get the ball to their leading and only scorer, Eric. Soccer at this age level usually consisted of having one or two good players on each team, and those players scored. Most kids were still growing into their bodies, and only a small few managed to grasp any more complicated soccer concepts. Lightning wasn't any different. Eric was their main scorer with the other team members feeding the ball to him, and, as expected, he received and moved the ball down the field, headed toward the goal. The opposing team wasn't so fortunate in their lineup, so Eric had scored four goals by the end of the first half.

Her halftime speech was short and sweet, and after conferring with Sam, she moved Eric to the midfield, so as not to run up the score. She hated teams that did that, and was rewarded as the other team scored two goals in the second half, but Lightning won! They gathered around her jumping up and down. "Great game, you guys. Way to play. I am so proud of you."

The parents had lined up on the field, two lines, London bridge style waiting for the kids to run underneath their arms, and they did, screaming and shouting all the way, receiving and giving high fives to each other and their parents. They left with their parents soon after, all but Shane. Joe had called her earlier, informing her that he wouldn't make it to the first game because he had work commitments that he couldn't reschedule, but he assured her he would be attending the remaining games. They'd previously exchanged cell numbers in case of an emergency with Shane.

"Great job coaching today, Reye," Sam said.

"Why thank you, Samuel, you were great assisting the new and magnificent coach."

Laughing, he put his arm around her shoulders and pulled her into a hug. "I'm sorry Stephen missed watching you coach."

"It's not a big deal," she said, feeling emotional all of a sudden, and not just because of the game. She felt lately that Stephen was putting distance between them and pulling away from her. She stayed in Sam's arms for a second more and then stepped away.

"I've got to drop Shane off at home. I'll see you later," she said. She picked up her bag of soccer gear and took it and Shane to her truck before Sam could see her tears.

Reye walked Shane to his front door and waited while he rooted around in his backpack for his key. The door opened before he found it, startling them both. Joe stood there, his eyes landing on Shane, before moving over to Reye, who couldn't read his expression.

"How was the game, Shane?" he asked, his eyes returning to Shane and giving him a smile, ruffling his hair as he entered the house.

"Great, Uncle Joe. I had two assists, didn't I, Ms. Reye? We won!"

"Yes, you did, you were great," Reye said into Shane's beaming face.

"I'm sorry I missed it, I had work today, but Ms. Reye gave me the schedule for the season and I'll plan on making the rest of them, okay, dude?"

"Okay, Uncle Joe," Shane said as his arms locked around Joe's waist in a tight hug.

"Well, I'll see you two after spring break. You guys have a good week, okay," Reye said.

"Okay. See ya, Ms. Reye."

"Reye, wait." Joe turned to Shane. "Let me talk to your coach for a second. I'll be right back, okay?"

"Sure," Shane said, skipping away.

Joe stepped out of the house and stood next to Reye. He was taller than she was, about the same height as Stephen. Reye joked that Stephen and Henri belonged to a fraternity filled with handsome men, and Joe fit in easily, too. He had shoulder-length blond hair, grey eyes, and a slim and athletic build. At this moment, he was also uncomfortable. It was written into his stance as his hands were shoved into his pockets and he trained his eyes to a spot above her head. She heard him take a deep breath. "I wanted to thank you for all that you are doing for Shane. He and I both appreciate it," he said.

Surprised and pleased, she responded. "You're welcome. He's a great kid. Have you heard from your sister?"

"No, not yet." He pushed a big breath out again. "I'm not finished. I also wanted to apologize to you for the things I said to you at the party and about you after that soccer game. I was just angry, have been that way for a while. The things I said were really directed at Stephen and were less about you. I don't like your boyfriend." He moved his eyes from hers to look off toward the street.

"My life hasn't been easy, getting through school, going on to college. Navigating through the foster care system left me really angry. I resent Stephen and those like him that are given so much, receive so much, without much effort, just lucky at birth. He even has you," he said, giving her a smile.

"Stephen's had to work hard, too, you know. He couldn't help who his parents are."

"You know what I mean," he countered, giving her another smile, smaller this time, a smile not perfect, but disarming nevertheless. "Defending him, huh, must be love, I can tell." He paused, looking at her intently now, his voice quiet and serious. "I'm only telling you this because of what you've done for Shane, and, indirectly, for me. I'm starting to like you."

"Tell me what?" she asked, fearing what he would say, but unable to resist knowing, like passing by an accident on the road and looking for something gruesome.

"He won't be there for you in the end. You do know that, don't you?"

"I'd better get going," Reye said.

"I don't mean to make you angry, and this isn't an attack on him. He's just not tough enough for you. He won't be strong enough in the end to stand up to the pressure from his parents. That's all."

"Thanks for the apology, but I really do need to get going." She walked down the steps to her car, getting away from something she'd begun to suspect.

"Yeah, see ya." His eyes followed her until she was gone.

Spring break in Cancun, really? What had he been thinking? He'd so outgrown the need to drink everything put before him and screw everything in sight a long time ago, since Reye, anyway. He'd gone to a party the first night they were here, but left after about thirty minutes, tiring quickly of the loud, blaring music and girls asking him to dance. He went back to the hotel. Henri and some of his other frat brothers were here having the time of their lives, women everywhere. But he wasn't interested, choosing instead to spend his days on the beach, his nights in his hotel room. He went snorkeling at Xel-Ha, a little cove about an hour and half away from the hotel, and rotated his time between lying on the beach, swimming and snorkeling, getting in some much needed sleep. It was beautiful here, blue, clear water, white sands . . . he should have brought Reye.

He felt bad about leaving her, about not attending her first soccer game, about not meeting her family, but he didn't want to promise more than he could give. Going to her game felt dishonest in some way, it would have indicated a commitment that he wasn't prepared to make. So he'd become a different type of jerk to her instead.

CHAPTER 13

Two weeks later, between classes and running late, a harried and tired Stephen rushed through the back door of his fraternity's house. He'd promised to leave a book for a frat brother at the house. The semester was quickly closing in on him, leaving him knee-deep in books with little time to spare. He entered the house, distracted, head down, moving fast, and ran smack into a body. "Sorry dude, my bad." he said, not aware of who he'd run into. Stephen stopped and looked up into a face made of stone. The face belonged to Joe. Standing next to Joe was an alarmed and wary Henri. He didn't get why Henri hung out with Joe, but as long as Joe stayed out of his way, he ignored their friendship. "Henri," he said as acknowledgment, stepping aside to allow room for Joe to pass. He would rather chew off his leg than hold a conversation with Joe. He looked away, hoping Joe would take the hint and leave. He didn't, but rather waited until Stephen's attention returned to him.

"What?" Stephen asked, not bothering to hide his dislike.

"Dude," Joe said, distaste marring his face, too. So they both didn't like each other. "You know if you're not serious about Reye, you should tell her."

"What the fuck did you just say to me?" Stephen asked.

"I said, if you're not serious about Reye, you should tell her. She doesn't deserve bullshit, she loves you, and you and I both know you're too much of a pussy to stand up to your parents for her."

"What the hell do you know about me and Reye?"

"We talk," Joe said calmly.

"You talk. What the hell does that mean? Are you chasing after my woman now, Joe?"

Joe continued to hold his gaze as Stephen moved in closer. "I know you don't have the guts to go against Mommy and Daddy for her. You and your easy life, always the smooth and successful one, but you are such a fake!"

"So this is about you being jealous of me?" Stephen angrily jabbed Joe in the chest as he posed the question.

"Are you kidding me? Jealous? Why would I be? You don't even appreciate what you have. Maybe Reye *would* be better off with me," Joe said and sneered.

Stephen stepped closer to him. "You need to back the fuck up, dude!"

"And if I don't?" Joe asked, moving forward. Henri squeezed in between them, grabbing Joe by the arm.

"That's enough! Let's go!" he said, hauling Joe out of the room and out through the back door.

"What are you doing?" Henri asked.

"You know I'm right, don't you?"

"Leave it alone," Henri said.

Stephen stood inside, steaming, processing the fact that Joe not only knew Reye, but had been talking to her. Joe had defended her, to him, of all people, and he'd stood there clueless. Reye hadn't mentioned a word to him. How the hell had that happened? He was angry and hurt. Was Reye interested in Joe? He'd never considered her with anyone but him.

School was forgotten; he needed to talk to Reye, and he needed to do so now. Dropping the books off as promised, he drove immediately over to her house, where he pulled up behind her truck and parked. She opened the door at his banging, surprised to see him angry. She moved to let him in, but he didn't move, just stood at the entrance.

"How the hell do you know Joe? And I don't mean from the frat party. You've talked to him since then, haven't you?"

"Are you coming in? I'm not going to have this conversation standing here. Either you come in and talk to me like an adult or you can leave."

"Answer the question Reye," he said as he entered her house, reducing the volume of his voice, but not by much.

She closed the door and turned to him. "Remember Shane from my class? Well, he is Joe's nephew, his sister's kid. I've been taking him home from the center and soccer practice." She looked at him, puzzled by this anger. "I didn't tell you because I remembered how you reacted before regarding Joe. I wanted to avoid all that. Anyway, Shane's mother left him, and Joe's been taking care of him since then. I took him home one day after soccer practice, because no one had shown up to pick him up. That's when I found out about Shane's mother and relationship to Joe. It's great what he's doing for Shane, and I wanted to help."

Silence greeted her explanation.

"So we talk. It's necessary, since I'm responsible for Shane sometimes. I agreed to bring Shane home, and he's apologized to me for his behavior at the party and game. I take it you ran into him again," she said. "What happened?"

"Nothing that I care to share."

"What do you mean 'care to share'? Talk to me, Stephen."

"No. You didn't tell me about Joe, I don't have to talk to you about him, either."

Men could be such kids sometime, she thought.

"You've got some nerve," she said, angry now at being questioned by him in this way, as if he had the right! They were casual the last time she'd checked. She marched over to stand in front of him, once again thankful for the similarities in their heights. She didn't have to look up to him; she looked him directly in his eyes.

"So I didn't tell you about Joe, but you keep secrets from me, too, Stephen. Was Beth in Cancun with you?" she asked, inwardly flinching at the initial reaction of recognition and shock that was visible on his face. It was there just for a second.

"Joe told me a lot of things, none of which I believed. He told me that you were seeing someone besides me, someone named Beth. He also told me that you wouldn't stay with me, that you would never pit yourself against your family for me. That Beth was your family's choice. Is that true?"

"Beth is an old friend from high school, nothing more. We grew up together in Dallas. Her family and mine are good friends."

"Did you see her when you went home?"

"Yes, at a couple of parties, but I also saw other friends from high school. She wasn't in Cancun with me. I went alone, spent the time there alone. There is nothing to this, Reye."

"There is nothing to Joe, either. He's Shane's uncle. Shane had started to miss the sessions after school and soccer practice, and I wanted to prevent him from quitting. He's come so far."

Then she asked him again, "Are you seeing someone else beside me?"

"No, Reye, I'm not." His anger dissipated as he ran his hands through his hair. "You and finishing this last semester are all that I can handle right now, all I want to handle," he said. He reached for her and drew her to him. She let go of the breath she had been holding. He kissed her, mouth and tongue pressing into hers.

She pulled back. "I love you," she said.

Silence hung in the air. She hadn't expected any response, but . . .

"Don't worry, I wasn't expecting you to say it back. I just wanted you to know."

"I know, Reye," he said. "I don't know what to say. In spite of what Joe said, I do care about you."

"I know."

"Don't let him bother you," he said, pulling her in for another kiss.

"Only if you don't," she said, leaning in to meet him.

Reye was just as impressed with Stephen's apartment complex the second time as she had been the first. She hadn't seen it since before Thanksgiving. That little fact, a persistent reminder of her place in his life, bothered her. She was going to have to do something about it eventually, but she wasn't going there now. She would make herself crazy worrying about it. To be fair to him, he'd never said they were exclusive. Never. Never had he promised more than what he'd given. It wasn't his fault that she wanted more, that she loved him.

She parked her truck in a visitor's slot near his home, next to a very new and nice Mercedes and not the low-end C class, either. She would only be there a second; she was just stopping by to pick up additional soccer gear that Stephen had given her as a contribution to her team. She walked up to his apartment, knocked in case Henri was home. No answer, so she used the key that Stephen had left for her and opened the door.

"Hello," she said, walking into the main living room.

"Hello," she heard in return, surprising her. Stephen hadn't mentioned that someone would be here. Walking toward the sound of voices, she entered the breakfast area to find two older women sitting at the kitchen table in conversation. They were drinking coffee and eating what looked like cookies. One brunette and one blonde, both looked to be in their late fifties. Both were impeccably dressed, straight from the pages of *Town & Country*.

They seemed equally surprised to see her.

"Who are you?" The blonde was giving Reye the once-over, clearly displeased with what she saw, her expression reflecting distaste.

"I'm Reye," she answered as politely as she could, extending her hand for a shake. It was ignored, and Reye withdrew it. She wished she had dressed better, but she was on her way to practice at the soccer fields. She'd taken to wearing the shorts from Stephen's high school with her t-shirts. She had them on now, St. Anna's Prep embroidered on the left hem. It was not her best look, but really, it was very comfortable and great for soccer practices.

"I'm Stephen's mother, and this is Henri's mother. We drove down yesterday to see the boys," the blonde said. Henri's mother gave Reye a warm smile.

"Who are you here to see?" Mrs. Stuart continued.

"Oh, I'm not here to see anyone. I needed to pick up something."

"How do you have a key?"

"I borrowed Stephen's. It's your Stephen that I'm friends with, although I know and like Henri, too."

"And how do you know Stephen?"

"I met him last year on a plane trip back from Dallas."

"I remember that trip. You've known Stephen that long?"

"Yes."

"He tutored you in school?"

"No," Reye said, baffled by the question. "Uhm, look, I came by to pick up some soccer balls. Stephen said I could borrow them."

"Yes, well, help yourself. Do you know where to find them?"

"Yes, I'll only be a minute." She moved to Stephen's room and walked into his closet. She found the balls in the back of his closet stuffed into a mesh bag, just as he had said they would be.

She closed the door to the closet and went back into the main room. Should she say goodbye?

Before she could debate the question, Stephen's mom entered the room and stood by the door, apparently waiting for her. Mrs. Stuart was looking her over head to toe again. Reye was sure she was equally unimpressed now as she had been during her entry. In turn, Reye was growing equally unimpressed with his mother. So she didn't like what she saw, but her rudeness was inexcusable.

"I found them," she said, lifting her hands to indicate the bag of balls she held.

"I see."

"Well, it was nice meeting you and Henri's mom."

"You know, Reye, Stephen has a good future in the law profession ahead of him."

"Yes, I know, he's a very good student. I assume he'll also make a good attorney." Mrs. Stuart continued on as if Reye hadn't spoken.

"I want only the best for him. Our family's law firm is one of the oldest in Dallas, and we have a certain reputation to uphold. He has certain expectations set before him. Do you understand what I'm saying?"

"I think so," she said, not really understanding, but wanting the conversation to end so she could get the hell out of there.

"Let me make it clearer to you, then. Stephen is to come home and take his place in the family firm. He is very talented, and, with the right woman at his side, he could make great strides in his life. Do you understand?"

"Yes, I do, and I'd really better go," Reye said, moving to the door. "Good bye, Mrs. Stuart."

The door was soundly closed behind her. *Well, that was informative,* Reye thought as she made her way to her truck. "What a pompous bitch."

Stephen was hunched over his books at the local Starbucks. He needed a break from the law library and Reye's; sometimes a change of scenery could give him a boost of energy.

His cell buzzed and he checked the caller info. His mom. "Hello, Mom."

"Stephen, did you forget I was going to be in town today?" Yes, he had.

"I'm sorry, I've been stuck with my head in the books all day. Where are you? I'll come to meet you."

"No, that's not necessary. I am at your apartment with Joyce."

"Oh, tell Miss Novak hello. Is Henri there?"

"No, it seems that both of you have abandoned your mothers today. But one of your friends stopped by."

"My friend?" Stephen racked his brain. Most of his friends knew he wasn't at home most of the time. He didn't recall giving the key to anyone. Oh, wait a minute.

"Reye," his mom said. "She stopped by to pick up some soccer balls. She's quite an attractive girl, your Reye. Is she from Dallas?"

"She's not my Reye, and no, she's not from Dallas."

"Well, I was surprised to meet her and equally surprised to see her wearing shorts from St. Anna's Prep school. I didn't know that they'd begun admitting girls? I thought you told me she was someone you tutored."

Had he said that? "She's a friend, Mom."

"Really?"

"Yes, really."

"You do realize what people expect of you when you join the firm?"

"I know."

"Reye seems nice enough for Austin, but the demands and expectations of someone with your future are somewhat different."

"I understand. Again, Reye and I are just friends. I hope you were pleasant to her."

"I don't like your meaning, Stephen. I'm always cordial to people I meet."

Stephen had seen his mother cordial, and it could freeze Hell. He probably should call Reye.

"I need to get back to my books."

"Sure, Joyce and I will be at the Four Seasons. We're leaving in the morning. I love you, and remember I only want the best for you. I want you to have the advantages that I didn't have growing up."

Not this again, thought Stephen. "If I don't see you before we leave, I'll see you in three weeks, for your graduation."

"Good bye, Mother," he said, disconnecting and sitting back in his chair, oblivious to the sounds around him. He didn't want to imagine the conversation between his mother and Reye, nor the shock. He'd forgotten he'd given her the key, and, more importantly, that his mom would be in town. He needed to talk to Reye. And say what? *Yes, my mother is correct. There is no future for us. You wouldn't fit in with me in Dallas.* His mother in her frustrating, intrusive way had brought that reality front and center. He'd go by Reye's later, recognizing that there wasn't ever going to be a good day to break up with her. He had dreaded this, had spent the better part of this semester feeling unsettled. He agreed with his mom; even though what he had with Reye was good, he had a lot he wanted to accomplish. He would move home, start work, and over time forget about Reye.

He would miss her. She'd become special to him, but he wasn't sure if that special would, could, last. Maybe someone else would come along and mean more.

Reye's truck was parked in her driveway. He pulled in behind her and walked to her door. He would miss this house. It was so like her, eclectic, fun, yet serious in the care she gave to it. The care she gave to those around her, the kids at the center, and him. He would miss all of that. He knocked and waited. He could hear movement inside, and, a few seconds later, she opened the door. She stood there looking at him, smiling.

"Hey," he said.

"Back at you," she said sassily, turning to let him in. He closed the door behind him, dropped his book bag, and went to take a seat on the couch. She joined him, pulling her legs up Indian-style.

"I heard you met my mother today," he said.

"Yes, I did. She was surprised to see me, didn't know anything about me." Anger was a quiet backdrop to her words. "Apparently she was under the impression that you were tutoring me."

"I hadn't told her about you because she can get way too interested in my life. She would have just harassed me to death. I told you from the beginning that dating you was new for me, it's not something I've done before."

"Almost a year ago. I remember, I just thought we'd passed that point, Stephen, somewhere this year. I did, at least. I mean, you spend most of your time here, practically live here. I thought I'd come to mean more to you. I thought we had something special."

"It did and you are, but you've finished with school and you have plans for your life. I'll be finished in another three weeks. I'm going back to Dallas, Reye, to a different life with a set of plans, goals, and expectations for me."

"What expectations? To marry a girl more like you? To be this great lawyer for the family firm?" Her anger quickly moved to the front.

"You and I both know how important my career and my family are to me. I've told you that often enough, and I can't believe you'd think this could, would, turn out any other way than with me leaving," he returned.

"You don't want to see me anymore? Is that what you're telling me, just like that?"

Stephen watched anger and hurt settle on her face, but continued.

"If you're honest with yourself, Reye, you knew it would end. I never told you anything different," he said, running his hands through his hair. "My world in Dallas is so different from here. Austin is a carefree place; all kinds of people are welcome. Dallas is different, old standards, old contacts, and it would be difficult to change that."

"You don't think I'm worth it?" she said, tears forming in her eyes. "Am I not worth fighting for?" she asked quietly.

"Come on, Reye, it's not a question of worth, and it's not about fighting, but if it were, I don't want to live my life fighting, a least not with my family. Don't make this harder than it is."

"I'm not trying to, but times have changed. I see a lot of multiracial couples around. We wouldn't be the first," she said, talking in earnest now, reading the word *no* written on his face. "We could take it slow if you want, I'd be willing to wait for a while until you do."

"Come on, Reye, I can't." He looked at her, watching a tear snake its way down her cheek.

He reached for her hand and looked into her eyes. "I'm sorry, Reye."

"You don't know it now, but you will come to regret this," she said.

He reached for her and pulled her onto his lap, moving his hand to cup her face and using his thumbs to brush her tears away.

"Look, Reye, what you feel for me will pass and I will be just a blip on your radar." He gave her a shaky smile, his eyes bright, too.

"Good bye, Stephen," she said and removed her body from his lap. "You can see yourself out, right?" she said, not bothering to hide her tears.

"Yeah," he responded, watching her walk away from him and down the hall to her room. He heard the door close. He continued to sit there for a while, willing himself to go. It was harder than he'd thought it would be. A few minutes later, he grabbed his book bag and left.

Sam stood outside of Reye's front door and rang the doorbell for the fourth time. He hadn't heard from her, she hadn't answered her cell, and he was worried. Her truck was parked in her drive. He looked around her many hiding places for her spare key and found it under a squirrel statue. That statue wore a cocky smile as it held a nut behind its back, reminding him of Reye. He unlocked the door and went in, looking around for signs of life. Quiet. He walked down the hall. Her door was closed, and when he opened it he found her asleep. She lay on her side, facing the door. He walked over to her and sat down on the bed.

"Reye," he said and lightly shook her. "Reye, it's me, Sam, your annoying big brother."

She stirred and looked at him. "Sam, what are you doing here?"

"Looking for you. You haven't answered my calls."

"I turned my cell off."

"For three days. Why, Reye? And why are you in bed? Are you sick?" He put his hand to her forehead, checking for signs of fever.

"Stephen came over," she said, and, just like that, her tears started again. The story of Stephen came pouring out, and, with it, her hurt. Sam looked around for tissue, noticing the multitude of used ones overflowing from the trash basket. He went to the bathroom and returned with another box.

"When did this happen?" he asked, thinking it through. "Let me guess, three days ago? Why didn't you call me?"

"I don't know, I didn't have the energy."

"Have you tried to call him?" She shook her head no. "I threw my SIM card away so I wouldn't be tempted to call him. I may be a weakling, but I refuse to beg."

"Have you eaten?"

"I'm not hungry."

"Come on, Reye, don't do this to yourself. If he didn't see that you were worth it, he's not worth you," Sam said, now angry on her behalf. Reye started to cry again. "Come on, baby girl. It will be all right. What about your time at the center? Have you spoken with them?"

"Yes."

"What about graduation? It's in a week. You know how much this means to Mom and Dad."

"I can't do it. I've already gotten my degree, I don't want to go through with the ceremony. Please call and explain for me, just tell them I'm sick."

"Okay, Reye, I will, calm down." Sam sat for a while with her until she'd fallen asleep.

He was worried; this was so unlike her. She needed to eat. He left her room and went to the kitchen in search of food, thinking to himself that if he ever saw Stephen again, he'd kick his ass from here to Dallas and back! Sam knew Reye loved him, could see it on her face whenever Stephen was near. Sam just thought he'd seen an answering love in Stephen's. He guessed he was wrong.

Reye woke up to the sound of someone knocking at her door. What day was it? She hadn't eaten in a while. She laid there waiting to see if the knocking would continue. Her stomach growled, bemoaning its hungry state. No further knocking, but she heard the door open and close and she sat up.

"Baby girl?" a voice sounded from her living room. Her dad was here.

"Hey, Dad, I'm in my room. I'll be there, give me two seconds." She stood, a little weak. *I really need to eat something,* she thought. She went to the bathroom to wash her face and brush her teeth.

She finished up in the bathroom and walked into the living room where her dad sat, watching something on ESPN. "Daddy, what are you doing here?" She went over to sit next to him on the couch.

"Sam called me and your mother. He told us that you didn't want to participate in your graduation ceremonies. You know we love you and we'll do whatever you want, but I needed to hear you explain why to me, why you would want to miss something you've worked so hard for."

"I know you're right, I know what it means to you and Mom. I've changed my mind, I'll attend the ceremonies. I didn't mean to worry you."

"What's wrong, Reye? Come here and talk to your dad. You know there is nothing you could do that would make me ashamed of you." She scooted over to him and he pulled her in close. She laid her head on his chest, starting to cry. She told him of meeting Stephen last year, of how they'd spent most of their time together and all the things they'd had in common, and his ending the relationship.

"You know you've always told me to be myself, that I should take chances, right, that someone would love me for me. When will someone take a chance on me?" Her voice broke and she started crying again. Her dad held her and let her finish. "I don't think I'm going to ever stop crying," she said, going for humor.

"So, how are you going to proceed, baby girl? Are you going to sleep your life away, lay around feeling sorry for yourself, or will you be the tough girl that I know and raised and get back in the game? I bet those children at the center miss you. I bet they love you." He sat silently for a second. "I know what it means to be hurt. Your mom wasn't my first time around the block," he said and smiled. "Give yourself time to feel sad. If you loved him like you say you do, it may hurt for a long time, but promise me you won't let it stop you from being the best you. You don't have to participate in the ceremonies, but you can't withdraw from life. Okay?" He squeezed her to his side. "Promise me you won't."

"I promise, Daddy."

"And if that young man was willing to let a great girl like you get away, then he wasn't worth you."

Stephen closed his test booklet and stood up to turn it in. He grabbed his bags and walked down the hall. That had been his last final. He was done! Graduation ceremonies were scheduled for next week. His parents and grandparents would be here, overjoyed and proud of him. He walked over to his car, unlocked it, and threw his bag in the backseat. He put the key in the ignition and sat there, staring out of the window. He missed Reye. It had hit him at different times during the day, a sharp ache, a hurt that left him unable to breathe for a few seconds sometimes. He had expected to miss her, just not quite this much. He hadn't seen or heard from her in about two weeks. She hadn't called and he'd expected her to, secretly wished she would. He guessed he'd really made it clear that he was moving on, and he would. He could do this, one day at time. It was for the best, right? One more week to get through and he could go home. He hoped that would be far enough away.

PART TWO

CHAPTER 14

Stephen—six months later

Stephen woke up in his bed next to an unidentified female and tried to pluck her name from his memory. Remembering he'd met her last night at a party, his mind went in search of a name. Christy? Maybe. Her blonde hair spread out on the pillow next to his as she lay sleeping on her stomach, her face turned away from him. He sat up, pulling with him the blanket that had been draped on his body and partially covering hers, leaving her bare. Nice tattoo, he thought, peering at an angel on her left butt cheek. Nice cheeks, he also thought, removing the blanket from his body. He dropped it over her. He looked around his room and found clothes, leading in a line from the bed to the bedroom door. He also saw used condoms and wine glasses scattered over the floor.

Not wanting to wake her, he slowly slid off the bed and stood up. She moved a little, moaning in her sleep while Stephen held his breath. Thankfully, she continued to sleep. Running his hand over his face, he looked around the room for his watch. What time was it? Noon, if the light from the windows were any indication. He had to stop doing this, partying and drinking, drinking and partying; it was getting old. In the beginning, he'd at least known something about the girls he brought back to his apartment; not that they were people he cared about, just warm bodies, people to use, to lose himself in. Rubbing his hand over his face again, he couldn't remember when he'd first broken his cardinal rule. Never bring women home! Now he was forced to see them in the morning. He hadn't even broken that rule for Reye, and she had meant something to him.

He found his watch. It was eleven-thirty, and lucky for him he had nowhere to be and no time to be there. He used the bathroom, taking note of the nearly empty box of condoms. It was comforting to know that even in his drunken state he'd practiced safe sex. He moved to stand in front of the sink and stared at his reflection in the mirror. He looked hung over and thinner. He'd lost weight, dark shadows had taken up permanent residence under his eyes, and he clearly hadn't shaved in a couple of days. He laughed sadly to himself. He was no longer Reye's golden one. He couldn't remember the last time he'd been outside, active. He spent most of his time inside at someone's party.

He'd been back home in Dallas for about six months now, found an apartment within the first two days of returning, and used money from his trust fund to purchase it. He'd given living at home with his parents a try, but that lasted for one day and one night. He'd felt locked in and antsy. He needed his own place, and he wanted to be alone. He found a gem in a new building downtown. It was a newly built condo. Since he'd left

Austin, he seemed caught in between three main emotional states—restlessness, anger, and sadness. His emotional turmoil made being around anyone for any length of time untenable.

"Hey, baby," said a soft voice behind him. He looked in the mirror as the woman with the angel tattoo stood behind him in her naked splendor. Pretty girl, he thought. "Why don't you come back to bed," she said, moving towards him and wrapping her arms around his waist. "You were great last night, except for the part when you called me Reye." Stephen stared at her refection in the mirror, nonplussed.

"Are you bisexual?" Stephen didn't respond. "It's okay, you know, being bisexual. I've had lots of friends who are. Was Reye your old boyfriend?"

He barked out a laugh, torn between horror and humor at her comment.

Not answering, he turned to face her. "I wish I could join you in bed, babe, but I've got to get to work."

Stephen hadn't been to work at his dad's office in six months either. He'd gone into the office a total of two days right after he'd returned home. He found that he couldn't sit still, let alone focus on studying for any bar exam.

"Maybe another time," he said, noting the annoyance on her face. "Why don't you go find your clothes? Give me a second here and I'll walk you out." She left and he turned to brush his teeth. He splashed water on his face and reached in the laundry for a pair of old jeans. His laundry overflowed; that which wasn't on the ground was stuffed into the hamper. He needed to have someone wash his clothes again. By the time he was done in the bathroom, Angel was dressed and waiting for him by the front door, looking more alive than he felt.

She reached up and placed a kiss on his lips. "Call me. I left my number on the counter in your kitchen. I had a good time," she said.

"Me, too," he said, even if he had only a vague recollection of the evening. Ushering her through the door and shutting it behind her, he leaned against the closed door. He had to stop doing this.

He walked over to the counter in his kitchen in search of his phone. He needed to check his calendar, knowing it would be empty. He looked around his apartment, which was also empty. He had a sofa and lamp in the living room and a bed in his bedroom. That was it. No kitchen table, or any tables for that matter. He usually ate standing up, if he ate at all. More and more frequently his diet consisted of liquids. Finding his phone, he checked his calendar, and, as he'd expected, there were no appointments. His phone rang, the caller ID identifying the caller as his mother. That one word had the power to make his blood boil and his anger come crashing back, always focused at her. He blamed her for his breakup with Reye. He'd listened to her, like a momma's boy, not wanting to disappoint, giving over to her concerns regarding Reye and what it would mean to his career and her expectations. Look where it had gotten him, lonely and alone.

"Hello, Mother, what can I do for you today?" Most of the time he avoided her, didn't go by the house or answer her calls, but today he was in a mood to punish, so he'd answered.

"Stephen, I'm glad you're answering your phone today."

Her comment was met with silence.

"Stephen?"

"What?" His tone dripped with disdain.

"We are hosting a dinner party tonight, one that you promised to attend. It would mean a lot to your dad, and don't think about backing out at the last minute. You've not attended one thing since you've been home. This dinner is very important for the firm."

Silence.

"Stephen, do you hear me?"

"What time?"

"Seven for cocktails, dinner will be served at eight."

Stephen hung up without saying goodbye, grabbing a beer from the refrigerator and taking a seat on the sofa. He had ESPN to catch up on.

～

Reye—six months later

Reye pulled up to an older, two-story house with a for sale sign standing in the yard and a foreclosure notice on the door. Getting out of her truck, she walked over to pull the sign up, beyond excited. This house was to be the location of the new non-profit she would head. It was an old-fashioned two-story home built in the 1940s and located about two blocks from the center. She and her dad had closed on the house yesterday. She was meeting him here for a walk-through, to make a list of the needed repairs and renovations, along with a timeline for getting them done. Her father had agreed to help her make it livable.

While she waited, she took a moment to reflect on all that she'd accomplished A.S., After Stephen. The breakup with him had left her heartbroken. Six months ago, she could barely get through the days; just thinking about Stephen could still make her cry, but now crying was limited to the privacy of her home. If loving someone could do that to a person, she didn't want any part of it ever again. Sam and her dad were working hard to convince her otherwise. Never was a long time, but nope, she was never falling in love again. No, thank you very much. From now on, she would give her time and her love to people who needed it, who would appreciate it and not throw it away because things got difficult. No more giving it away to golden beautiful men with great bodies, great hands, great mouths, and who knew how to use them. Or who were smart and funny, or . . . Enough already, she told herself, shaking her head, wanting to erase his image from her mind. He still haunted her thoughts, though. It had been six months and she still felt unusually hurt, used, and alone.

She walked back to her truck and leaned against it, waiting for her dad. It had taken her weeks to stop crying, but somehow she had. She'd learned to cope by plunging headlong into work at the center. She'd accepted the offer to work, foregoing teaching in the public school system, hoping she'd have the freedom to try new ideas.

The center's administration had recognized and was committed to providing good quality after-school and child care. They'd asked her to help develop a good summer program at a time when she'd needed a mission. Working on a shoestring budget, using the center as the home base, she'd put together the basic framework of a summer school, using the children who had attended the aftercare program to start. Most of their parents worked during the day and were more than willing to turn them over to her for the summer, a much more attractive alternative to keeping them home alone to watch television all day long. They had gotten to know Reye through the aftercare program and as coach of the soccer team and felt comfortable with her, excited even.

Using her paycheck to subsidize more than a few trips, she filled the kids' days with any and all types of activities designed to keep them, and herself, occupied. She signed them up for a swim team through a local neighborhood association. Swim practice began at six most mornings, so Reye borrowed the center's van and picked the kids up early, leaving her home around five a.m. Swim meets were on Saturday and took up most of the day, but that was okay by her. They visited any and all museums in the city and the surrounding areas. They went to an endless list of parks, movies, and libraries.

She spent time working with them on their soccer skills as they continued to play in the summer league, and she promised she'd coach again in the fall. She pushed them to read, to practice their writing, and to improve their math skills. There would be no chance this summer of them forgetting what they had learned the previous year. If a parent needed a babysitter, she was available. She kept herself busy, and, in the process, stumbled upon her dream job, her passion. Working with the children was exhausting sometimes, but she loved it, loved them, loved seeing them exposed to new things and ideas. She loved watching them grow. Six months ago she had plowed all her emotional energy into this program. It had been her salvation, the kids her saviors, and she'd grown up a little on the way.

She'd learned that it was okay to love, painful sometimes, but okay, and to love completely. She didn't regret her love for Stephen, but going forward she would require more from her men; they would have to love her, too.

She looked up from her musings to see her dad's truck pull in behind her. She met him as he got out of his truck. He grabbed her in a great, big hug, lifting her off of the ground.

"So, baby girl, are you ready to get started? I think your house needs more than a little work."

"I agree, but I think its needs are mostly cosmetic. The structure is sound, good bones as they say. The prior owner, before losing it to foreclosure, had the foundation reconstructed."

"Well, do you have the key and your clipboard ready?"

"I do, sir," she said, bringing forth old memories of her and her dad repairing and restoring homes together. She'd spent many a summer and holiday following him around, trying to keep up and jotting down all the things he shouted to her. He loved this type of work. She didn't have the same passion for it, but she'd learned to appreciate the transformation that hard work could bring.

Later on that evening Stephen parked outside his parents' home. Earlier his dad had called and cautiously reminded him to attend. He missed talking to his dad, and it hurt to see the disappointment in his eyes resulting from the current state of his life. He'd been a little disappointed that his dad hadn't pushed him more to find out what was wrong, but equally grateful for being left alone.

He continued to sit in his car, contemplating the scene inside. Judging from the number of cars, it was quite a gathering. He got out of the car and walked up to the front door. Taking a deep breath, he opened the door and went in.

The dinner party appeared to be in progress. Men and women his parents' age stood around in various groups discussing who knew what. His mother excused herself and walked over to greet him.

"Hello, Stephen," she said, lifting her face for a kiss. Instead, he ignored her. He liked the way her face looked in shock at his snub in front of her friends. He could be mean sometimes. These were the friends he had to give up Reye for, a bunch of snobs. He ignored his mother and walked over to the sideboard looking for something to eat, realizing that he hadn't eaten today. The expression on his face must have reflected how he felt because people in the party parted like he was Moses and they the Red Sea. He didn't smile as he picked up a plate and filled it with something small and adorably edible. He left the room, going upstairs to his old room, where he and his food sat in a chair and watched a basketball game.

He must have fallen asleep, waking up a couple of hours later to a much quieter house. He sat up just as his mother entered, anger lining her face.

"How dare you make me look like a fool. You should have stayed home."

"What?" Anger simmered just below the surface of his composure. "I did what you asked. You wanted me here, so I'm here," he shouted.

"Keep your voice down. What is wrong with you, all that money spent on your education and you're wasting it. All you do is sit around all day feeling sorry for yourself. When you're not chasing girls, drinking, and partying, that is!"

"What? Now you're disappointed in your son? Is that it? Aren't I dating and fucking the right shade of girls for you?"

"You will not talk to me in that manner. See, that's what dating women who aren't your kind does for you!"

"You don't say another word about Reye. I stopped seeing her for you and Dad and the suffocating expectations.you've set for me. So you can go to hell!"

"You didn't stop seeing her because I said so. When have you ever done anything other than what you wanted? I've never been able to make you do something unless you wanted to. So stop blaming me for your leaving her. I'm sick of it!"

He pushed past her and stormed down the stairs. His dad stepped out of the study. His face was unsure, worried.

"What is going on here? Why are you shouting at your mother?" Stephen didn't respond.

"Stephen. What's all this about?"

"You really don't know? You should ask your wife," Stephen said, continuing his march out of the front door, slamming it behind him. He got into his car, squealed out of the drive, and drove away. He stopped at a light, fuming, his mother's words reverberating in his head.

She was right, of course. It wasn't her fault, not really. He was really angry at himself for being a wimp, for not standing up for something that meant so much to him. He sat at the light absorbing that realization. All this time, he'd been drinking and angry at himself, punishing himself for his treatment of Reye. His only redemption was that at the time, he hadn't realized that she'd meant so much to him.

Later on that night, he sat alone on the sofa in his apartment, holding a bottled water. He couldn't bring himself to get another beer. He was done with that. It was dark in the room, save for the lights from the Dallas skyline that twinkled as he watched them through the windows of his apartment. He listened to music, something by John Meyer that reminded him of his time spent, like this, with Reye. He missed those nights, missed her. Nights spent with her on her couch, lights out, except for a candle or two, listening to music and each other. Mostly she talked and he listened. He stared out at the city and recalled the earlier confrontation he'd had with his mom and dad. He shouldn't have said those things to her. He hadn't meant them, he loved her. Sure, he felt pressure from her, but ultimately it had been his decision to end it with Reye, not his mother's. Joe had called him a coward, and he had been. He'd chosen the path of least resistance, or so it had seemed like it at the time. He hadn't counted on the pain he'd later feel, along with the regrets. He'd been the coward, the one that wasn't willing to be uncomfortable or to lose his favor as the golden boy. He could have, she'd asked him to, and he'd walked away, he'd let her down, and he'd regretted it immensely.

His doorbell rang. Some brave soul coming to visit the lion in his den, he thought sadly to himself. He'd been a wounded lion with a thorn in its paw that bit the heads of those who ventured near to help. Another regret. Since he'd been home, he'd insulted or offended just about anyone who was close to him or came close to him. He turned on the light next to his sofa and went to answer the door. It was his dad. He opened the door and his dad entered.

"This is the first time I've seen your new place," he said. "It's nice, a little sparse, but nice."

"Yes, it is. Can I get you something to drink?"

"I'll take a bottled water, if you have one."

"I do." Stephen went to the kitchen and grabbed a bottle from the refrigerator, returning to find his dad gazing out the window.

"This is a nice view."

"It was the main reason I bought the apartment," Stephen said, handing the bottle of water to his dad. "Dad, let me say that I'm sorry. I shouldn't have said those things to Mom today. I'll go by and apologize tomorrow. I was angrier than I'd realized."

"You know, son, I had a talk with your mother after you left. I had no idea that you were dating someone in Austin last year or that she'd meant so much to you. You never said. I thought you would eventually settle down with Beth, thought you liked her. I was surprised by the outburst today, but it explains your behavior since you've been home, your not being at the office."

"It's not your or Mom's fault," Stephen said. Taking a deep breath and starting at the beginning, he told his dad about Reye, how they met and why she had become special to him. He'd become emotional during the telling, stopping several times to regain his composure. It was the first time he'd talked to anyone since their breakup. His dad listened without interruption or comment until he'd finished.

"You know, son, when I was eighteen, before I met your mother, there was a girl that I had grown up with, a beautiful African-American girl, Anna. Her dad worked for your grandfather, doing odd jobs around our house. It was a different time back then. We played together, long past the time that we should have. We went to different high schools, but she would come over to the house to help her dad from time to time. She was beautiful, and at eighteen, no one could have told me anything. Anyway, I wanted to marry her, and told anyone that would listen to me. Can you imagine her father's response, and your grandfather's? He would not hear of such a thing, and if he could have shot me, he would have." His dad was quiet for a minute, lost in his own thoughts. "Anyway, her family moved away abruptly and I searched all over town and the surrounding areas for her. Of course your grandfather knew where they'd moved, but he wouldn't tell me. I was angry with him for a long time after that. I went on to college, met and fell in love with your mother. I don't know if Anna and I could have withstood the challenges we would have faced during those times. I'm telling you this to say that I understand what you feel. I know that anger and sadness that can come from letting someone you love leave." Stephen sat looking at his dad, his eyes filling with tears again.

His dad continued. "Here's the way I see it. You've got choices. You can blame your mother and yourself until you are old and grey, or you can recognize the wrong and either try to make it right or move on. That decision has to be yours. It's been what, six months? Do you think it's worth going back to see if she would be willing to try again? Women can be unforgiving sometimes. If she loved you as much as you thought, don't you think you should try?"

"I don't know."

His dad looked at him intently. "I also need you at the firm. You've got to take the bar exam and pass it so you can get on with your life whether or not you work it out with her. She really might not be willing to take a chance on you again if you're unemployed," he said with a chuckle.

Stephen gave him a watery smile.

"I'd better get home. You know your mother will be calling anytime now." He stood up and started to walk to the front door. Stephen followed, reaching out to grab his dad in a hug.

"Thank you," he said.

"You're welcome. I'll see you bright and early Monday morning at the office."

"Yes, I'll be there."

Reye sat behind her desk in her office at the center and reread the invitation a second time. "You will be honored at the Twenty-fifth Foundation and Christmas Charity Gala to be held on December 23 for your outstanding contributions to the lives of Texas children." The ball was to be held in Dallas at the Grand Hotel, one of the finest hotels in Dallas, six weeks away. She'd been nominated by Susan and the center's board of directors for her work with the kids in both the after-school and summer programs. She was beyond honored. Hell, she should be the one honoring them. She looked out of her window, reflecting again on the hurt Stephen caused.

Dallas, huh? What were the chances of running into him, anyway? She hadn't heard from him, even after the breakup. Well, in all fairness, she didn't know if he'd tried to call or not. She had thrown her SIM card away and later traded her number for a new one. She hadn't wanted to run the risk of calling and begging him to come back to her; once had been enough. Looking back at that day still caused her to wince in pain.

The problem with cell phones was that you didn't really have to learn anyone's number anymore. After the cell was gone, she'd regretted not memorizing his number, but it had saved him from her. She could laugh now about driving by his apartment, driving by the law school in hopes of seeing him, but it wasn't funny at the time.

Apparently it had been just about sex for him. To be fair to him, he'd never told her he loved her. He never lied to her by promising her anything. She still loved him, though, she didn't lie to herself about that. She was still angry, but at least the urge to see him had dwindled. She put the invitation on the bulletin board behind her back and put the date into her phone.

She wasn't going to Dallas alone, that was for damn sure. The chance of running into him was small, but she could use the company nonetheless. She thought of calling Joe, but Joe had a girlfriend now. Actually, Joe had numerous girlfriends, too many for her to keep up with. Reye and Joe had become good friends, united in the purpose of making sure Shane stayed on track.

She could always call Sam, who held her when she cried, dragged her out of the house to the movies, played soccer with her, and had even been willing to go to the mall, which he hated with a passion. He'd seen her at her worst, and she trusted him.

She picked up her phone and dialed.

"Hey, baby girl." She liked that the men in her life called her that; it made her feel loved, and, since Stephen, she had needed mucho love.

"Hello, big brother," she responded, looking out of the window again. "You won't believe this, but because of my work here with the kids, I was nominated for an award for outstanding volunteer in Texas."

"Why wouldn't I believe that?" he asked. "Even I've noticed how hard you been working on behalf of those little rugrats."

"Well, I am to be honored, along with others like me in Dallas, at this ball. I don't want to go by myself. Would you go with me?" She hoped she sounded upbeat. "It's on December 23, and I know you aren't teaching then. Plus I feel an obligation to help the women in Austin get a break from you and your infinite charms."

"I'm sure they appreciate your efforts on their behalf." He chuckled. His voice changed from playful to serious. "Dallas, huh?"

"Yeah, Dallas. I'm a big girl, Sam, or at least I've learned to be." She knew where he was going with this line of questioning. "And anyways, Dallas is a big city. I'm sure I'm not in the same social circles as Stephen, and I can't imagine him attending a charity event. I'm good. I just wanted someone to hang with. I didn't want to attend as the hard worker for kids, the girl who is giving her life up for her career. You know the one, with no life as evidenced by her lack of a date or significant other."

"Have you told Mom and Dad?"

"Nope, you're the first. I'm calling them next. I am going to downplay it. I don't want them to get worked up over it."

"Well, they are proud of you, and, in case I've forgotten to say it, so am I. You had me worried there for a while, but you pulled it together, so yes, I will be your escort to your prom." She could hear the laughter in his voice.

"Thanks. I'll call you back with more details. See you soon."

CHAPTER 15

Stephen leaned back against the kitchen sink, sipping from a bottle of water, his reward for having cleaned his apartment today. He was proud of the progress he'd made in his life over the last few weeks. That disastrous fight with his mom and the subsequent talk with his dad had allowed him to lance a wound he'd kept hidden from himself. One he'd created. Slowly, finally, he'd started to get his life back on track, now studying for the bar exam, running daily to get his body back in shape, and working at his dad's law firm. With a bit of luck, he might just have a chance with Reye again.

He remained standing in the kitchen, taking in the changes recently made to it and to the rest of his apartment. It had started one day a few weeks ago with a simple cleaning. He needed to bring order to chaos. Other more basic needs followed. Finding something clean to wear turned into purchasing a washer and dryer so he could wash clothes. Finding something to eat led to stocking the refrigerator with something other than beer, and growing tired of take-out required cooking, which required dishes, pots, and pans. He also broke down and bought some more furniture. He'd had some shopping to do.

As a way to spend time with his mom, seeking to mend the rift that he'd created between them, he'd let her drag him all over town looking for furniture. They'd fought initially over where they would shop. His mom with her high-end taste and money to match wanted to pay for everything, but he'd refused, needing the autonomy that came from paying for his own things, being his own man. So they'd agreed to a moderately priced store that offered good quality furniture, preferably wood with clean, simple lines.

He acquiesced over the accessorizing. He didn't get the need for it, nor did he care. He picked out only one item for himself, a frame to hold a picture of him and Reye taken at the second soccer game played between their teams. In the picture, a smiling Reye stood with her foot on the ball, leaning into his chest, trying to move around him. He, with a matching grin, stood behind her, his hands on her hips. Using your hands was illegal in soccer, but he hadn't cared. He was supposed to have been guarding her, preventing her from moving up field. A member of Reye's team had captured the shot and had given it to her. He'd taken it, intending to make a copy, but had never gotten around to giving it back. Prior to the frame purchase, he'd kept it in the drawer of his nightstand, taking it out when he was alone and feeling sorry for himself. Now it was framed and prominently displayed next to his bed. He'd moved his box of condoms to the drawer, where they would remain for now. He'd chosen to forego sex for a while. As much as he wanted the release that a woman could offer, they weren't the body that he craved. So, until he'd resolved this thing with Reye, either to put a period to the end of them or to move forward if she were willing, he would remain celibate.

Finishing his water, he threw the bottle into the recycle bin and walked over to the couch and sat. He found a basketball game on TV and leaned back, lifting his feet to the ottoman in front of him, relaxed and more content than he'd felt in a long, long, time.

Saturday morning a week later found Stephen nearing the end of his morning jog, mentally compiling a Christmas list, bemoaning the hurried passage of the holiday season. Christmas was but a few days away, catching him unprepared. No time today either for the mall. Maybe tomorrow, he thought. The next destination after his run would be to the office for a couple of hours and then on to join his dad and a client in the afternoon for a round of golf. His day would end with his required attendance tonight at a charitable gala the firm had purchased tables for or underwritten, he wasn't sure of the details. No getting out of that; he was still in make-up mode with his parents.

Actually a large part of the trust and estate business required schmoozing, getting to know the players in Dallas, building relationships. So, going forward, he would be expected to attend balls, dances, dinners, parties, dinner parties, and golf, endless golf. Golf he could do. Although it wasn't his best sport, he wasn't a shankapotamus either. He'd grown up in one of the older country clubs in Dallas, and his parents held memberships at one more.

One more block and he was done, finally. He stopped outside of his apartment building, catching his breath and looking around him, taking in others who were running, walking, or heading to the neighborhood Starbucks for a different kind of pick-me-up. He caught the eye of several women while running who had thrown smiles his way.

Opening the main door of his apartment building, he looked into the face of Henri, who appeared to be leaving. Henri's face looked into his, undergoing several changes before settling on wariness. He looked like someone not sure where the next punch would land. Stephen had become familiar with that expression lately, having seen it on quite a few of his friends' faces.

"Dude," he said. "How've you been?"

"Fine," Henri responded, stepping away from the door and moving toward a less active place on the sidewalk.

"Do you live around here?" Stephen ran through his memory for any recollections of the last time he'd seen Henri. More importantly, Stephen wondered what he had said that warranted this cool response from his former roommate and best friend.

"No, I was here visiting a friend."

"Oh, I purchased an apartment here. Didn't know if you knew that."

"Yeah, I did," Henri said, offering nothing further.

Stephen chuckled a little. "So, let me apologize for my behavior, whenever it occurred. I don't remember the specifics, but I do know that I haven't been in a good place for a while. So I'm sure I've said something to you that I need to apologize for. My bad, man, it wasn't meant to harm you. It seems that I've said something to hurt just about everyone I care about." He extended his hand again to Henri.

Henri's expression cleared, a smile forming on his lips as he reached to accept Stephen's hand. Stephen pulled him in for a hug. "I'm sorry, you were always a good friend of mine, I still consider you one," he said. "What have you been up to?"

"Nothing much, working at my dad's business, starting from ground up. How about you?"

"I'm studying for the bar exam finally, working for my dad, too, and, as you can see, or more likely smell, I'm trying to get in shape again."

"Hey, I'm glad for you. You had me worried for a while, I'm glad you're back."

"Me, too," he said, smiling.

Reye finished the final touches to her makeup and stood back to look at herself. Sam was waiting for her in the living room. As a treat they'd upgraded their room to a suite, two bedrooms and one sitting room.

Perfect, she thought, examining herself in the mirror. The dress she'd purchased fit like a second skin, made perfectly for her athletic body. It a long white column with silver undertones, the color contrasting beautifully against the brown of her skin. Her locks, which she'd always worn short, shined and sparkled tonight, framing her face. She'd borrowed some of her mother's dangling diamond earrings and a pair of silver high-heeled sandals, lifting her six-foot frame higher. Reye had practiced walking in them, wanting to feel comfortable and not like some little girl playing dress-up in her mother's shoes. "You clean up well," she said to the mirror, turning at the sound of knocking at the door. Opening it for Sam, she absorbed his reaction. It was a salve for her bruised psyche. She appreciated a positive male response, even if it was from her brother.

"Wow, you look fantastic," he said, walking into the room and taking her hands in his. "Are you ready?"

"Yes." She stepped closer to him and placed a kiss on his cheek. "Let's go," she said, grabbing her purse, making sure she had her room key. She followed him out of the room, and they stepped on to the elevators to take them downstairs to the ballroom. The gala coordinator had wanted the honorees to arrive early to be seated at the head tables, located front and center.

Stephen sat in his car, knee-deep in a long line of other expensive cars waiting for the valet to reach them, regretting his decision not to park the car himself in the hotel's parking garage. It would have been faster. The golf outing earlier had lasted longer than he'd anticipated, forcing him to rush to be here on time. He had not looked forward to this evening.

Finally a young valet, decked out in the required dress of black pants and white shirt, stood outside, opening the door for him to exit. "Good evening, sir," he piped, all energy as he handed a valet stub to Stephen, who'd slipped out of the car, removed his tux jacket from the back seat and slid it on. Stephen walked through the hotel's doors.

This was one of the more exclusive hotels in town, and, as he'd expected, it was very much understated, adopting the less-is-more philosophy. He entered the doors and spotted a group of women who, judging by their attire, were headed in the same direction as he. All were attractive and about his age, dressed to appeal to the available men attending. Their gowns cuddled their bodies, laying open some very nice assets to those interested in assessing. He received a few sly and shy smiles, which he politely returned. He wanted in and out of this gig, the quicker the better.

Outside the main ballroom doors, two long tables covered in white floor-length tablecloths waited for guests to receive their table assignments. Seated behind the tables were four ladies about his mother's age. The three girls in front of him were helped first, and he walked over to the last woman. She was dressed in a sequined blue number that covered her arms and neck, reminding him of that woman who was in *Mad Money*. She smiled and looked up at him. "May I help you?"

"Yes, I am Stephen Stuart with Stuart & Stuart law firm," he said politely.

She took a moment to locate the firm's name. "You are at table six," she said, handing him a program.

"Thank you," he said, smiling. He proceeded to the entry doors leading into the ballroom. It was opened by a hostess, a young woman with red lips and an equally red dress. A beauty, she was a slim brunette with enhanced breasts, and he'd seen enough to know. She looked him over and smiled, her eyes signaling to him that she thought he was her match in the beauty department. He was. He returned that smile and followed her to his table, which was located in the front of the room. What was the point of underwriting these events if you couldn't be seen as the great benefactors that you were? And you couldn't do that from the tables located in the back. He looked over and nodded to his parents, who were seated at the first of two tables reserved for his firm. The second table held two empty chairs, for him and a date, which he hadn't found and didn't bring. He thanked the beauty in red and sat down, smiling in acknowledgement at those seated at the table with him.

In the front of the room, two tables extended from each side of the podium. He supposed that was the seating for the honorees. An older lady, dressed in a black sequined gown trimmed in black fur around the neck, stood at the podium in front, talking, providing the audience with the reason for being here tonight. He sat back, his gaze moving around, taking in the ballroom, amazed. Every table was full. He was surprised by the popularity of events like these. He'd expected less. Christmas was only two days away; perhaps the size of the crowd was due to the holidays and related festivities. This was one form of entertainment, not his preference, but he'd admit that the food was probably excellent, the drinks were free, and the company rich.

Stephen turned his attention back to the woman speaking. "We are here to honor the outstanding volunteers of Texas. They have been nominated by their respective organizations for exhibiting heart and dedication to their causes and for persevering long after the lights are turned out." Stephen glanced briefly over the honorees located to the left of the speaker, his inspection interrupted by the waiters delivering the salad course. The speaker continued. "Our first honoree is younger than most, having just received her teaching degree from the university." Catcalls filled the air as the crowd cheered; they all loved the university. Waiting until the room was again quiet, she continued. "Reye Jackson has been nominated by the East River Community Center, where she has worked tirelessly with their after-school program. Her biggest accomplishment was the start up of a new and unique approach to their summer care program. I would like you to stand with me as I invite Reye to join me at the podium."

Reye stood up and walked over to join the speaker. "Let's give Reye an applause that demonstrates our appreciation of what she has done for children in Austin, Texas."

Shocked and stunned, Stephen stared, standing up to clap along with everyone else, not really aware of doing so. She was beautiful, better than he'd committed to memory. Her hair was still short and spiky, but she seemed taller. Heels, he guessed. The body he'd spent the better part of a year getting to know was still perfect. Her smile knocked the air from his lungs, sucker-punched him, leaving him shaken and dazed. He sat down before the others had finished clapping. Smiling, she moved to stand in front of the podium, adjusting the mike to accommodate her height, and said confidently, her smile huge, eyes shining, "Thank you for this wonderful honor. Believe me, if you all were given the chance to work with these kids, it would be you instead of me on the receiving end of this award tonight. Those kids make you believe that anything is possible, and if it isn't, you feel compelled to do all within your power to make it so. They have been my saviors, and I love them tremendously. Thank you again." She held the plaque up and smiled, stepping away from the podium.

The speaker said, "Please, let's give one more round of applause for Ms. Jackson." Stephen remained seated, his eyes following her as she moved back to her seat, and moved over to the person, male, seated next to her. It was Sam, whose eyes met his with a look that was sharp enough to cut glass. Stephen didn't blame him, recalling Sam's talk to him months before on the soccer field about Reye. He understood the anger he saw in her brother's eyes. He deserved it. His gaze swung back to Reye, who was now looking down, reading the plaque. Either she didn't know he was here, or she wanted to avoid him.

He was slightly aware of the waiter removing the salads and placing the main course before him. His mind now scattered, he wondered what he should do. He needed to talk to her, but how? What would he say? Thoughts ran like ants in search of food through his mind. Shit, he planned on going to Austin, talking to her in private, not here in front of all these people, but he didn't want her to leave without talking to her. God, he'd missed her. All of the unsettled feelings from the past six months hit him, surprising him with their force. He sat back against his chair, tugging at the tie at his neck, needing to breathe.

The speaker had moved on to introduce the other honorees. People stood and clapped for each one, and so did he, but his body was just going through the motions. His mind had separated entirely from it. Finally and thankfully the program portion of the evening ended. People were getting up from their tables, to mingle, dance, and seek the bar for stronger libations. He looked again at the table where Reye and Sam sat. Reye was engaged in conversation with a woman seated next to her. She laughed. He stood up, deciding to go over and congratulate her.

He turned to step away from his table and bumped into his dad, who was now standing in front of him, blocking his path. Leaning his head back, he looked into his son's face. Stephen didn't know what his dad saw there. "Are you well, son?"

"Yes, I am," he answered, finding understanding in his dad's eyes.

"Your mother remembered Reye from their meeting and pointed her out to me. She is a beautiful girl. I can see why you're taken with her."

"Yes, she is."

"I was on my way over to the honorees table to congratulate and thank them for their hard work. Would you like to join me?" Stephen, surprised by his dad's request, agreed. It would be nice to have a buffer.

Starting at the end of the table, they congratulated the other honorees, slowly making their way towards Reye. The crowd to meet and thank the honorees was larger than Stephen anticipated, so it took some time to reach her. She stood with Sam, his arm around her shoulders as they talked to an elderly couple, her back to him. The couple moved away, and Stephen touched her elbow, watching as she turned to him, her widening eyes giving away her surprise at seeing him. Her smile faltered, disappeared, and returned, all in the span of two seconds.

"Ms. Jackson, I wanted to personally congratulate you for your volunteer efforts. Stephen's told me about your work at the center and on the soccer fields," said the elder Stuart, reaching for Reye's hands. Her eyes swung to his dad's, surprised again as her hands disappeared, lost between his father's. "Stephen has told me so much about you."

Reye looked between them, unsure. "Thank you," she said.

"You remember my son, Stephen?"

"Sure I do," she said, accepting Stephen's hand, her eyes hard, at odds with her smile.

Reye turned back to the elder Stuart. "Mr. Stuart, this is my brother Sam," she said.

"It is a pleasure meeting you sir," Sam said, accepting the older Stuart's hand.

"Will you be staying in Dallas for the holidays?" Mr. Stuart asked them.

"No, sir, we are going to go back to Austin. We usually spend the holidays with our family," Sam replied.

"Well, it has been a pleasure meeting you, Ms. Jackson. I look forward to seeing you again soon."

"Thank you, sir," she said, not sure of his meaning.

Reye turned and began speaking to the next person in line before Stephen could say another word.

"Do you need a minute?" Sam asked her during a break.

"No, I'm fine, but I do want to find the ladies' room for a second. I'll be right back," she said.

Sam's eyes were hard. "He's not worth you, Reye."

"I know, it was just a shock to see him again. Give me a second, okay? I'll run to the restroom and then I'll be back," she said, laying a hand on his arm. He stepped back, allowing her to pass.

She strode through the ballroom, returning smiles as she made her way out the doors. Why him and why now? What happened to all the cute, cutting remarks she'd prepared to say when and if she saw him again? They'd all vanished from her head. And why did he have to look so good? Ugh! His eyes were still the striking blue she saw most nights in her dreams. He was still fine, especially so in that tux, still golden. But he'd left her, he'd had someone else while he was with her. *Remember that, Reye,* she said to herself. She marched out of the main door and down the hallway with her head up as she went in search of the bathroom. There were so many people, she thought, changing her mind and direction, deciding to go to her room instead. She needed privacy. She turned to walk to the main part of the hotel where the main elevators were located and heard her name. She'd have recognized that voice anywhere. Stephen walked toward her. Pretending like she hadn't heard him, she walked faster until she reached the elevators and pushed the button.

"Hey," he said as he stopped next to her, looking both uncertain and nervous, his hands in his pockets. That was a new look for him, she'd never seen him nervous or uncertain.

"Hey."

He took another step closer to her. "You look beautiful tonight."

"Thank you."

"Congratulations on the award. I guess you took the job at the center."

"Thank you again, and yes, I did." The elevator had arrived. Two teenagers disembarked and she stepped in. So did Stephen, along with an older couple. She pushed the button for the eighth floor.

"Would you push number ten?" the other couple asked.

"Sure," she said. The door closed.

Reye and Stephen watched as the elevator took them nonstop up to her floor. The doors opened and she stepped out. Stephen followed.

"Where are you going?"

"I need to talk to you," he said.

"Maybe another time. I need to get back, Sam's waiting for me."

"Give me a second."

Not wanting to argue in the hallway, she turned and walked to her room. He was behind her. *What are you doing,* she silently asked herself, but opened the door to her room, holding it open for him.

She entered, faced him, arms folded across her chest. "Okay, I'm listening," she said.

"Look, Reye, I'm sorry for the way I left things. I had planned to come to Austin after the New Year to find you to tell you that I loved you then, and still do. It just took some time for me to figure that out, to realize that I want you in my life," he said.

"Okay, thanks, I've heard you. Now what?"

"I was hoping we could start over. Could we talk, get together before you leave?"

She shook her head. "Nope. Been there, done that. Would you leave now?" She reached for the door handle and opened it.

"Reye," he said again.

"What, Stephen? I need to get back, would you please just leave?" Her voice was firm, her expression set.

He looked at her, searching her face for an inkling of forgiveness. Seeing nothing, he decided to leave. He'd give her a little time and try to talk to her later. The evening was still young, or so he hoped.

Sam was surprised to find Reye coming out of the room as he opened the door. He surely hadn't expected to find her dry-eyed and in the process of returning downstairs.

"Sam, I was on my way back."

"Oh. I saw Stephen getting off of the elevator and got a little worried," he said.

"Don't be. I had given some consideration to running upstairs to cry my heart out, but you know what, I've had enough of that, no more tears for me. He wanted out, he walked away, remember."

"Yeah, I do, but I wasn't sure you did."

Stephen had returned to the ballroom and was immediately accosted by his mom. "I wondered where you went to. I saw you and your dad talking with Reye."

"Yes, we were."

"She is a beautiful girl," she said, her attempt to demonstrate, if not her approval of Reye, at least not her opposition.

"Yes, she is."

They both looked over as Reye and Sam returned to their table, taking their seats, engaging in conversation with the people sitting next to them.

Later on that night, Stephen watched Reye and Sam walk to the dance floor, the band playing some tune he didn't recognize. Deciding to ask her to dance, he headed in the direction of the dance floor. His dad stepped in front of him again, and he almost fell over him. What was up with his dad?

"Take some advice from your old man. Give her some time. You are going to have to reintroduce yourself to her and let her know that you are serious about her this time. You are serious about her, aren't you?"

"Of course I am."

"How serious? Do you want to marry her?"

Stephen didn't have an answer for that. He was at a loss for words. He hadn't given any thought to what would happen beyond Reye agreeing to see him again. What did he want from her ultimately?

"I think you owe it her to be sure of what you want from her before you do this again. Don't you?"

He slowly nodded. He looked over at Reye, dancing and laughing, her head back as she gave Sam one of her favorite smiles, wide and open, eyes dancing. Just as sure as he knew his name, he knew he loved her and wanted her permanently in his life. He would do what was necessary to have her again.

"I can tell from your face that you've answered my question. Good luck then."

"Thanks, Dad. Knowing Reye like I do, I'm going to need it." He laughed with his dad, but his gaze was still focused on her.

$\Longrightarrow$

Toward the end of the evening, Stephen sat at his table waiting for yet another song to end. He'd not given up yet, so he'd sat and watched and waited. Reye and Sam were finishing yet another dance. He was determined to talk to her again before she left. The evening was winding to a close and fewer people remained. Now seemed like a good time, so Stephen stood and walked over to her table.

"Would you dance with me, Reye?"

She sat there for several seconds, not looking at him, her gaze focused on her lap. After a few more seconds, he thought she wasn't going to answer, but she looked up and met his eyes. She nodded. He reached for her hand and led her to the dance floor. He pulled her into his arms, lifting her arms and placed them around his neck, moving his hand to her waist as he pulled her in to him. He took a second to stand there, holding her, not moving, just getting re-acclimated to the feel of her body next to his. It had been so long since he had held her, and it brought back so many memories for him. "Are we going to dance or just stand here?" she asked, breaking his reverie.

He laughed softly and started moving in tune with the music. It was a slow song so he didn't have to concentrate on his moves, just her. She danced with her cheek pressed next to his, his mouth next to her ear.

"Reye," he said.

"Yes," she answered, a little breathlessly.

"I miss you."

"Don't."

He paused for a second. "I love you." His voice was sincere, his hands tightening around her as he felt her start to pull away.

"Just listen, please," he said. "Will you just listen to me?"

For several seconds there was silence as he and Reye moved slowly to the music of the band. "Okay," she said finally. He pulled her closer, slowing to move with the music. "I want to see you again. I realize you're angry, and you have every reason to be, but I want the chance to make it up to you." She pulled one of her arms from around his neck. He grabbed her wrist before she could pull away completely, holding it near his face as he continued talking, his voice earnest. "Don't answer right now, just think about it. Okay?"

She pulled her head back to look him in his eyes. The eyes looking back at her were intense, sincere, and hungry. Her body, the traitor, began to respond to his nearness. They both stopped moving, all pretense of dancing gone.

"Look, Stephen," she said. "I'll think about it, but I don't know if I'm willing to risk myself like that again, or if you're worth it. Should I take the chance that you might change your mind down the line if things get too difficult? What if you encounter others who don't approve of us, what then?"

"Shsssh," he said placing his finger to her lips. "How about we start again? Take it slow if you want, until you're comfortable with me, us," he said.

"I don't know. I'll think about it, and don't push me."
They were quiet for a few minutes. Realizing that they'd
stopped dancing, they began moving slowly to the music
again. "I'm really tired. Do you mind if we stop?"

"Sure," he said trying not to sound disappointed,
adjusting his face into a smile that didn't quite reach his
eyes. He didn't know what he expected her to say, but this
wasn't it.

He took her hand again and led her back to her table.
Once they'd arrived, she turned to him and said, "Thanks
for the dance, Stephen. See ya around."

"Yeah. See ya, Reye. I'll be in touch." He looked over
at Sam, who sat intently watching them. "Good night,
Sam," he said and turned and left. He walked over to say
goodbye to his parents and left the ballroom for good. He
needed some air and space, somewhere he could be alone,
to lick his wounds. He saw the red dressed beauty
walking towards him, stepping in front of him before he
reached the main doors.

"What's your hurry?" she purred through pouting
lips.

"Long night," he said, giving her a tight smile as he
walked past her and continued on out through the door.

Sam looked over at Reye as she sat in the passenger
side of his Grey Ghost, staring out of the window. Grey
Ghost was the name he'd given to his white Escalade, a
graduation gift. He and Reye were now on the road

driving down I-35 towards Austin. They'd left the gala, returned to the room, packed, and checked out, stopping only for Reye's favorite Starbucks drink.

Earlier he'd been shocked to see Stephen walking into the ballroom. Reye hadn't seem him enter, and Sam had been grateful for life's small wonders. She was nervous enough without the ex showing up. He'd watched them on the dance floor and was struck by how beautiful they were together. They made a striking couple, Reye with her brown skin against her white dress next to Stephen in his tux, with his golden boy looks. They'd turned heads. Apparently they'd forgotten that dancing was required on a dance floor, because they'd stood still, talking and looking intently at each other, as if they were the only two people in the room. He knew, had known all along, that Stephen was serious about Reye, that he loved her. He also knew he would have a hell of a time convincing Reye that her golden boy was for real this time. But he hoped Stephen was successful. Reye had become singularly focused on her job, to the exclusion of a personal life. And that worried him. He looked over at Reye out of the corner of his eye.

"After all we've been through, you're not going tell me what Stephen said to you?"

Reye was quiet for a few minutes, staring out of the window at the passing dark landscape. "He said he loved me, he wants to see me again, wants us to be together and would I please think about it. He is willing to go slow, blah, blah, blah, if that's what I need," she said flatly.

"Well, what do you think?"

She turned to face him. "I don't know. Why should I? He'll just hurt me again. He thinks he misses me, and he might. We were good together, and I don't just mean the sex. But I've learned that I need more than that. What if he tires of the hassles that may come with being with me? What then? I do love him still, but you of all people saw what I was like after he left. Why would I willingly do that to myself again?"

"You *do* still love him, and that's a place to start. Right, Reye?"

"Yeah, I do, but what's love got to do with it?" She laughed.

"Maybe you should just wait and see. He might surprise you."

"Maybe, we'll see."

CHAPTER 16

Christmas Day found the Jackson clan together again. Reye loved her family dearly, but the noise level they created when they were together was overwhelming sometimes. Or maybe it was just her. Since leaving Dallas, she had been weepy and fretful. She looked around the room, taking in the wrapping paper scattered everywhere, along with a multitude of gifts, the conclusion to the family's gift-exchanging ritual. Leaving the family room, she went in search of quiet. Grabbing her jacket from the hall closet, she walked through the kitchen, inadvertently interrupting a conversation between Sam and her mother. "Don't mind me, I just need some air," she said, opening the back door and stepping out onto the deck.

"Hey, baby girl. You needed some peace and quiet, too?" her dad asked. He'd settled back into his favorite lounger on the deck, cup of coffee in hand.

She was like her dad in so many ways. "What are you doing outside?"

"I'm just sitting out here watching the stars, taking in this quiet evening, enjoying God's day. What brings you out?"

"The same," Reye answered.

"Come over and tell me about your trip to Dallas. Did you have a good time?"

Reye located a chair and pulled it over to him while looking around for something to prop her feet on. Not finding anything, she took off her shoes and settled her feet on her dad's legs.

"Yes. The ceremony was very nice, very grand." She overemphasized the word like she was the Queen of England. Her dad chuckled. "We, the recipients, were given the red carpet treatment, a beautiful suite, fabulous dinner, a plaque, and a standing ovation. I've never felt so appreciated. All kidding aside, it was great, Dad." She waited a minute before nonchalantly adding, "I ran into Stephen. You remember him, don't you?"

"Sure, the young man from Dallas that went to the law school here?"

"Yep, that's him. I think their family's firm helped to sponsor the event."

"Really."

"Yep, and guess what?" Reye decided she needed to talk about this with someone other than Sam. She loved her sister-in-laws and her mom, but she'd never felt close enough to discuss Stephen with them. But her dad, he knew firsthand what Stephen had meant to her.

"What?"

"He wants to see me again. He say's he realizes that he loves me and made a mistake in leaving."

"Huh," he grunted. "Well, what do you know," he said, glancing at her face. "What do you think?"

"I don't know. I've done nothing but think about this since I've been home. I'm tired of thinking."

"Do you still love him?"

"Unfortunately, I think so. What does that say about me? That after all my tears and grief, I'm actually giving him further consideration. See, Dad, I've always told you I'm the weak link in this family's chain."

Her dad chuckled and she joined in. "Loving someone doesn't make you weak, baby girl. It actually takes more than a bit of courage to put yourself in someone else's hands, to risk."

"Yeah," she said.

"Yeah," he said, mocking her, but continuing to talk. "Love is sometimes unexplainable, certainly unpredictable, and a whole lot irrational. It goes beyond what you can see to what you feel, and it's scary. But if you find that someone, it is so worth it. Your mom was worth it for me," he said, smiling at her. They sat in silence for a long time, looking out at the night sky.

"You know what, Dad?" she said. "I don't have to do anything right now, do I? I can wait and see what he does, can't I?"

"You can do whatever you want, baby girl," he said, looking at her.

"I love you, Dad." She leaned over to give him a hug.

"I love you, too."

Stephen sat in his dad's office reviewing documents from an estate for which the firm had been named executor. One of their long-standing clients had died early this week, leaving behind a large fortune to be distributed to his family and local charities. It was one of the services provided by their firm, a timely and thorough transfer of assets in accordance to the client's direction, usually a will or trust. They were in the beginning stages of the process, and depending on the size of an estate, it might take years to complete the process.

His dad was giving him a large chunk of it to work through. Stephen, having gained experience from his summers spent working at the office, understood what was required. In addition to having a law degree, Stephen held an undergraduate degree in finance, another advantage in the trust and estate business. It was now nine-thirty, and they'd been working in his dad's office since the firm officially shut down at five. His dad had agreed to spend tonight completing the preliminary review so that Stephen could take tomorrow, Friday, off. He was going to Austin.

"Your first trip to Austin?"

"Yes, sir. I thought about leaving on Saturday, but I'm getting a bit anxious."

He looked at Stephen, proud of the man he was becoming. "Well, good luck."

"I'll need it."

Unfortunately, the office called, and Stephen went in for a short time Friday morning, so he'd arrived in Austin around three in the afternoon. He'd booked a hotel close to the university, dropped his bags off, and had changed into jeans and a t-shirt, leaving his hotel in search of Reye. His first destination was the center where she worked. He was headed there now, taking in the city as he drove. Austin was so different from Dallas. It was more laid back compared to Dallas' rat-on-a-treadmill pace. It was slower here, and slow was good sometimes.

Stephen turned into the parking lot of the center, where Reye spent a large chunk of her time, filled with regrets. He was regretful that he'd never been to this place before, that he'd never helped her coach, and that he'd been stingy with his time on things that had mattered to her. He'd felt supremely sad that she'd left thinking their relationship had been just sex. It hadn't, he'd just been clueless at the time. No use crying over spilled milk, his grandmother liked to say, so he pushed ahead.

He walked up to the center, noting the kids around it, standing and hanging out. He gave a nod to the group of boys clumped together working at looking cool and indifferent. The indifferent part needed more work. He opened the door and walked in, taking a second to look around. The information desk was located a few steps away. He walked over, making eye contact with an older woman, short, with a short afro talking on the telephone. He stood next to her, waiting for her to finish the conversation.

She looked up, smiling at him, holding a finger, the age-old sign for wait, shaking her head as she listened to the person on the other end.

"Girl, let me call you later, there's a gentlemen at the desk that needs my assistance. I'll call you back in a minute." Stephen gave her a huge smile, hoping his charm would aid him in finding Reye.

"Can I help you?"

"Yes, I am looking for Reye Jackson. She works here in the aftercare and summer care programs."

"I'm sorry, son, I didn't catch your name?"

"Stephen Stuart."

"Is she expecting you?"

"No, I was hoping to surprise her."

"Well, Stephen Stuart, you've just missed her." His smile stayed in place, but his eyes dimmed a bit. Of course Susan knew who *he* was. So this was the face that belonged to Reye's Stephen. He was indeed handsome, tall, with a beautiful pair of blue eyes, a thick head of black hair, and a smile that had probably gotten a lot of women in trouble. She also knew what he'd meant to Reye and the hurt he'd left behind. Men! She loved them dearly, but they could wreak some havoc, leaving plenty of destruction in their wake.

"Do you know where she is?" he asked, his question bringing her back from her musings.

She hoped she wouldn't regret this later. "On Friday afternoons, Reye is usually at soccer practice with her team. They meet at the soccer fields located at Henderson and Third. Do you know where that is?"

"Yes."

"She left about thirty minutes ago, so you better get a move on. They practice for an hour. If you miss her there, she and her dad have been working on restoring a house for the new non-profit. That address is 9234 Henderson, which is not far from the soccer fields."

"Thank you," he said, his eyes reflecting surprise.

"I love Reye like she was my daughter, and she has given so much to the children here. I want her to be happy, and if you ever hurt her again, I'll personally come looking for you." Her smile was broad, but he believed she meant business.

"I won't, and thanks again. I'd better get moving. Thank you . . ."

"Susan," she said, "Dr. Susan Houston, Reye's boss." She extended her hand for him to shake.

"Nice meeting you, Dr. Houston, hope to see you more often," he said, accepting her hand. He gave her another one of his smiles as he backed away from the desk and walked out the door.

The fields were located fairly close to the center, within five minutes or so. This neighborhood was mixed, Hispanics, African-Americans, whites, some Asians. He pulled in to the parking lot of the soccer fields and got out of his car. There were three fields, sitting side by side. He spotted Reye on the field farthest from him. The other two fields were being used by adults, playing as if they were representing their country for the world cup. He was glad he'd taken the time to change.

The kids were divided into two lines standing side by side, facing the soccer goals, practicing their shooting. Reye stood in the middle of the goal; large goalie gloves covered her hands as she stood catching the balls while giving instructions to the children as they took their shots. One of the kids' shot hit her in her chest. It was caught easily and rolled back to him. Stephen walked over to stand next to the goal. She glanced over at him, surprised.

"Where did you come from? And how did you know where I'd be?"

"I stopped by the center and Susan told me you were here. Can I help?"

"Sure. I guess you could be the goalie. It'll give me more time to work with the kids. We are working on striking the ball correctly."

The kids had stopped and were watching them intently. She called them over to her. "Kids, this is going to be our goalie for today. His name is Mr. Stephen." He looked out into ten or more assessing pairs of eyes.

"Hi," he said, "I'm a friend of your coach. I met her last year when I played soccer against her." The children's eyes swung back to Reye. "I love soccer, and I started playing when I was your age and continued to play all through high school," he continued.

"Let's take a water break and then we'll start again," Reye said to them. The kids took off like bullets to the side of the field that held their water bottles.

"So, how was your Christmas?"

"Fine. I spent it with my family, as usual. Yours?"

"It was good."

"How long are you going to be in town?"

"The weekend. I thought I might talk you in to a movie or maybe you would have dinner with me?"

"I wish I could, but I usually help my dad on the weekends and I have a soccer game with the kids tomorrow."

"Maybe I could help. I came to see you, so I don't mind hanging and helping you and your dad."

"Maybe. We'll talk after practice," she said, walking away. She moved to stand in front of the kids, who were back in line, ready to resume the kicking drill.

"Ready when you are," she said, turning to look at him. He'd forgone the use of gloves and assumed the goalie position, waiting for the first kick. The kids were much more enthusiastic in their kicks with him in the goal. Stephen was impressed by some of their techniques, and he told them so. He listened as Reye offered instruction and further demonstration to the children. She was a good coach, he thought to himself.

After about what seemed like fifty kicks on goal, Reye called the kids over to her. They formed a circle around her. "Are you all ready for tomorrow's game?"

"YES!" her team shouted as Stephen walked towards them.

After noticing Stephen, Shondra raised her hand. "Is he going to be there?"

"I don't know. If there aren't any other questions," Reye said, extending her hand out in front, little hands piled in on top of hers.

"One, two, three, Lightning," the children chanted.

"Don't forget to take your water bottles and balls home," Reye reminded them as she stood watching them leave. Stephen stood next to her.

"So what time and where is your game tomorrow?" he asked.

"It's at 9:00 a.m. over at the Riverside fields, why?"

"I'd like to help."

She turned and moved to pick up the cones and other soccer-related gear. He dogged her steps, helping her.

"Do you usually eat before you work with your dad?"

"Sometimes, but I hadn't planned to tonight. I'd planned on going there after practice."

"Can I see your house? Susan gave me the address, but I'm not sure how to get there."

Reye gave him directions as they walked backed to their vehicles. "I'll meet you over there," she said.

"Okay. See ya later."

The house was within five minutes of the field. He pulled up to the two-story home, parking behind a large truck. Probably Reye's dad, he thought, turning off the ignition and taking a moment to look around. Pretty yellow paint on the main parts, trimmed in white, large porch, with a yard that was neatly trimmed. It would make a nice home for children. No sign of Reye's truck, though. The lights were on in the house, so he got out and walked to the door, which stood open behind a screened door.

"Hello," he called out, ringing the doorbell. He could hear music softly playing in the house, jazz maybe, something instrumental. He heard someone walking towards the door. A very tall older African-American man stood before him. He was tall, taller than Stephen by about three inches, and built like an oak tree.

"Can I help you?"

"You must be Reye's dad. Mr. Jackson, right?" No response. "You don't know me, but I'm a friend of your daughter's. My name is Stephen Stuart. I'm in town for the weekend and wanted to see Reye's new project. I just left her at the soccer fields. She said she was on her way."

"I know who you are," said Mr. Jackson, his expression still stern.

That wasn't the response he was expecting. "May I come in, sir?"

"Sure." He backed up to allow Stephen entrance.

He and Mr. Jackson stood in the foyer taking stock of each other. No time like the present to lay it out on the line, Stephen thought. "Sir, I met your daughter last year when I was in my last year of law school. We dated most of the year, but I didn't meet many of her friends or family. I don't imagine you have a good opinion of me."

"Should I have a good opinion of you?"

"No, sir, you shouldn't. I didn't treat Reye as well as I should have, which I regret. All I can say in my defense is that dating Reye was a new experience for me and affected me in a way I wasn't prepared for. I saw her again at the awards dinner in Dallas last weekend, but I would like you to know that even before then, I had made up my mind to try and make amends to her, sir. I didn't realize until later that I loved her, which I've since told her. I would like to marry her, sir, if she agrees. I've not told her that yet."

Mr. Jackson looked him over and smiled slightly. "Is that so?"

"Yes, sir."

"Well, you will have your work cut out for you."

"Don't I know it, sir," he said, chuckling.

"Make sure this is what you want. I won't have her hurt again," Mr. Jackson said, all seriousness, looking more than a little frightening.

"No, sir, I'm serious. It won't happen again."

"Well, good, then, you can start winning Reye's favor by helping me replace the sheetrock that has a hole in it in the kitchen."

"Sure," Stephen said, following Mr. Jackson. "If you don't mind me saying so, meeting you was easier than I thought."

"Well, I've got to tell you that I love my daughter, and watching her after you left was hard. As a parent it is always difficult to see your children hurt, especially if it is your only girl. But your leaving brought good things for her. Life usually does. If you'd stayed, she might have put her career and ambitions on hold. Ambitions I'm not sure she knew she held." He stopped and placed his hand on a section of sheetrock. "Grab that end of this sheet," he told Stephen. They walked it over to an empty spot where a portion of the wall had been. "Can you hold that in place?"

"Sure," he said. Reye's dad continued talking. "Your leaving forced her to do something with herself, giving her efforts to those children. This house and the non-profit were an indirect result of that hurt, and it could very well be her life's work. So, as far as I see it, it's all good." He grabbed his nail gun and nailed the sheet into place. He stepped back and looked over the wall. "I'll need to tape this later. Reye and I have done most of the work in here. She purchased the property with my help.

Now all we have left to do is paint. I hope you don't mind getting dirty."

"No, I don't mind. I'll be here on weekends to see her, so I will be available to help whenever you need me."

Her dad looked at him, reassessing him. "Serious, are you." It was more a statement than question. "Where are you staying?" Mr. Jackson asked.

"At a hotel near downtown."

"Every weekend?"

"Yes, sir."

"Well, we can't have that. Tell you what, when you are in town, plan on staying with me and my wife. But we don't need to tell Reye that just yet. This way you can get to know her mother and me, and we'll have a chance to get to know you."

"Are you sure you don't mind?"

"No, we don't mind. In fact on Sundays we have a customary standing breakfast with our children, those that are in town and can make it. The wife starts cooking around nine. Why don't you come over this Sunday morning? Reye will be there. Here is my card, my home number and address are there. Call if you get lost."

"Thank you, sir, I will."

"We'd better get started painting."

The two of them worked in companionable silence for the rest of the evening, talking about Stephen's future plans and family. Before he knew it, it was ten and they had worked through all of the bedrooms and the hallway upstairs. All that remained was the main room downstairs. There was still no sign of Reye. Mr. Jackson had gathered all of the paint supplies they'd used and was in the process of cleaning them. "Well, it looks like Reye must have gotten tied up. This isn't like her," Mr. Jackson said as his cell phone rang. He looked at the caller ID. "Here she is. Hey, Reye," he answered, his face again showing no expression as he listened. "We were just finishing up and getting ready to leave," he said. Stephen left the room, giving him privacy for his conversation with Reye.

He was a little hurt that she skipped tonight. After all, he'd come to Austin to see her; the least she could do was cooperate. He laughed at himself, shaking his head, he was so full of it sometimes. He would be the one who needed to make the effort for a while. He wanted this, but he knew it wouldn't be easy. Even so, he didn't want to contemplate her not forgiving him. He would see her tomorrow at her team's game, and, with any luck, he would talk her into having dinner with him. He hadn't taken her out much when they'd been together. Mostly they had spent time at her house, gone to an occasional movie here or there, and dinner had been mostly pick-up or delivery. He should have made more of an effort to treat her as more than a warm body. But man, she wasn't just a warm body—although he really loved her body— she had been more, and he felt remorse that she'd never known that.

He turned as Mr. Jackson entered the room. "Well, son, it seems Reye got tied up and wasn't able to make it over after all. She say's she's sorry about that."

"No problem. I'd better get going. It has been a pleasure meeting you, Mr. Jackson," he said, extending his hand, which was captured in a firm handshake. "I look forward to seeing you and your wife on Sunday," he said.

"Same here, son." Mr. Jackson clapped Stephen hard on the back as they walked to the front door. "Chin up," he said.

"Yes, sir. Good night, Mr. Jackson."

He went through the front door, down the sidewalk to his car, got in, and drove away. He had planned to go directly to his hotel, but he'd ended up heading back towards the university and towards Reye's house. He found it just as he'd remembered. Planted flowers were in the front beds of the house, an explosion of purples, yellows, and pinks. She'd always taken care of her home; he'd at least helped her with that on occasion. Taking a deep breath, he drove away.

CHAPTER 17

Saturday morning came early for Reye. She was tired, not having slept well the night before, her conscience had worked her over pretty good for ditching Stephen. Between those feelings of remorse and remembering the goods times they'd shared last year, she'd tossed and turned most of the night away before finally drifting off to sleep at around two a.m. The alarm had gone off at six, leaving her feeling more than a little punch drunk and in need of a strong cup of joe. Her team's soccer game was scheduled to start at nine this morning, and she preferred to get to the fields at least thirty minutes before the kids arrived. She'd asked the parents to have the kids at the fields at least thirty minutes before each game.

Apparently her conscience wasn't done with her yet as she fought off another round of guilt at leaving him alone with her dad. It was inexcusable, except that her anger and hurt would show itself when she least expected it, like a permanent virus that lived in its host and attacked when the defenses were low. To appease her conscience, she promised herself to apologize the next time she saw him.

She walked to the kitchen for a cup of coffee, made in her brand spanking new coffee maker, the crème dé la crème of coffee makers, complete with timer, courtesy of her brother Jack and his family. Before this gift, she'd used a hand-me-down from her mother. She eagerly set her new machine to brew each morning, waking her up to the strong, addictive aroma of her favorite coffee blend. Standing in the kitchen with her cup in her hand, she contemplated Stephen again. It would be so easy to give in to him now, she wanted to badly since returning from Dallas, her fingers itching to touch the body that she'd grown to love. She'd worshiped religiously at that area of skin, just below his waist and abs, a smooth stretch of highway leading to one of his best assets, and her absolute favorite part of him. She loved the spot on his neck below his right ear, and she missed curling into his chest after a night spent making love to him.

Those days when she felt low and needed a lift she would pull from her memory a night spent with him where he, in his usual way, had taken control of her body like a man possessed. She totally loved it. He could ask anything of her, and he had, and she did her damndest to not disappoint. Giving yourself completely to someone, now that was some scary shit. Not having them feel the same, and learning to live without them, had been on the edge of terrifying. But she'd lived to tell the tale.

She finished her coffee, placing her cup in the sink. She'd better get dressed and put her mind on the game. She'd just stepped out of the shower when she heard her doorbell. It couldn't be anyone but Sam. She paid dearly for having him as her assistant coach, stopping by to get his eat and drink on whenever he wanted to, or to pick up groceries. "No, just a second," she screamed as she went to put on her robe and walked to the door. She looked out of the peephole to find Stephen standing there. She stepped back, surprised. What was he doing here? *Okay, don't panic, breathe, girl.* She opened the door about two inches, peering out at him. He stood on her porch, looking like a god. He wore black shorts that stopped just above his knees and a snug-fitting black shirt that clung tightly to his upper body in a way that was truly criminal. A baseball cap turned backwards, also black, resided on his head. The most damaging part of his ensemble was that smile, her favorite, the slightly wicked one, the one that had talked her into plenty.

"What are you doing here?"

"I thought maybe you could use some help dragging your soccer gear over to the field before the game."

As excuses went, it wasn't great, but he continued wearing that smile, so it worked. "I also brought you some coffee." He held up a cup of Starbucks close to the door for her to see. "Your favorite, a tall white chocolate mocha with whip." Okay, so he'd remembered her favorite drink. Opening the door fully, she stepped back, allowing him entrance. "Come in. You caught me just getting out of the shower, so could you wait here while I change?" She closed the front door behind him, taking a few steps toward her room before turning around, walking back to him and taking the coffee from his hand. "Thank you," she said, heading to her room.

"This was so not a good thing Reye, you can't just roll over and play dead whenever you see him," she said to her weaker self. "I know," her weaker self replied to the stronger self, who didn't always stick around when she needed her. Hurriedly she put on her shorts, shirt, socks, and tennis shoes. She had gotten the soccer balls and small cones that made up her training gear together and had loaded them into the truck last night. All that remained to be added were the water and sports drinks.

"Hey, Stephen," she called out from her room. She walked into her closet in search of her cap.

"You called," he replied, leaning into the doorframe, a forearm on each side of the door. She turned to see him standing at the entrance of her bedroom door and it brought forth a rush of memories of times spent with him in this room. He would sometimes follow her when she went in search of something, and it always led to a minor delay for them both. When she'd turned and found him standing there, for a moment she just stared at him, processing some of those memories. It took a couple of seconds for her to pull it together. The smile he had worn when she called him had turned into something else entirely, maybe matching the desire she was sure was evident on her face.

"Would you grab that ice chest in the kitchen and put it in my truck. It's for the game," she said.

"Sure," he said, turning to do her bidding.

"Thank you. Oh, and Stephen . . ."

"Yes?" He turned to her again, looking at her, his face now a study in neutrality.

"I wanted to apologize for last night. You know, me sending you to the house and then not showing up. Anyway, I meant for you to meet my dad without me, but I didn't intend to not show up at all. I'm sorry for standing you up."

She looked him in the eye and continued. "It's just that seeing you at practice kind of caught me off guard. Knowing you came specifically to see me sort of rattled me."

"You shouldn't be surprised. I told you I would."

"Yeah, I know. It still surprised me, though."

"Don't worry about it," he said, smiling again. "I didn't expect you to be easy." She read both sincerity and earnestness in his expression. "I m just grateful that you're willing to listen."

"Okay," she said.

They both continued to look at each other a second or two more. Reye realized that she needed to get moving. "Well, I'd better finish." He left to retrieve the ice chest and she quickly grabbed her hat and followed him into the front of the house.

As she entered the living room, he was walking towards the front door, pulling the ice chest along behind him.

"Are you ready?"

"Just need to get my keys."

"I'll just load this in your truck."

"Sure, thanks. Hey, do you want to ride to the game together?" As soon as the words left her mouth, she could have kicked herself.

"Are you sure?" he asked, sensing her hesitation.

"It's no big deal. You're here to help, and there is no point in us riding in separate cars. We are, after all, going to the same place. Right?"

"Sure." They both walked out the front door, Reye locking up behind them.

Who would have thought he would have shown up to help her out today? She was nervous at having him with her, coaching while he watched. He'd let her talk non-stop about her strategy on the drive over. More than anything he could have done monetarily or physically, his showing up did more to move her back into his arms than anything. Once they arrived at the fields, he followed her instructions and set up the cones like she wanted. After the kids arrived, he kicked the ball back and forth with them, helping them to warm up. She was nervous, but because he knew soccer, she felt calmer having him here. He was a good listener, had been even in the earlier days when they laid in the dark talking about their days. He had always listened to her.

Sam arrived not long after, and hadn't seemed surprised to see Stephen. He and Stephen shook hands and talked for a while, about who knew what. She was sure her dad had called Sam the night before and given him the 411. Sam and her dad had bonded with each other during their "save-the-Reye" campaign after Stephen's departure.

After the game, which her team won, Stephen watched her walk over to him and Sam after having made sure all of her kids were going home with a parent. She looked great in her coaching attire. He'd always loved her in shorts, his second favorite clothing item of hers; her birthday suit being his favorite, of course. Watching her give instructions to the kids had his body temperature rising. Who knew, maybe he could talk her into playing coach with him one day. He liked this side of her, the coach, the caregiver. It was nice to know, for future child-rearing purposes, that'd she make a great mother. He imagined she'd want children of her own, of their own, after they were married, that is.

He had been surprised by Sam's response to him. Reye's brother had been welcoming, throwing him for a loop. He had expected an adversary, but instead he'd been blown away by Sam's hospitality. Maybe he knew something that Stephen didn't; whatever, it was encouraging to know that someone was rooting for him. Reye stopped in front of him and Sam.

"What are you two smiling about?"

"Nothing much, just admiring a beautiful girl," Sam said.

Reye rolled her eyes and looked over at Stephen. "Are you ready to go?"

"Oh, you two came together?" Sam asked, clearly surprised.

"Yes," they said in unison. Stephen, with his eyes on Reye, said, "I went by her house this morning, thinking she might need some help with the game. She let me tag along."

"Okay, then. Well, good game, Reye, I'll see you later," Sam said.

"Sure. Bye, Sam," Reye said.

"See you around, Stephen." Sam stuck out his hand for a fist bump.

"Yeah. You, too."

Reye and Stephen watched him walk away before getting into Reye's truck. They didn't talk much on the way back.

Reye pulled into her driveway. Stephen's car was parked out front, exactly where they'd left it.

"Let me help you load everything into the house," he said.

"Sure, grab the cooler and I'll grab my soccer bag." They walked to the front door, and Reye opened it for Stephen and followed him in. He rolled the ice chest into the kitchen while she stood by the front door waiting for him to return. This wasn't the ending he had envisioned.

"Would you like to get some lunch?"

"No, thanks. But thanks again for helping me with the game. I'm tired, so I am going to take the rest of the day to clean up my home and get some rest."

"Sure, no problem. Well, until next time. Take care."

"Yeah. You, too," she said as she opened the door to let him pass through.

With a final wave, she closed the door.

Disappointed, he walked to his car. The upside, he reminded himself, was that he'd gotten to spend the morning with her. Baby steps, he reminded himself. She was worth it.

Stephen checked out of his hotel early Sunday morning, feeling optimistic. He was headed over to Reye's parents' house for breakfast and to meet her mother. He dressed in casual slacks and a collared shirt, deciding to forgo his jeans. He needed to make a good impression. Reye had spoken of her mother both with fondness and with a little bit of frustration from what she'd considered her mother's constant pushing. Hell, he'd trade his for hers any day of the week. Mothers, his and hers, were alike in wanting their kids to be successful, also alike in how their kids responded and were affected by that pushing. Funny that their parents were similar; both he and Reye felt a special kinship with their fathers and a loving, albeit a little distant, relationship with their mothers.

He drove into a newer subdivision, built within the last ten years by the looks of it, located in the north part of town. He'd mapped the address, and here he was pulling up alongside a light pink two-story brick home. No sign of Reye's truck, though, as he parked in the empty driveway and walked to the front door. He rang the doorbell. The door was opened by an older, shorter version of Reye, minus the locks; long strands of beautiful brown hair fell around her face.

"You must be Stephen. Please come in. My husband told me to expect you for breakfast this morning. We've had breakfast here since the kids started leaving home, living on their own. It was our way of keeping our home open for them, and they make it over when they can. Children can get so busy with their own lives, and sometimes it's the only chance we get to see them. I bet your mother understands what I mean." During her talk, she walked him through the living room and on to the kitchen. Their home was lovely, done in yellows and blues; he'd located the source of Reye's love of color. Reye's mom reached the kitchen and stopped. "It's only you and Reye this morning. Have a seat. I can finish cooking while we get to know each other. Would you like something to drink? I have coffee, several juices—orange, apple, or cranberry—and milk."

"Sure, I'd like a glass of orange juice." He watched as she reached into the refrigeration behind her, poured juice into a glass, and handed it to him.

"Thank you," Stephen said, taking in the large spacious kitchen. To his right was a large table that looked large enough to seat eight or nine. Mrs. Jackson had indicated the bar stools for him to sit on. It put him in front of her and the grill as she was preparing what appeared to be pancakes. His stomach rumbled. She heard, and they both smiled.

"So, my husband tells me you met Reye last year before school started?"

"Yes, I did."

"He also told me you spent quite a bit of time with her, what, almost the whole year? Is that correct?"

"That's correct, yes."

"We haven't met you? A year is a long time. So tell me about yourself. You live in Dallas now?"

"Yes, I was born and reared there. My family has a law firm that has survived four generations. I was in Austin completing the last year of law school when I met your daughter. I've recently taken the bar exam and I've started working with my dad in Dallas. I've purchased an apartment there, and most of my time is spent at the firm, getting to know the business."

"I see. So what brings you back to Austin?" This woman was amazing. She was grilling him while mixing the ingredients for pancakes from scratch. She pulled a griddle from underneath the counter and placed it over the stove.

She stopped in her food preparation, waiting for his answer. He cleared his throat. "Actually, your daughter is the reason why I'm here. Reye and I were in a relationship last year, and after law school ended I broke up with her."

"I see. So you're telling me that this relationship ended because you had to go home to Dallas?"

"Yes and no."

She was looking at him the way his old schoolteachers did when they knew he'd done something, waiting for him to tell them the truth. It took all of his concentration not to squirm. He looked into her eyes. "Honestly, Mrs. Jackson, at the time I felt that maybe the differences in our races would be a problem. I hadn't dated outside of my race before, so it kinda took me by surprise. I didn't do a very good job of dealing with it. It wasn't just her race that confused me, she confused me, and I wasn't ready and didn't handle it well. But she captured me, and, in spite of all I knew, I fell in love. It took me a while to come to terms with it. I'm sorry for the hurt I caused her." He hadn't broken eye contact with Mrs. Jackson through his diatribe, surprising himself with his heartfelt plea. "Sorry for the long explanation," he said, smiling sheepishly.

She smiled in return. "No, I appreciate your candor. Reye is my only daughter, and I only want the best for her. She pushes against me sometimes, most times, in fact, but I love her and don't want to see her hurt. Thank you for explaining."

"Mom, where are you?" Reye's voice alerted them to her presence. She walked into the kitchen and stopped, looking over at Stephen, surprised. "I thought that was your car parked in the drive."

"Hey, Reye, let me pour you some coffee," her mom said.

"Reye," Stephen said, taking a sip of his orange juice and giving her a smile.

"Uh, good morning, Mom. I didn't know we were having company."

"Your dad invited him, and I didn't want to spoil the surprise."

"Have a seat, I'm almost done. Stephen was just talking about his reasons for returning to Austin," Mrs. Jackson said, turning her back to them, finishing her breakfast preparations.

"I'm surprised to see you here," she said to him, not knowing what to make of her mother's comment.

"Well, your dad invited me, and I hadn't met your mother, so I accepted the invitation. You look great," he said, giving her a thorough once-over, causing her temperature to rise just a little.

"I'm going to go to church after breakfast."

She looked gorgeous in a tailored black suit that hugged her curves. She had on pumps that put her at eye level with him. He loved her hair, which always made her look sexy to him. He wished he could pull her over to him now, kiss her, hold her; he'd missed that.

Mr. and Mrs. Jackson both called them to the table, where they talked about the changes that Stephen and her dad were able to complete to the house on Friday night and what repairs were remaining.

"If you need any help with any legal work, I'm available. Our firm works with lots of charities and foundations. Maybe next weekend I could take you to dinner and we could discuss it," Stephen said. Reye smiled at his attempt to book a date with her.

After breakfast, Stephen thanked Reye's folks and said goodbye to them. He and Reye walked out the front door. He was heading back to Dallas and she was going to church. Reye followed him to his car and stood nearby as he opened the door but didn't get in. He turned to her. "So, your parents have been having breakfast every Sunday morning before you and I met?"

"Yes."

"Did you miss most of them when we were together?"

"Not all of them, but the bulk of them, yes."

"You never asked me to go."

"Honestly, I didn't think you were interested, and I didn't want to push for fear of scaring you off," she said and gave a fake, half-hearted laugh. She turned to look off down the street.

"I'm sorry," he said, bringing her eyes back to his.

"No worries, mate," she said and smiled at him, a smile that didn't quite reach her eyes nor camouflage the hurt he saw in them.

He leaned in and touched his lips softly to hers, letting them settle there for a moment. He'd surprised her with his kiss. He heard it in her intake of air, the tensing of her body. He pulled back slowly and smiled. "Thanks for letting me hang out with you this weekend. Can I call you this week?"

"Sure," she said, more than a little flustered. "Give me your phone," she said, holding out her hand to him. He pulled it out of his pocket and handed it to her. "Just like old times," she said, remembering their first meeting at the airport. She programmed her number into the phone and handed it back to him.

He leaned in and kissed her again.

"I'll call you this week, and see you next weekend."

"Okay," she said as she watched him get into his car and drive away.

The following weeks took on a routine for Stephen. He would put in long hours at the firm during the week in compensation for his time spent in Austin on the weekends. In Austin he would help Reye with soccer practice and her games. He'd had gotten to know the kids on her team and their parents, who teased him, calling him the coach's boyfriend. He took heart from the knowledge that Reye never corrected them. He spent most Friday nights and some Saturdays working with Reye's dad over at the new house.

She was slowly coming around to having him in her life again. So far, though, she'd mostly watched him, but she was beginning to smile and act more spontaneously around him, be less guarded. But it was clearly going to be on him for a while. How long, he had no clue. She had been surprised to find him staying at her parents home. They treated him like their long-lost son, putting him up in Reye's brother Frank's old room, giving him a key for when he was late getting into Austin, and neither of them had told Reye of his living arrangements.

She found out, though. It happened on his fourth weekend in Austin, at the end of a month of trips. As usual, he'd helped her earlier that Saturday afternoon with her team's game. And, as usual, she continued to refuse dinners, lunches, or any other outings with him. She thanked him as always for helping with the game and sent him on his way. He'd spent some time in the city with some of his friends from law school for a couple of hours and then drove over to her parents' home.

Saturday nights were movie nights at the Jackson household. They would rent several movies for the three of them to watch together. Mrs. Jackson would make popcorn and margaritas, a combination he wouldn't have put together but that actually worked. The Jacksons sat in their recliners that were reserved for TV watching and he'd taken the floor. They agreed to watch a thriller, and, about halfway into the movie, Reye entered, needing to pick up something from her dad. She'd found the three of them engrossed in their movie. He'd seen her enter, remaining quiet as he watched his presence register on her face. He watched her taking in the scene; her eyes moved to look at him, laying on his back, head propped and resting on a pillow, popcorn bowl sitting on his stomach, margarita in hand, watching the movie.

"Oh, Reye, we didn't hear you come in," Mr. Jackson said, pausing the movie and acting like having him here was an everyday occurrence. They all looked up at her. "I don't know if I told you, but Stephen is staying with us on the weekends now. There's no use in him wasting all his money on a hotel. I thought this way he could get to know us and we could get to know him." Stephen watched her drop down into a chair, looking over at him again, speechless. He gave her a large smile, tears in his eyes as he fought against laughter.

Her family had somehow become co-conspirators in his quest to win her back. He had met all of her older brothers and their families. Most of her brothers had made their way to Austin to check him out. It was subtle at first, but that usually gave way to full interrogations by first one brother and then another. He understood their need to meet and assure themselves of his commitment to Reye. He had gotten to know and like her family very much. He wanted her to get to know his.

He was starting into his third month of making the trek to Austin to see Reye. He pushed aside any worries that she might not ever forgive him, or risk herself for him again. He didn't want to contemplate a life without her in it, wasn't anywhere near ready to give up on them.

He was sitting in his apartment, looking out the windows at the cityscape, contemplating the upcoming weekend. Tomorrow was Friday and he would be leaving later than usual for Austin. He had a meeting in Dallas that he had to attend in the late afternoon, so he wouldn't be getting on the road until after eight, at best. He pulled out his cell to call Reye and let her know. She answered on the first ring.

"Hey."

"Hey, yourself," she responded, her voice low and sexy. Listening to her on the phone was one of the highlights of his life, and yet also one of the hardest experiences for him. Staying with her family hadn't allowed for much of anything physical happening between them, and he hadn't pushed it. He wanted her to know that although he loved her body and the physical part of their relationship, he loved other aspects of her as well. But he paid a price for it. He needed lots of cold showers and long runs to reduce his longing for her body. Hearing her on the telephone left him constantly hard. He forced his mind back to their conversation. "How was your day?"

"Fine, and yours?"

"Long, as usual," he sighed.

"Poor baby," she said, and he heard a smile and teasing in her voice.

He chuckled. "Listen, I've got a meeting tomorrow in the afternoon at the office that I have to make, so I won't be leaving until late. In all likelihood, I won't see you until Saturday morning at the game. I made reservations at a hotel instead of staying with your parents. I didn't want to disturb them again. What time is the game?"

"Twelve, but I was thinking that you could stay here with me this weekend instead of at my parents."

He sat up, snapping to complete attention.

"Stephen, did you hear me?"

"Yeah, I did. Are you sure? Be sure, Reye, because if I get anywhere near you, alone . . . I'm not sure of the consequences. Is this what you want?"

"Come and stay with me, Stephen. I know what I'm asking you to do. The last few weeks have been murder on me, too. But I needed to be sure."

"And are you?"

"Yes, I am." He was quiet for a long time. "Stephen? Are you there?"

"Yes, I'm here, and yes, there is a God." He heard her laugh on the other end. "It's been so long."

"I know, for me, too. Call me when you get on the road?"

"I will," he said. "And get some rest. You are going to need it."

"I hope so. Love you."

His breath caught. "Reye," he said and paused. "Did you just tell me you loved me?"

"Yeah, I did. I never stopped, really."

"I didn't think you would ever say that to me again."

"I didn't think so, either."

"I love you, too." Both were quiet on the phone as their declarations sank in.

"See you tomorrow?"

"Yeah, see you tomorrow."

Stephen hung up the phone and sat in silence taking in Reye's words.

━━═

Reye sat on the couch Friday shuffling through the TV channels, waiting for Stephen to arrive. It was about midnight now. He'd called about nine to say that he was on the way, so he should be there any minute. There went her plans for a romantic evening. She'd driven herself crazy throughout the day. What to wear? Did she want candles? What about dinner? So here she sat in old shorts and a t-shirt, curled up on the couch waiting for him.

He'd surprised her with his tenacity. Sure, she knew he had that quality. He wouldn't have gotten to where he was today without it, but she'd never thought to have Stephen's exclusive focus turned on her. He loved her and she believed him, finally. It was evident in his commitment to coming to see her, to getting to know her parents, and to helping her with her kids and her work. So, after his last visit, she decided to commit to him again. She loved him. She'd just needed proof that he returned her feelings this time. Getting to know his parents was the one last hurdle they needed to clear, but at this point she was willing to give him the benefit of the doubt. Plus she needed to touch him, to feel him, in her. These last few weeks had felt like the longest in her life. She'd probably self destruct if he so much as kissed her.

She heard a car outside and went to look out the window. It was Stephen, in that shiny BMW of his. She went to the door and opened it, watching as he walked towards her. He looked tired, a GQ model in rumpled business wear, tall, lean, and golden. All hers. His pretty blue eyes were level with hers as he walked to stand in front of her. His hand moved to the back of her neck, pulling her into him for a soft, easy kiss. She opened at his touch and his tongue moved in to reacquaint itself with hers. She moaned, breaking the kiss.

"I have thought of you and nothing else all day, woman. Move over, let me in." She moved to allow him entrance and locked the door behind them. He dropped his bag and lifted his arms above his head in a stretch.

"Tired?" she asked as she watched him.

"A little," he said, lowering his arms and turning towards her.

"Hungry? Thirsty?"

"Nope," he answered, sliding his hands into his pants pockets.

"I was just watching TV, waiting for you to get here," she said as she walked back to the couch. She sat down and picked up the remote. "There's nothing on TV."

He followed her, taking the remote from her hand and turning off the TV. He kicked off his shoes, pulled his shirt from the waistband of his pants, and walked to stand directly in front of her, bending until he was at eye-level. Cradling her face in his hands, he kissed her hard. He was hot and hungry and she responded immediately, her need equal to his. He continued the onslaught in her mouth and those wonderful, long fingers moved lower until they found her breasts through her t-shirt. He took one in each hand, re-introducing himself to their shape and feel. She wasn't wearing a bra, which made him ache more. He moved his hands under her shirt to touch skin. He circled her nipples and she moaned and squirmed, her body lifting to his. Stopping, he stood up and pulled her to stand with him. He turned, grabbed her hand, and led the way to her bedroom, discarding clothes along the way. He pushed her to lie on the bed, moving over on top of her. Once again his mouth settled over hers in a kiss so hot, it was a surprise the sheets didn't instantaneously go up in flames.

"I'm going to apologize in advance at how short this will be. It's been a long time, babe," he said.

He felt her smile against his lips. She put her arms around his neck and pulled him down to her. Her hands moved over his body, finding what she'd missed and tracing the shape and hardness of him. He moaned into her mouth. Pushing her legs apart, he positioned his body between them. His single-mindedness had returned. She lifted her hips to allow him entrance. Both were lost in the feel and sensation of each other. He lifted his head and looked at her, waiting until her eyes opened. He pushed into her. Holding on to her hips, he pushed once, twice, and he was close; three times, and he couldn't hold back any longer. He came immediately and he gave over to the sensation of it, finally arriving home. He realized, as her body clutched him tightly, that she'd come, too. When he could breathe, he lifted his head and looked into her eyes. She was smiling. He smiled softly. "That was quick, huh?" He watched her smile turn into laughter. When their laughter died down, he captured her face between his hands again. "I love you," he said and took her lips in a soft and tender kiss. "Marry me?"

He could tell he'd surprised her. The catch in her breath gave it away, so he pulled back and looked into her eyes. "Marry me, Reye," he said again.

"Are you sure?"

"Never been surer," he whispered to her.

"Then yes."

He kissed her again and again, soft kisses on her lips, her cheeks, her eyelids. He was still inside her, still connected to her when he felt her hips lift, communicating her need again. His body answered, growing hard. He would go slowly this time. She was so warm, wet, wonderful, and his. Their hands sought and found each other, and with his eyes open he watched her react to him as he moved slowly in and out of her, fighting against his desire in order to prolong hers.

He continued as he felt her tighten around him. Her head moved slowly from side to side and she moaned as her second orgasm hit her. He could feel it; gritting his teeth, he fought against the need to follow. Not yet. After letting that orgasm run through her, he started again, moving slowly in and out, again, slowly in and out, again, relentless in his desire to pleasure her. Once more, he felt her moving toward another climax. He picked up his pace, letting go of the rein he'd placed on his desire, pumping into her faster and faster. His arms tightened around her, holding her in place, and once more she came, tightening around him. He was lost as he came, too, his body shaking in pleasure.

His breathing slowed and he loosened his arms, turning to lie on his back, pulling her to drape over him. She lay limply across his body, worn out as he reached to cover them. He moved his hand to run over her short dreads and took in her face with its smooth brown skin, shapely nose, and sexy full lips. He released a big breath and watched her eyes close and her breathing slow. God, he loved her, and he closed his eyes, thankful for another chance to be here with her.

Reye lay curled next to Stephen in the early hours of the morning. She slept most of the night; she had been busy with the kids this week, and that, coupled with making love to Stephen, had knocked her out. She watched him sleep. One of his eyes opened and he gave her a slow smile, pulling her closer to him. "What are you looking at?" he said, his voice low and gravelly from sleep.

She shrugged her shoulders, a silly smile on her face.

He waited for her to look at him, running her hand over his face. "I need you to do one favor for me."

"What?"

"I need you to come to Dallas and meet my parents. I know you met my mom here, and my dad at the gala, but I would like for you to spend some time with them and get to know them. I don't have to have their approval, but they do approve, Reye. They want me to be happy. I need you to see that they do. I don't want anything in the future to come between us, ever again."

"Your mom is okay? With us?"

"Yes, she is, but even if she wasn't, I am, and you need to be sure of that."

"I am. I've watched you since Dallas, and I know how much I mean to you. But yes, I will meet them. But it only matters that you want to marry me."

"I love you," he said, reaching for her again.

CHAPTER 18

Spring break was the first available time Reye had to venture to Dallas with Stephen. He still had to work, but he'd planned to leave early some evenings to show her around Dallas. Reye was used to fending for herself, and brought along a stash of books, reading she could always do, anywhere. He'd come down to Austin Saturday afternoon, returning Sunday with her in tow.

"This is home," he said, opening the door to his apartment and standing aside, waiting for her to enter first. She stepped in, taking a moment to look around, to soak it all in. It was a beautiful place, similar to his old place in Austin. Wood flooring led into a spacious, and beautifully decorated, main living area. A large fireplace anchored the room, taking up almost one wall, surrounded by a large, expensive, and inviting leather sofa. She walked across the floor to stand in front of the tall ceiling windows that looked over downtown Dallas.

"What is with you and windows?" She admired the beautiful view, her face and hands pressed against the glass.

He walked over to stand behind her, his hands covering hers. "You should see it at night. It's great. One of the main reasons I purchased this place. Come on, let me give you the guided tour," he said reaching for her hand. "As you can see, this is the living room, and that is the famous couch filled with misery, where I spent many nights sitting thinking of you, missing you," he said, pulling her to him, capturing her face between his hands, kissing her. They stayed there for a moment, lost in each other. Reye pulled back first.

"Tour, remember," she said, laughing.

He pulled her along behind him, moving toward the kitchen and breakfast area. "Here is an area you should pay particular attention to. It could be a great place for you to practice your culinary talents, to the delight of your future husband." he said, laughing at the expression on her face. "Just kidding." He turned and pointed to a closed door off from the kitchen. "And through that door is the area that holds the washer and dryer, where if you wanted to put your domestic talents to use, you could wash clothes for a person who will be living with you in the future. But I don't suppose you'll wash for me, either, huh?"

"How about we wash and cook for each other?"

"Maybe," he said, smiling. He turned and she followed him to the second bedroom, which had been converted to an office. A desk sat with a computer on it, and a small couch stood against one wall. The remaining walls were flanked with floor-to-ceiling bookshelves, where a set of law books stood in silent sentry alone on one shelf. "For all those books you love to read," he said. "There is a bathroom through that door."

"Very nice," she said approvingly.

"Now for the most important room in the house, or at least my favorite room now that you're here," he said, towing her back quickly through the living room and through a door that held the master bedroom. It was large, with the same king-size bed from his old apartment in Austin. There were floor-to-ceiling windows in here as well. He stood by the door and watched her look over the room. She walked to gaze out of the windows before moving to stand in front of one of the nightstands, where a picture of them sat. She picked it up, recognizing it immediately from the second game played between their teams. In the picture they both looked happy, playful, and in tune with each other. As she looked over the picture he came to stand behind her, putting his arms around her waist, laying his head in the crook of her shoulder, looking at the picture with her.

"You kept this?" she asked. "I wondered what happened to it."

"Yep."

"I meant a lot to you, huh?"

"You have no idea, but yeah, you did. It just took me a while to see it. I left you, knowing that I cared about you, but not sure that it was love. Did I learn different. That was a hard six months for me, here without you. I hadn't told you about that time, have I?"

"No," she said, continuing to stare at the picture.

"I partied and drank mostly, trying to appease the hurt, but that didn't work. I bought this apartment because I couldn't stand being around anyone, especially my mom, who I considered responsible for my breakup with you. I'd distanced myself from my friends and slept around quite a bit."

"You were unhappy, huh? Good, I wasn't alone," she said and smiled.

"Nope, I was there, too. Anyway, after a loud argument with my mom and a talk with my dad, I began to realize that I was the sole person responsible for our breakup. But honestly, Reye, I didn't realize until later that you'd come to mean so much to me. I'd never been in love before, so I didn't know until you weren't there that it was love that I'd felt."

He was quiet, holding her, leaning his head on her shoulder as they continued to look at the picture of them. "I'd take that picture out when I started to really miss you. Like some lovesick kid, which I guess I was."

She turned in his arms to face him, tears in her eyes. His hand moved to capture her face. "I love you so much it scares me sometimes, but I guess you know all about that," he said.

She put the picture down, turned to him again, and kissed him, her tears falling from her eyes.

"I'm glad you came back for me."

"Me, too."

"Are you ready?" He was holding her hand in his as they sat in his car outside of what appeared to be a expensive and exclusive restaurant in the city. He and Reye were to meet his parents here for dinner. He was dressed in a black suit, white shirt, and blue tie, and she in a black halter dress that cinched at the waist and flowed outward. She looked both hot and elegant. At least that was how Stephen had described her as she stepped out of the bedroom, black sandals gracing her feet. She was more than a little apprehensive about this dinner, but they needed to put it behind them.

"I'm ready," she responded, looking over at the face and body she needed as much as she needed air.

"Let's go," he said, both of them climbed from his car. He walked around and took her hand in his, leading her to the front entry. They were met by the hostess, a willowy blonde who ran her eyes fondly over Stephen and a little less so over Reye. "How can I help you?"

"We are meeting the Stuart party for dinner," Stephen replied.

She looked down the list on the podium that sat before her to confirm the reservation.

"They've arrived. Follow me, please, and I'll take you to them." She gave Stephen another smile. By now, Reye had gotten used to women and their admiration of him. She understood its source and was neither annoyed nor worried by it. She was confident in his desire and love for her. They trailed along behind her, and Reye took a moment to admire the restaurant. This was apparently where the prominent and elite were served. Being a part of his life meant she would have to get used to places like this. There were beautiful white tablecloths gracing tables filled with sparkling and shining silver and glass. The patrons sat, coifed, expensively dressed, and looking beautiful around tables that were well spaced, allowing for privacy.

They reached the table where the elder Stuart stood, having spotted them entering. He was impressed by Stephen's choice in Reye. She was beautiful, and he didn't think she had any idea of her beauty, which was refreshing. He was proud of his son and his choices, from following the law to picking his bride.

They reached the table. "Reye, you remember my dad?"

"Yes, hello, Mr. Stuart," she said, extending her hand for him to shake, which he dismissed by pulling her in for a hug. Stephen's mother stood beside her husband, a smile fixed on her face.

"You remember my mother?" Reye stepped back from the senior Stuart and extended her hand to his mother, which she accepted. "Please call me Claire," she said as they all took their seats.

"How was your drive from Austin?" Claire asked.

"It was fine."

"I hope Stephen didn't drive his usual fast speed with you in the car," she continued.

"No, he was fine," Reye answered, smiling.

The wine steward appeared at the table to take their wine request. Mr. Stuart made the selections and then turned his attention to Reye. "So, Stephen tells me that you've purchased a house in Austin to serve as the site of your new aftercare and summer programs. Is that right?"

"Yes, sir. I'm not sure how much Stephen has told you about the program."

"He's told me that it was not your typical program."

"That's right, sir. I've spent this summer developing an idea that came from my mother. I'm the only girl and the baby of five children, and I can always remember her being around, picking us up after school, overseeing our homework, trotting us around to our sports practices and other extra-curricular activities. In the summers it was track."

"It sounds like what Claire did for Stephen as he grew up. Isn't that right, Claire?"

"Yes, it's what parents do for their children," she said.

"Purchasing the house was part of my decision to take the summer program in a different direction, away from a center setting, to mimic more of a home setting environment for the children. I want them to have something like the ones Stephen and I grew up in."

"It sounds like you appreciate your mother."

"I didn't always, but working with the kids has helped me to see her in a different light. I think I understand her better, and I certainly appreciate her more. I understand now why she pushed us so hard. Although we still disagree on many things, I know that she only wanted the best in life for me, and pushing us was her way of insuring our success. She gave us the kind of care that I'm trying to give to my students when they are away from their parents."

The waiter interrupted her, and they stopped to place their dinner orders.

"So that's more than you probably wanted to know about my program," she said and smiled, reaching for her wine glass.

"You know, Reye, it's hard for children to recognize why their parents do what they do. It's innate that we want more for our children, that we want them to bypass all of our old hurts and live differently. So I appreciate that you understand your mother's desire. It's what we mothers do, even if sometimes very badly, very ineptly," she concluded, giving Reye a tentative smile.

Was that a peace offering? Reye decided to interpret it as such, she returned his mother's smile.

The food arrived and they got down to the business of eating it, all of them continuing to discuss their respective lives.

She looked over to Stephen, who gave her a smile. She loved this man, and as scary as that was, she wouldn't want to be anywhere else but here with him, braving his mother and anyone else who had a problem with them.

He found and squeezed her hand under the table.

They finished dinner, followed by dessert and coffee.

"Thank you for a wonderful evening," Reye said, giving a hug again to the elder Stuart. They were all standing in the foyer, preparing to leave. She turned and was taken in to the arms of his mother.

"It was nice meeting you, and I look forward to getting to know you better," Claire said.

"Me, too," she said.

She and Stephen left the restaurant and walked to his car, her hand in his. Before she could get in, he tugged her into his arms, leaning in to give her a soft, thorough kiss. "Not too bad?"

"Nope," she said against his lips.

"Thank you."

"Anytime," she said and kissed him again.

It was Saturday night, the last night in Dallas as Stephen would deliver Reye back to Austin tomorrow. She would miss him, had gotten used to seeing him again every day, touching him, talking to him whenever she wanted. They lay on his couch now, he on his back, minus a shirt, in just his jeans, while she stretched out on top. It was dark in the room except for the lights of the city through the windows of his living room. She so got his fondness for floor-to-ceiling windows now; it was beautiful at night. A thousand tiny lights twinkled back at her, and it was relaxing, soothing, and comforting. She dreaded having to leave tomorrow. Everything had gone perfectly here; seeing his parents again was more than she hoped it would be. She just had one remaining question burning a hole in her head. Where would they live after they married? What would she have to give up? She'd just gotten to the place where she felt like she was supposed to be, needed to be. She didn't want to give that up, but she wasn't giving up him, either. They'd set a wedding date for August.

"Stephen, I've been thinking," she said, looking into his face as he laid there with his eyes closed. He was one fine man. Opening one eye, he looked at her.

"Yeah," he answered distractedly, his hands that had been resting quietly at her back started to roam.

"Have you given any thought to where we would live after we get married?"

"Why don't you tell me what you think we should do and I'll let you know if I like it," he said, his hands now having moved on from her back to trail lower.

"Be serious."

"I'm very serious," he said, his lips finding her neck, placing small kisses there. He turned her over onto her back before his lips started their downward descent to her breasts. She continued talking, trying not to focus on his hands and mouth.

"I know how important your family is to you, but I was thinking that since I'm just starting the center, you could find a job at a law firm in Austin, work there for a while until I get the program off the ground. Then when we start to have babies, I'd be willing to move back here to live while you work with your family's firm. Your dad is still fairly young, right? He wouldn't need you for a while yet."

"Lift your hips," he said, sliding her shorts and underwear down her legs.

"Stephen, are you even listening to me?" She was slowly losing her focus, succumbing to the ministrations of his hands and mouth.

"I hear you loud and clear. Do you want my answer now?" He was opening the button of his jeans, lowering the zipper, lifting himself away from her to push them and his boxers down his legs and off. He grabbed her around the waist, rolling them off the couch and onto the floor. He took the brunt of the fall with his body when they landed, before turning her, so he was now back on top.

"Have I told you lately that I love you?" He was wearing that wicked smile of his, her favorite, while pushing her legs apart, settling between them.

She clamped her legs around his thighs, holding him in place until his eyes found hers. "What?"

"Before you go any further, tell me what you think of my solution."

He reached behind his back to unlock her legs, moving them further up to surround his waist. Then his hands moved to cup her hips, lifting her as he pushed into her body.

He paused until her slightly unfocused eyes opened to his. "I think I like your idea, Ms. Jackson. I'm happy wherever you are, and don't you ever forget that," he said, his breath catching, as he pulled out of her only to slowly push back in, hard, just like she liked it.

She moaned.

"Reye," he said, sliding out and pushing back into her again. Harder.

"Stephen," she said pleadingly.

He stopped moving, waited until her eyes found his. He said now, all seriousness, "I like your plan, had already come to a similar conclusion myself, and talked to my dad about it. We'll make it work, I promise," he said, slowly pulling out of her body, but not completely withdrawing, "Okay, babe, are we good now?" She nodded while he pushed back in to her body.

"Yes . . . okay . . . stop talking . . . please," she murmured, pulling his mouth down to hers.

"Please what, Reye?" he whispered against her lips, remembering when he'd first posed that question to her a long time ago. He smiled against her mouth, content to be here, wherever she was, forever.

ABOUT THE AUTHOR

Ruthie resides in Austin, Texas with her husband and two teenage children. She holds a bachelor's degree in economics from Clark College and a master's degree in economics from the University of Texas in Austin. She worked for more than a decade in the banking industry before turning her love for writing into a second career.

Ruthie enjoys being a mom, gardening, traveling, and reading. Reye's Gold is her debut novel.

2010 Mass Market Titles

January

Show Me The Sun
Miriam Shumba
ISBN: 978-158571-405-6
$6.99

Promises of Forever
Celya Bowers
ISBN: 978-1-58571-380-6
$6.99

February

Love Out Of Order
Nicole Green
ISBN: 978-1-58571-381-3
$6.99

Unclear and Present Danger
Michele Cameron
ISBN: 978-158571-408-7
$6.99

March

Stolen Jewels
Michele Sudler
ISBN: 978-158571-409-4
$6.99

Not Quite Right
Tammy Williams
ISBN: 978-158571-410-0
$6.99

April

Oak Bluffs
Joan Early
ISBN: 978-1-58571-379-0
$6.99

Crossing The Line
Bernice Layton
ISBN: 978-158571-412-4
$6.99

How To Kill Your Husband
Keith Walker
ISBN: 978-158571-421-6
$6.99

May

The Business of Love
Cheris F. Hodges
ISBN: 978-158571-373-8
$6.99

Wayward Dreams
Gail McFarland
ISBN: 978-158571-422-3
$6.99

June

The Doctor's Wife
Mildred Riley
ISBN: 978-158571-424-7
$6.99

Mixed Reality
Chamein Canton
ISBN: 978-158571-423-0
$6.99

2010 Mass Market Titles (continued)

July

Blue Interlude
Keisha Mennefee
ISBN: 978-158571-378-3
$6.99

Always You
Crystal Hubbard
ISBN: 978-158571-371-4
$6.99

Unbeweavable
Katrina Spencer
ISBN: 978-158571-426-1
$6.99

August

Small Sensations
Crystal V. Rhodes
ISBN: 978-158571-376-9
$6.99

Let's Get It On
Dyanne Davis
ISBN: 978-158571-416-2
$6.99

September

Unconditional
A.C. Arthur
ISBN: 978-158571-413-1
$6.99

Swan
Africa Fine
ISBN: 978-158571-377-6
$6.99$6.99

October

Friends in Need
Joan Early
ISBN:978-1-58571-428-5
$6.99

Against the Wind
Gwynne Forster
ISBN:978-158571-429-2
$6.99

That Which Has Horns
Miriam Shumba
ISBN:978-1-58571-430-8
$6.99

November

A Good Dude
Keith Walker
ISBN:978-1-58571-431-5
$6.99

Reye's Gold
Ruthie Robinson
ISBN:978-1-58571-432-2
$6.99

December

Still Waters...
Crystal V. Rhodes
ISBN:978-1-58571-433-9
$6.99

Burn
Crystal Hubbard
ISBN: 978-1-58571-406-3
$6.99

Other Genesis Press, Inc. Titles

Other Genesis Press, Inc. Titles (continued)

Other Genesis Press, Inc. Titles (continued)

Other Genesis Press, Inc. Titles (continued)

Other Genesis Press, Inc. Titles (continued)

Naked Soul	Gwynne Forster	$8.95
Never Say Never	Michele Cameron	$6.99
Next to Last Chance	Louisa Dixon	$24.95
No Apologies	Seressia Glass	$8.95
No Commitment Required	Seressia Glass	$8.95
No Regrets	Mildred E. Riley	$8.95
Not His Type	Chamein Canton	$6.99
Nowhere to Run	Gay G. Gunn	$10.95
O Bed! O Breakfast!	Rob Kuehnle	$14.95
Object of His Desire	A.C. Arthur	$8.95
Office Policy	A.C. Arthur	$9.95
Once in a Blue Moon	Dorianne Cole	$9.95
One Day at a Time	Bella McFarland	$8.95
One of These Days	Michele Sudler	$9.95
Outside Chance	Louisa Dixon	$24.95
Passion	T.T. Henderson	$10.95
Passion's Blood	Cherif Fortin	$22.95
Passion's Furies	AlTonya Washington	$6.99
Passion's Journey	Wanda Y. Thomas	$8.95
Past Promises	Jahmel West	$8.95
Path of Fire	T.T. Henderson	$8.95
Path of Thorns	Annetta P. Lee	$9.95
Peace Be Still	Colette Haywood	$12.95
Picture Perfect	Reon Carter	$8.95
Playing for Keeps	Stephanie Salinas	$8.95
Pride & Joi	Gay G. Gunn	$8.95
Promises Made	Bernice Layton	$6.99
Promises to Keep	Alicia Wiggins	$8.95
Quiet Storm	Donna Hill	$10.95
Reckless Surrender	Rochelle Alers	$6.95
Red Polka Dot in a World Full of Plaid	Varian Johnson	$12.95
Red Sky	Renee Alexis	$6.99
Reluctant Captive	Joyce Jackson	$8.95
Rendezvous With Fate	Jeanne Sumerix	$8.95
Revelations	Cheris F. Hodges	$8.95
Rivers of the Soul	Leslie Esdaile	$8.95
Rocky Mountain Romance	Kathleen Suzanne	$8.95
Rooms of the Heart	Donna Hill	$8.95
Rough on Rats and Tough on Cats	Chris Parker	$12.95
Save Me	Africa Fine	$6.99

Other Genesis Press, Inc. Titles (continued)

Other Genesis Press, Inc. Titles (continued)

The Missing Link	Charlyne Dickerson	$8.95
The Mission	Pamela Leigh Starr	$6.99
The More Things Change	Chamein Canton	$6.99
The Perfect Frame	Beverly Clark	$9.95
The Price of Love	Sinclair LeBeau	$8.95
The Smoking Life	Ilene Barth	$29.95
The Words of the Pitcher	Kei Swanson	$8.95
Things Forbidden	Maryam Diaab	$6.99
This Life Isn't Perfect Holla	Sandra Foy	$6.99
Three Doors Down	Michele Sudler	$6.99
Three Wishes	Seressia Glass	$8.95
Ties That Bind	Kathleen Suzanne	$8.95
Tiger Woods	Libby Hughes	$5.95
Time Is of the Essence	Angie Daniels	$9.95
Timeless Devotion	Bella McFarland	$9.95
Tomorrow's Promise	Leslie Esdaile	$8.95
Truly Inseparable	Wanda Y. Thomas	$8.95
Two Sides to Every Story	Dyanne Davis	$9.95
Unbreak My Heart	Dar Tomlinson	$8.95
Uncommon Prayer	Kenneth Swanson	$9.95
Unconditional Love	Alicia Wiggins	$8.95
Unconditional	A.C. Arthur	$9.95
Undying Love	Renee Alexis	$6.99
Until Death Do Us Part	Susan Paul	$8.95
Vows of Passion	Bella McFarland	$9.95
Waiting for Mr. Darcy	Chamein Canton	$6.99
Waiting in the Shadows	Michele Sudler	$6.99
Wedding Gown	Dyanne Davis	$8.95
What's Under Benjamin's Bed	Sandra Schaffer	$8.95
When a Man Loves a Woman	LaConnie Taylor-Jones	$6.99
When Dreams Float	Dorothy Elizabeth Love	$8.95
When I'm With You	LaConnie Taylor-Jones	$6.99
When Lightning Strikes	Michele Cameron	$6.99
Where I Want To Be	Maryam Diaab	$6.99
Whispers in the Night	Dorothy Elizabeth Love	$8.95
Whispers in the Sand	LaFlorya Gauthier	$10.95
Who's That Lady?	Andrea Jackson	$9.95
Wild Ravens	AlTonya Washington	$9.95
Yesterday Is Gone	Beverly Clark	$10.95
Yesterday's Dreams, Tomorrow's Promises	Reon Laudat	$8.95
Your Precious Love	Sinclair LeBeau	$8.95

Order Form

Mail to: Genesis Press, Inc.
P.O. Box 101
Columbus, MS 39703

Name _____
Address _____
City/State _____ Zip _____
Telephone _____

Ship to (if different from above)
Name _____
Address _____
City/State _____ Zip _____
Telephone _____

Credit Card Information
Credit Card # _____ ☐ Visa ☐ Mastercard
Expiration Date (mm/yy) _____ ☐ AmEx ☐ Discover

Qty.	Author	Title	Price	Total

Use this order form, or call 1-888-INDIGO-1	**Total for books** _____
	Shipping and handling:
	  $5 first two books,
	  $1 each additional book _____
	Total S & H _____
	Total amount enclosed _____
	Mississippi residents add 7% sales tax